TO THE
EMERALD
CITY

# Munchkinland

Rush Margins

ILLSWATER

WEND HARDINGS

THE CLOTH
HILLS

YELLOW
BRICK
ROAD

WATERSLIP

Qhoyre

Bengda

SALT
HELDS

Encounter Day

WATERSLIP

The Hex

# ELPHIE

## ALSO BY GREGORY MAGUIRE

### FICTION
*A Wild Winter Swan*
*Hiddensee*
*After Alice*
*The Next Queen of Heaven*
*Lost*
*Mirror Mirror*
*Confessions of an Ugly Stepsister*

### THE WICKED YEARS
*Wicked*
*Son of a Witch*
*A Lion Among Men*
*Out of Oz*

### ANOTHER DAY
*The Brides of Maracoor*
*The Witch of Maracoor*
*The Oracle of Maracoor*

### NONFICTION
*Making Mischief: A Maurice Sendak Appreciation*

### FOR YOUNGER READERS
*Cress Watercress*
*Matchless*
*Egg & Spoon*
*What-the-Dickens*
*Missing Sisters*
*The Good Liar*
*Leaping Beauty*

# ELPHIE

## A
## WICKED
## CHILDHOOD

## GREGORY
## MAGUIRE

WILLIAM MORROW

*An Imprint of* HarperCollins*Publishers*

FIRST EDITION

Designed by Bonni Leon-Berman

Library of Congress Cataloging-in-Publication Data

Names: Maguire, Gregory, author. | Maguire, Gregory. Wicked.
Title: Elphie : a Wicked childhood / Gregory Maguire.
Description: First edition. | New York, NY : William Morrow, 2024. |
 Summary: "What happened to young Elphaba before her witchy powers
 took hold in Wicked? Almost 30 years after publication of the original
 novel, for the first time Gregory Maguire reveals the story of prickly
 young Elphie, the future Wicked Witch of the West"—Provided by publisher.
Identifiers: LCCN 2024005381 | ISBN 9780063377011 (hardcover) | ISBN
 9780063377035 (e-pub)
Subjects: LCGFT: Fantasy fiction. | Novels.
Classification: LCC PS3563.A3535 E47 2024 | DDC 813/.54—dc23/
 eng/20240212
LC record available at https://lccn.loc.gov/2024005381

ISBN 978-0-06-344582-6
ISBN 978-0-06-337701-1 (hardcover deluxe limited edition)

25 26 27 28 29  RTLO  10 9 8 7 6 5 4 3 2 1

*For Idina Menzel and for Cynthia Erivo*

*and for all the Elphabas, past and to come*

Pursue the authentic—decide first
what is authentic,
then go after it with all your heart.
Your heart, that place
you don't even think of cleaning out.
That closet stuffed with savage mementos.

*—Louise Erdrich, from "Advice to Myself"*

# CONTENTS

PART ONE

# ENCOUNTER DAY

# 1

War in the air, and yet the air is soft. Rotting jasmine and ripe skunk cabbage. Frogs in the sawgrass marsh. The basso profundo statement of a water buffalo, out of sight somewhere upstream. From farther off, a *pock-pockity-pock*. Not rain, but human hands skittering across drumheads of alligator hide. It sounds random unless you know the grammar. Just a *pockity-pockity*, while dawn drifts in like an afterthought.

Some of the family take this in. Most do not. The father sunk in his devotions, eyes closed, fingers moving over prayer beads. The mother at her daily rinse, naked to the waist, while a mist stands stationary above the sliding water. Mist speckled with midges that glint and vanish.

The older child is lollygagging on a blanket set squarely in the mud. She's no baby, she can poke about when she wants. She can run when she remembers about running. At the age of three and spare change, maybe four. Certainly old enough. Though often she just sits, sucking her thumb and looking about her. She does this whenever her parents are distracted, which means frequently. She looks as if she is supervising the world, though like any child she is merely curious.

Some children are more alert than others. This girl is one of them. Elphie, the Nanny calls her. Elphie, get down from there. Elphie, mind your tongue. Elphie, get your finger out of—Elphie.

A green child in a green green world. Maybe green is as invisible to her as concepts of time, gravity, justice. She's only a child on a blanket. Through the haze the sun bleeds, a wound leaking through gauze. She hears the dip of paddles from some unseen canoe down the river.

Two bugs meet on the satin edging of her cotton playground but as they're of different congregations they pass by without acknowledgment. One is the color of new-split bamboo and the other wetly black.

The mother, the father, the child, and Nanny. Also the team of bearers and guides.

Something has caused this day to lift out of the morass of everyness. The girl hears a cry across the water, a human cry, as of someone startled. The sound of a human being set upon by some unimaginable aspect of the morning.

Her father concentrates his grip on his beads and screws his eyes more tightly closed. Her mother shifts a shawl to cover one of her breasts, but only one; even on a dangerous morning something might be seducible. Nanny comes to squat upon the far edge of Elphie's blanket. She finds Elphie's hand and holds it without remark. This as much for her own comfort as for the child's, Elphie being the kind of person who doesn't elicit the consoling gesture.

War is in the air. She has caught the hint, though she can't yet know what war is. She takes her thumb out of her mouth and dries it along the smooth, smudged blanket. Nanny says, "Oh, I think that was a morning dove, don't you?" A lie about what peace sounds like. If there is such a thing. Elphie glances at Nanny but keeps her own counsel. Well, that's a bit rich; Elphie has no counsel to keep at the time. She will come to know Nanny as something of a failure.

The black bug has gotten interested in a loose pink thread on the blanket. Elphie watches it. "Oooh, the nasty," says Nanny, and flicks it away. "This *place*. And its *bugs*. Melena, dress yourself. Even the backlands abhor a harlot."

Elphie won't remember any of this actual talking. She is slow to speak herself, according to family legend. But with what other tool does she have to consider the start of everything? Words, words alone, and the lustrous peril of the wicked world.

# 2

About those teeth. Some still whisper that Elphie was born with snake dentures. If so, maybe that's why her mother has dragged Nanny along on this mission to Quadling Country: to wet-nurse the new baby the way she did Elphie. *Somebody* has to. Though the younger child's gums are soft and pink and normal, and the baby teeth poking through are little gems of standard design.

Melena has always valued her assets, especially now that her portfolio is limited to what's left of her personal allure. A few better gowns and a fine embonpoint, which signals social capital in some circles—for instance, those of Colwen Grounds, her childhood home in Munchkinland. And, yes, all right, point taken: Melena has sidestepped the oversight of her family these four years and counting. But that formative influence, apparently, she hasn't *quite* escaped. Attitude, poise. The confidence of her breeding. Now, a fine bosom is nearly all she has left, or so she concludes when the sour cloud shadows her.

Elphie has no memory of harboring daggered pincers within her mean little smile. Her second-growth teeth have come in unnaturally early, and more conventionally shaped. She won't remember having pulled out her own milk teeth when they got loose. (Perhaps no one else risked putting a hand inside Elphie's mouth.)

Nanny always says, "Don't kiss the baby, Elphie. You might scare it." There *is* that. The baby in its swaddles, the baby in its sling hung from the bough of a moss palmetto. Going on two years old, but slow to grow. Small and immobile, like a much younger child. A lump of sweet silence beneath the mosquito netting. "Jaguars don't care for the smell of moss palm fruit, so she's safe there. The monkeys can't undo knots to get her out of her nest. Don't worry about her."

Worry doesn't enter into it. Maybe dimly remembering her sharp milk teeth, Elphie has thought of chewing the strings so as to make the bothersome creature more accessible to thieving monkeys. After all, they take everything else that isn't tied down or caged.

# 3

A baby sister hanging in a tree. A mouth of forgotten razor teeth. An ambush sniffed in the air of a swamp morning. A father preparing for a meeting with the indigenous heathen of these parts. A distracted mother, put-upon and aggrieved, forgetting why she's fled her cushy family environs for this career of mildewy motherhood in Quadling Country. A nanny whose only asset is her indispensability. The world beyond the blanket. Green dripping from green, shrieking birds, silent snakes. The billion enterprises of the bug nation. A cry in the mist, a curious silence. The day is launched upon its inevitabilities.

"I don't believe they even *heard* that," mutters Nanny, shrugging at Frex and Melena, praying and preening. She tries to draw the green child closer, but Elphie can't abide the cloying touch.

But is her father even present at this moment? Or has he already left for his meeting with the elders of the tribe? Has her mother—what? Not gone with him, surely; she isn't interested in missionary work. Maybe Nanny has taken Melena aside. Maybe it isn't even the same day. One morning stands out and makes all the others recede. Catch a glint of sun on a single stone in the riverbed, and that's all you can see, not the other stones nesting against it.

Beneath a tree lies a kind of broad flat dish, two-thirds the height of Elphie. Hammered yellow of some sort, light and strong. A platter with beveled edges to catch the gravy. Not so hard to lift. A sort of suctioning sound as it comes away from the grass. Heave and drop, heave and drop, to make the world go *clop clop clop*.

She gives it a push to see if it will roll, and it does, heading downhill. It revolves in tightening circles and makes a metallic echo when it clangs to the ground. Someone hollers at her.

But few pay attention to her. Father—Frex, Frexspar, originally Frexispar Togue; Guv'nor Pastor, *Papa*—Father seldom looks up from his devotions—Elphie will have few memories of him even speaking to her until after the death of her mother. So it probably isn't Father. Maybe at this moment he isn't even around. Nor has Melena Thropp clucked a warning. Melena is a hen who doesn't mother her chicks.

Elphie alone. Elphie in the wilderness.

Most likely it's Nanny, whose voice caws and grates like a dawn scissorjay. Background noise.

Or—wait, there are occasionally a few others in the entourage, now and then. A local guide named Severin, probably hardly more than a teenager but good with navigation. He has a companion who takes the second paddle when Father needs to be ferried to a camp meeting at some other marsh-landing. The friend chews some kind of beetle that turns his teeth charcoal. Elphie tucks her own smile inside her lips so as not to provoke a return grin from that boy.

Then, also, there is Boozy. Not her real name—that's just how her name in Qua'ati sounds upon Munchkinlander ears. Boozy, an itinerant cook. She travels with the party when she wants, disappears for days on end when she's had enough. Elphie will never know if Boozy is twenty years younger than Nanny, or maybe older; the child doesn't know about years yet. Or about growing up.

But a presence, our Boozy; yes indeed. She's made an impression. Decades later, Ephie might have drawn her likeness, had she any talent for trailing ink off the nib of a quill. Boozy's forehead is tall and her glossy hair is yanked back along her scalp, clamped under a band of marshberry cord. The cook's top lip frills, one side of it going wryly up and down. As if she once made the soup *way* too hot and wrinkled herself permanently. Elphie's memory of Boozy at this stage is warmer than most. Maybe Elphie's command of Qua'ati—the tongue of the Quadlings—is weaker than her grasp of Boozy-speak. A kind of pidgin-Boozy.

People come and go in this party. In a list of dramatis personae in a theater program they'd be identified only as "the fisherman," "the seer," "the spice lady," "the chieftain," "the sewing circle." No one would have a proper name. Walk-on parts mostly. But Boozy is a fixture, and so are Severin and his ash-smiled companion—yes, his name is Snapper, that's it—and Nanny. And of course Elphie and her parents, Frex and Melena. No one else of significance, unless you pick up on the thin pleated cry of a baby annoyance. Elphie often forgets about that one, hanging in a tree. They call her Nessarose. A pretty name for a pretty sorry scrap of child.

# 4

elena on some morning or other, probably not the one in question. All days begin the same, at the bank of the river, wherever their camp might be pitched alongside it. At this point in the undertaking the missionaries don't bother going inland. The waterway provides an abundance of fish and also of marsh people drifting by, so it's a practical place for her husband to net converts to the faith.

Also, the river affords an escape route in case of a native resistance. Not that it has been needed. Melena and Frex have found that the Quadlings, a peaceable lot, raise their weapons only against predators like jaguars, marsh jackals, that sort. If Quadling locals don't like you, they mostly try to shout you off their settlement. The worst punishment is a brief if humiliating incarceration in bamboo cages. Nonetheless, ever prudent, the Munchkinlander mission keeps canoes at the ready, should Quadling hospitality evaporate.

Canoes for emergency evacuation, and a few devices of defense, including the shield of faith—an actual shield, made of pale worked bronze. A gift of several bishops relieved not to have felt a personal calling to establish themselves in such a hardship post. The shield is a spiritual artifact whose ornamental breast dazzles. It's said to be functional: it could provide cover for a mother and two small children, if they crouched close.

This length of black silk water might be the main river, called Waterslip. But perhaps not. Hereabouts, Quadling Country is threaded with several dozen channels, slight or substantial, all running into and out of Waterslip, braiding and dividing too frequently to be charted. Even the locals don't bother naming the courses, relying on instinct for orientation.

Melena isn't certain what her husband thinks about her return from Colwen Grounds last year, hauling the sad new infant and dragging along Nanny to care for it. Colwen Grounds, Melena's childhood home, theater of birth and death the same day. Good riddance to sweet rubbish. Melena is silent about it while her husband broods. But Melena has never been strong at imagining the viewpoints of other people. She can't bear to anticipate any viewpoint her healthy first child might take eventually, while her second child won't live long enough for the question to arise. So Melena, ill-trained at introspection, finds confounding the chain of events that has led her to this exile, this Frog Holiday, this evacuation from everything she's known before.

She has left home twice. The first, eloping with Frex to the harsh outback of Wend Hardings, Munchkinland, where Elphie was born. Sheep-shit country. Then, having returned to her family's demesne for the birth of her second daughter, she managed to slip away again. It would be the final retreat, though that hasn't been proven yet—Melena is still alive.

They don't give her much credit, her relatives. In a way Melena can't blame them. So she has a strolling eye—where's the crime in that? Everyone's got a pretty little flaw hidden behind the party smile and the better shoes. Hers is only loneliness, she decides, taking longer than necessary to wash herself in attractive poses of public dishabille. A need to be seen. By men. So what?

Yes, she has a husband. How her family disapproved of such a fervent man with so few prospects! An Eminence of Munchkinland, her grandfather, always intended a better match for Melena than some itinerant preacher.

Frexspar the Godly: A tall man, especially compared to old-stock

Munchkinland farmers, those barrelly folk whose chins rarely grow four feet above the soil. In contrast, Frex is a ladder, an apple rake. Melena had clung to him more out of the thrill of scandalizing her parents and grandfather than out of love. She realized this sometime during their first mission as a married couple, when Frex was assigned to Wend Hardings in the rubbly outback of Munchkinland.

Anyway, she approves of her own loyalty. Which is loyalty as she defines it, a bespoke virtue cut to her needs. She isn't beyond taking a man now and then when he piques her curiosity. She is always any community's most attractive attractive nuisance.

But Wend Hardings toughened her up, even before the green creature came along. And since then, Melena has stuck the course, oh, they can say that much for strut-about Melena Thropp. Other women might have fled back to their ancestral homes. Or disappeared in the night, leaving behind the tainted baby to be looked after by someone else. By the father, if he is up to it. (Frex is decidedly not.) No, Melena had bit her lower lip and done calculations of a moral sort, and decided that while she couldn't bring herself to cozen the poisoned infant with cuddles and coos, she could, in fact, stick to her post. The wife of a missionary.

The first few years with Baby Elphaba were a trial. The bleating of sheep the primary lullaby. Nanny was hard persuaded to keep around; she'd visit but then she'd flee. Having been threatened that any stray comment she might let drop back at Colwen Grounds about Elphie's condition would be cause for abrupt dismissal without references, she complied. Nanny had kept her word, even if she'd been inconstant in her tenure that first couple of years. Elphie was more or less a secret back home, at least as to the particulars of her complexion.

There will be other things Melena remembers about this day

on the banks of an unnamed stretch of a sly, grease-green river in some outback beyond Qhoyre, the provincial capital. But she's struck a pose, so let's relish her a silent moment longer. The lift of her left arm, a sponge tracing water from her elbow to the side of her exposed breast. The poise of that woman, the satin butter of her skin. A perfect beauty, a perfect target.

Maybe she's totally vain and that's the sum of it. Or maybe this is only how she's seen and how she seems. Whose memories are these anyway? Perhaps just the river's.

## 5

Someone has brought Nanny a something. A dish of threads to repair a bonnet. A bowl of breakfast soup, hot and oily and snaily. Someone has brought Nanny a something. And put it on a campstool of some sort.

The someone is Boozy but she's fussing in the kitchen tent. It's unclear if she has cottoned on to a sense of approaching menace. What about Melena? And Frexspar? Maybe the good man has left already. And if Nanny was alarmed, she's let it pass. She's hied herself off to find tweezers to work a sliver of wood out of her thumb. Everyone else is engaged in adult enterprises.

Or perhaps Elphie's skittishness is only a mood of the river. Lurking in the mist that hides some peril signaled by that startled shout, that midvowel muffled in midair.

Tipping over whatever Nanny has set down, Elphie claims the stool underneath it. It's light enough to carry. She goes over to where the baby hangs in the tree. Maybe it's not quite accurate to call it a baby, but it has suffered what is sometimes called "failure to thrive," so it isn't much larger than it was a year ago. The thing can't move by itself much, so it's no fun to play with. It's a severed item, a fragment of childhood. Elphie pokes it from underneath with a ladle—the bowl end, so not to hurt it, just make it laugh or cry or something. The baby murmurs in the quietest of responses. A natural stoic. What a tiresome creature. And everyone flapping around it all the time, because it can do nothing for itself except soil its nappies. And everyone fussing. And everyone holding it all the time because it can't hold itself, really. All it can do is stare,

stare accusingly, and sometimes babble some babble. A sugar tit, a pacifier of some sort, is tied with a cord to its ankle. No problem of this strangling her, though, because she can't reach for it or even roll herself over. She's an immobile plug of a baby. She stays put.

Elphie thinks the creature is issuing some kind of message. Urgent syllables that everyone else thinks are mistakes. Elphie knows better. The infant is trying to magic itself whole. Fixed. Necessary. Loveable. It isn't going to work, though. Such a shame.

They talk about Elphie outgrowing her condition. Change, change. Later, she will realize they have sat her there day after day, hoping to bleach her with sunlight, like stained sheets. But of the infant they never suggest such a miracle. It will not walk. It can never balance. It won't grow strength because there is no place to put it.

Maybe they're being kind, to keep the infant from developing unanswerable hopes. Maybe they think she won't reach her next birthday. Or maybe their low expectations of Nessa will prompt her to come around, eventually. To prove them wrong.

The big sister throws the ladle down. If she only had a couple more inches she could . . . she might . . . No one else is around. Severin and Snapper are down by the water, whispering and scuttling with bent knees. Then Severin stands thigh-deep in some rushes, hooting his own secret language, and cupping his ears, as if to listen for an echo. He's distracted. It's easy for Elphie to steal into the side tent where her father practices his orations. She drags at one of his heavy stupid books. The way Boozy carries Nessarose around sometimes, on her head—Elphie tries that, balancing the book upon her scalp.

She wobbles across the camp. She clomps the volume upon the flat cap of the stool. She scrambles upon it. Learning does give one such a lift. The tome provides just enough height.

Elphie pushes up from the bottom against the infant. The way she's done with the ladle, only now she can use both her hands. She tips the creature through the netting and out of its hammock. It slips down into the crux of Elphie's arms and gurgles at the adventure. Nessarose rarely smiles at Elphie, so if the big sister is capable of remorse, this will be the moment. But Elphie is nothing if not determined, even when she determines herself wrong.

She puts Nessa under her arms, against her hip, its head facing the grass and its little legs pointing generally skyward. A tilting fish, astonished to find itself swimming in midair. The baby kicks a little. Elphie scuttles downslope like a monkey with a purloined savory. Where can we put her?

# 6

Now Frex. About him. At the best of times it's hard to know what men are thinking, or even if they do think. Pious Frexspar, as much in love with his own high calling as with his daring claim on Melena Thropp, beloved of her grandfather the Eminence, one Peerless Thropp of Munchkinland.

Claim? It was nearly an abduction. Operettas have been embroidered upon feebler tissue than this. Frexispar Togue, spawn of a dissipated branch of the Togue clan that settled in the slopes of the Pertha Hills. (Cider vinegar people, and it showed.) Frexspar, related to some better-heeled Togue cousins still swanning about in the vicinity of Colwen Grounds. Visiting these wealthier relatives, pious young Frex was hoping to cadge a bursary from them to underwrite a year's missionary effort in the Wend Hardings. His entreaties fell on deaf ears—the Togues near Colwen Grounds never underwrote nonsense that couldn't improve their social standing.

Still, Frex was garrisoned with those pinch-pursed relatives on the day an invitation arrived. The annual ball to benefit the local almshouse. Might Frex tag along with his cousins? He might. Such a comedy, he thought, but dusted his own cuffs, a plan in mind.

Because of course the gentry would make an appearance at a charitable fête.

Sure enough, the Eminence, Peerless Thropp, in all his Eminent Throppiness, presided. Colwen Grounds was his estate, after all. He was the token moneybags, the local title—beribboned, bespectacled, bewigged, and bewildered. Lady Partra, his canny daughter and helpmeet, steered him by the elbow through silk-hung salons. Into his ear Lady Partra murmured the names of people the old man had known for decades so he could appear to recognize them when they approached in the reception line, curtseying and paying their homages. Allegiances. Tributes. Hypocrisies. The regular horseshit.

As Frex approached, Lady Partra murmured to her father, "I don't know this one, he's a cringing sort, likely to be earnest, watch out for him." She wrinkled her nose. "Of the trades, no doubt." Her own husband, Roman, eclipsed by ceremony and happy enough to skedaddle, loitered outside in the forecourt, feeding carrots to the arriving horses.

At Peerless Thropp's other shoulder, his granddaughter, gorgeous Melena, hitched up her bodice apparatus. She prinked the rose on her shoulder, and like gobbets of blood, three petals fell off onto the floor at her feet. Frex noticed them. He would one day think they represented Melena's three children. Each one a cause of sorrow. Melena will not think this herself because by the time the third baby happens along, she won't have the wherewithal to remember petals; she dies in childbirth.

Lady Partra smiled first, encouragingly. She had no name to put forward into her father's ear. The Eminent Thropp said, "Eh, what is this?" as if a street dog had come into the queue and was waiting permission to advance.

Behind Frex, the senior cousin Togue intervened. "Upon my word, I precede thee, Cousin Frexspar." The more sanctimonious in that set still using *thee* and *thou*, affectedly, to prove a point.

"Ah," said Lady Partra, and sotto voce to her father, "The sugar beet merchant, Lotronius Togue, and some rural relation of his, no doubt. If my nose tells true."

"Call me Frexspar," said the young man, his teeth white with holiness, his hair a little long for the sultry season. He wasted no time. "Your Eminence, if you will, I should like to tender an application for your patronage."

"What is your cause?" asked the old man, forgetting his obligations to the next thirty people in the queue.

Lady Partra beamed with vacuous generosity though her voice became steely. "Not now, young man."

"I have no other now," said Frex, which he felt was a grand and important thing to say. And totally impromptu.

"Please, let me; I shall hear the cause," said Melena. And, oh fool Lady Partra, oh fool her old father, they allowed Melena to wander away with this unfinished but good-looking man of broad shoulders and spindly arms. With an expression hungry for a donation.

But the senior Thropps, the Eminence and his devoted daughter, Lady Partra, didn't realize they'd just donated the family heiress to a bounty hunter.

What did Melena Thropp see in Frex? Liberty. What did he see in her—he who relished his spiritual sight over any capacity of earthly observation? Did he even notice Melena's eyes darting out under her cultivated eyelashes, over her augmented blush? But how could he not notice her? Even a blind man can often see the truth.

Pivoting about the small chamber to which they've repaired. The novice minister is intense and looming. His better clothes (he doesn't have "best" clothes) can't conceal a sugar beet odor from his skin—there's no access to pomades in cousin Togue's strict household. Melena is excited by this and her nostrils flare. Frex responds to flaring nostrils (who doesn't?). They talk about the needs of the hinterlands. They both talk with enthusiasm, and neither realizes they are referring to different sorts of hinterlands.

Before the weekend is out Melena will have brokered for Frex a financial contribution, because the Eminent Thropp decides he'd best pay the young man to go away, to keep him from buzzing about the forecourt of Colwen Grounds uninvited.

Away goes the young man, under cover of night. With some cash. Away goes Peerless Thropp's granddaughter with him. Frex-spar has just enough authority of his office to be able to marry couples and so he marries himself to Melena Thropp. They light out for dismal, rural, weedy Wend Hardings. A district southwest of Colwen Grounds, where the Cloth Hills share a border with Quadling Country. Frex and Melena honeymoon in Wend Hardings. They endure their spiritual awakenings, such as they are, in Wend Hardings. Stony breakfasts, leaden dusks. As Frex dives ever deeper into persuasions of a more spiritual nature, Melena experiments with being casual in her approach to marital vows.

A this one, a that one. A traveling salesman. A goatherd from the scrubby slopes. A fetching Quadling glassblower who has come north on his way to complain about improprieties being taken against his home-scape back south, but who is mesmerized first by Melena and then, perhaps, by Frex himself. You could call it an affair along modern lines. Well, Frex *is* good-looking if you can get past the superiority of his calling—and he uses his brooding mien to attract both the penitents and their pittances. Then when this Turtle Heart, a sort of seer from the ruby fields under the waters of Quadling Country, remembers his original mission, he leaves the Wend Hardings cottage in the village of Rush Margins and eventually arrives at Colwen Grounds. Where the poor rube is murdered. Suppose he must not have been much of a seer. You can't make this stuff up.

Elphie had already been born. Inside a clock, of all things. Capped by a mechanical dragon kitted out with mechanical incisors. But nobody talks of this. Nanny wasn't there, Turtle Heart hadn't yet come and gone, Boozy hadn't been thought up, Melena had been out of her skull from chewing pinlobble leaves for the pain, and Frex was away on the circuit. Nobody but Elphie knew about the swinging pendulum, the way it slices time into ribbons, and Elphie—well, she may have been born with all those shark teeth in her mouth, but if she also had a sharp tongue on her first night on this earth, she kept it to herself.

# 7

The three whose names Elphie will be able to recall are viv-idly present. Boozy the itinerant cook; Severin and Snapper, the navigators. The other attendants may have skived off into the overgrowth. If the navigators are on-site, then her father must be, too. He doesn't take the canoe out on his own. So where is he?

Snapper is a mere adjacency to Severin; he won't yield up his secrets, if he has any. He sports a shadow of hair on his upper lip suggesting a distant drop of northern or western blood. If Severin moves this way, Snapper moves that. Related, or friends?—or they may merely be co-workers for the duration, hired from the day-laborer yard in Qhoyre.

Snapper giggles a bit. He sings while paddling, scaring off the serpents and charming the passengers. Songs through his mid-night teeth. It is nearly all Elphie will recall of Snapper.

Severin. The older, the alpha of the two. Here he is. Moving with more grace on trees and on water than he does on the ground. Not all that surprising; many clan communities live in settlements slung in the candelabra branches of oakanthus or teak baobabs. Most able-limbed adult Quadlings swing, climb, pace, and leap. The stealth of the jaguar, the poise of the cobra.

Having heard the *pock-pockity* hint of unwelcome guests ap-proaching, Severin had got one arm looped about a branch, one bare foot flexed against the trunk. His ear is trained for the per-cussion of drumheads, for human voices imitating river birds. He knows stealth communication when he hears it. He knows a little about what this party of pale missionaries is about. He is a loyal employee and he's no turncoat, but neither is he a convert to their cause. (Spreading the gospel of unionism among the already sufficiently spiritual.) Severin holds his job with honor, and not just for the pay. He's responsible for the women and children in this vulnerable party, not to mention the guilt-harried minister himself, Brother Frex. However much penitential suffering these foreigners need to endure in order to atone, Severin won't allow it to be served up to them on the spear or with the rifle.

Oh, yes, the Quadlings have rifles, sometimes. They had firsthand experience of firing arms from the spelunkers and mineralogists who descended upon them five years ago. Nominally to find a way to lay down a brick road to link the provincial swamps with Qhoyre, the putative capital. But honestly? To suss out where scooping out the underswamp mud would reveal the more lucrative seams of ruby. (The exportation of which, to be sure, would be rendered that much easier if a road existed.) The Quadlings are just as noble as any other race, and just as pliable with cash. Some foreign explorers went back to the Emerald City with tentative maps and treaties for development rights. The venturers left behind rifles, the odd fatal cough, and a new appetite for just a little—a little *more*—that will never, ever, ever be slaked. A new economy of—agglomeration.

The senior porter shifts his feet, cranes his neck in another direction. Here the sounds of spattered raindrops speak their coordinates more accurately. Closer than Severin has guessed. And he knows that the approaching group has not come with picnic baskets. It's time to sound the alarm more broadly.

He swings to another limb and coo-coos in semaphore to Boozy. Ah, but now she's picked up on the warning herself, she's no fool. She's forsaken her breakfast stew and is rolling up her family totems in a shawl, in case she needs to abandon her employers.

The semaphored messages of the support staff go something like
this—

— brute gang on its way, round the river bend, under the string-
   magnolia canopy. (That is Severin.)
— and what they want with these stupid people (Boozy.)
— where the mouthy man, where is the wife? (Severin.)
— who cares, who cares, what they doing here, why they coming
   here?
— find the holy man, Boozy! (a pause.) They quiet now. Snapper,
   what's this?

Snapper doesn't answer, he's begun listening, pressing his ex-
tended palm flat against the tree trunk. Then he speaks in that
sing-tune way.

— Severin! They have more coming along behind, and are waiting them to catch up, to gather before attack.
— how many there, how many more coming?
— I don't do numbers. Just: *more*. There's time.
— maybe they mean us to hear and to get out first?
— maybe, but why so many? Two elders with axes and an argument could scare these holy busybodies away.

Boozy has salvaged the most important parts of her supplies.
The rest she can come back for if she gets the chance. She scans
the encampment for her employers as she draws knots in her bun-
dles.

— but why they take up rage against these fool **Munchkinland**
   people? (Boozy)

Severin has left the tree and begun to holler for Melena. She bolts from her tent at his tone of voice, grasping the gravity of the moment if not the reason for alarm. Lacing herself up, she hisses for Nanny. Running in circles, these people. Snapper scurries into the near undergrowth to see if he can find out where Frexspar has gone—relief of his bowels, probably. Boozy tries one more time.

— what they do so wrong, Severin?
— wife is from family of status. It is her house that murder the young prophet Turtle Heart. Last year. Someone has found it out at last, and this war party comes to make vengeance.
— Turtle Heart, who he, small life, who cares so much, why his death provoke more death? There are children here, Severin. Where are the failed children?

Nanny has fallen in a faint on the grass. Melena is screaming because Elphie has wandered off. The child is in no danger of drowning, as she won't go near the shore of the river, but where is she? And Snapper has underestimated how long they have before encounter. And the mission group is too far from the berthed canoes to make an escape now.

The attack launches with a single falsetto aria followed by a chorale of high shrieks, while the air is perforated with whistling arrows. The sun starts to rise over the bank of mist. The incoming canoes draw themselves visible, emerging against the testimonial glass of the water.

# 8

The delegation lifts up out of the reeds, head and shoulders, this one this one this one and more of them. Spears and several guns, a raised knife or two. Alarums chanted in a triad, nasal and dronelike. It feels like five thousand of them but it's only a dozen or so. Twice the number of the missionary party, anyway; or twice twice.

This isn't a courtesy call. An adolescent Quadling waterboy lately serving the Thropp family—no, not Severin or Snapper, someone else—shouts in alarm. His bad luck to be nearest where the warriors emerge from the mist. He is felled with a thrown implement, maybe a slingshot stone. He sinks backward with surprising grace, crimson arcing over his chest as he drops, a blood rainbow. He dies elegant but anonymous.

The missionary party can raise no defense. Frex is missing. Even the famous ornamental shield is missing. Melena has bound herself in a boudoir wrap with a cord around the waist. She calls for her children as she lurches past Nanny, who has managed to get herself to her hands and knees. The Quadling guides raise their arms in the air and shout warnings to the marauders, though mildly. It's a gesture both of "Stop, you villain!" and "No harm intended to you," an ambivalent message of the sort that Quadlings tolerate better than most.

Boozy tries to haul Nanny to her feet. Severin pushes forward. He's brave, you have to admit, with that incidental boy gurgling his last in the grass eighty feet away. But the assailants keep coming up. Not in a rush, as on a battle plain of old, but almost casually. Now thumping on a barrel drum slung on someone's hip, to drive the warriors forward, to terrify the foreigners further.

Severin and Snapper wave their arms behind them, signaling to Melena, Nanny, Boozy, to anyone else in the party, that they should fall back, escape into the undergrowth. Even if the missionaries aren't totally defenseless. Frex harbors a gun. But it's locked in his minister's chest along with other tools of the trade, the unguents, blessed stones, water, and sacred texts. Frex has the key. Frex has the key to everything. Frex is not here.

Something, then, something like this:

— What for, what can you want, these strange strangers that I guide are already breaking up camp, they're moving. (This is Severin, his voice more high-pitched than usual, while trying to project sobriety and calm.)

— Clear off, we take what we need, save yourself. (The boss of the avengers, answering Severin.)

— You don't touch them, you leave them alone.

— It's that woman's family who murdered Turtle Heart, our ambassador. Yes, that woman. The hysteric. Can you get her to shut up? We'd rather not kill her entirely but mercy, the noise.

— Maybe her family did it but she didn't. She had nothing to do with whatever happened to your Turtle Heart.

— These people are the advance edge, the chisel point that splits the stone. It's all too clear. This is our answer to the entrepreneurs: we will not yield. The overlords are coming for rubies, they are coming to rule. They will overset the waterlands. I'm not talking to you, you toady. Out, men, spread out, up to the bulrushes there and the water wheat over there, left and right.

The men run, separating themselves one from the other like players on a field, a pinching strategy. Melena whirls, for once without worrying whether she is spinning attractively or awkwardly. "The baby! And Elphie!" she cries. "Nanny, get Nessa!"

The men swoop close upon Melena, near enough to abduct her; her knees buckle but she manages to keep from crumpling to the ground. They surround her, crowd her, though don't touch her. Nanny is at last on her feet. Her agility augmented by this crisis, she rushes at the marauders. She hammers at their shoulders with a pair of tweezers. A knitting needle from her apron pocket proves more useful for getting to Melena's side. Boozy is keening and wringing her hands—perhaps a touch theatrically, it must be said. Severin and Snapper fall into hand-to-hand combat with the newcomers. Though the Quadling hired guides are, so far, being treated as lightly as possible.

Before long the rest of the missionary's entourage, its straggling Quadling bearers and aides, has disappeared in the underbrush. Frex is missing. Elphie is missing. Nessa is presumably napping aloft in her bassinet. While Nanny, Melena, Snapper, and Severin are packed tightly, back to back, surrounded by a wreath of pointing spears.

Boozy returns to packing up her cookware. Suddenly she shows little interest in what's happening in the middle of the camp. Spoons bundled with spoons, two knives wrapped in plantain leaves to help them keep their sharp opinions to themselves.

# 9

oozy's name is Bouze'ezi. The word derives from the concept known as "dust on the soup." To a house-proud Munchkinlander, this sounds like criminal slovenliness. But to Quadlings, it suggests an attitude of sacred serenity toward one's ancestors. Dust on the soup: even a boiling broth would settle itself in order to apprehend the seraphic dead. A state of readiness, a patience for revelation. A setting of priorities, divine over domestic.

It's a pretty notion. Though perhaps not the right name for Boozy, dust on the soup in her case being more like a dubious recipe for leftovers.

Or maybe this is shortchanging Boozy. Bouze'ezi. Here she is, in this moment of almost comic dreadfulness. She's carrying on while her Quadling colleagues and two of her foreign employers are corralled mere yards from her cooking tent. Frex is on walkabout, which is unlike him. Though Melena and Nanny haven't yet noticed the baby's hammock is empty, they're aware that Elphie's blanket is devoid of Elphie.

No one calls Elphie's name again, in the hopes she will stay where she must be hiding.

The menacing party draws nearer, the spears jabbing without yet poking. Severin's bravado is going nowhere. It falls to Boozy to sort things out.

— Why you pester these people, they mean nothing to anyone, how could they, they are just big dung beetles! (Boozy's longest spoken sentence since anyone in this party has met her.)

— What is she saying, is she selling us out? (Nanny.)

— Go argue with the ones who actually killed your kinsman Turtle Heart, not with these stupid people!

— Did she just call us stupid? (Nanny again, who has picked up
more Qua'ati than she's realized.)

— We need to solve the equation. (The chief of the sortie.) These
termites will eat our home and our lives out from under us
unless we show them the cost. A life for each life. It is too bad
but we have no choice. Stop your squealing, cook. We will not
harm you. We need one of them. The lowest of them, in fact.
It is only a gesture.

— But you already brought down that boy at the riverbank.
(Boozy.)

— That was an accident.

— I won't tell.

— It has to be one of the Munchkinlanders. We can be merciful.
Who is the least valued?


It isn't for Boozy to say.
Severin speaks.


— Boozy, where is Frex's shield? It was right there on the slope.
Has he taken it with him wherever he went? Did he know this
was going to happen? Has he abandoned his family?


Boozy bites her crimped lip. She thinks it improves her looks by
concealing her mild deformity when in fact she seems deranged,
as if she is eating herself. But dust on the soup; something settles;
in her courage and awkwardness she puts her hand on Melena's
shoulder and talks to the chief over Severin's attempts at negoti-
ation.

— It is all as it should be. (Boozy, primed for argument, now lets loose.) You've come to terrify this family and its retainers. You've done your job. No one needs to know that you didn't slay any of *them*. You killed one of your own. Let that boy's death count as a sacrifice. It will put these people in greater debt to you. It will prove your greater strength—that you could have killed the highborn daughter or her wag-tongue husband, and you didn't. They stink with chagrin and shame. You bloom in mastery and honor. You have already achieved what you came for, to show them whose land this is. Rely on your own scales and weights, not theirs. You shall go away triumphant.

Boozy steps forward. She opens her hands and drops a wooden cooking spoon into the grass; she lifts her chin and sings a threnody. She has never known Turtle Heart nor anything about his original and ill-fated mission, but she sings for him, a song to put him to rest though his body is dropped in some ditch in a Colwen Grounds dung yard.

When she's done, she brushes the aggressors aside and steps toward the threatened group. She attaches herself to the mission group as one of them. Severin grasps her hand, as if they have just finished a binding ceremony.

— You do our brother Turtle Heart proud. (The chief.) We will not slay. All right. We will fall back. But not without proof of our engagement here. We will take one of the children. There are two of them, we understand. Bring them forward and we will take one, and they can have the other, and we will be done here.
— What the hell are you all talking about? (Melena.)
— We will take one of the children.
— Is that the word for *children*? Did he say *children*?

# 10

Melena considers letting her lapels fall open a little. She stops herself though. Words come out of her mouth that she hasn't anticipated.

"Severin," she gabbles, "tell them not the children. Tell them to take me."

"You just want a night off from babysitting, and you hardly lift a finger as it is," says Nanny. She is deranged with fear. No one replies to her.

Though Melena has always liked being on display, here she is as few have seen her before. In this rare moment she's found her footing—briefly. Pity it won't be noticed except by these who will never mention it. Melena's words mean little to Severin and to Snapper, because in their world, what mother wouldn't say the same? While Nanny could never give witness because the question would then arise, *Why didn't* you *offer in Melena's place?*

When Elphaba was born, Melena had sent back word to her family at Colwen Grounds from the hardscrabble hamlet in Wend Hardings. She'd written: "Don't come to find me. I left willingly, I left as a free agent. But send Nanny—I need some help." Grudgingly, Melena's grandfather had granted her request. Melena was his only grandchild, after all. So Nanny had readied herself for the severities of the gorse-bushed, scree-sloped wastebasket called Rush Margins. Arrived tutting, fussing, scheming. Any diplomatic contact between the generations of the Thropp line was conducted by Nanny, or Cattery Spunge as she was known when out of nanny drag and back in mufti.

But Nanny is a domestic, and she hasn't ever forgotten it. Elphie and Nessa are her charges but not her children. It's not her *place* to offer to be their stand-in. Putting on airs even to suggest such a transaction. Above her station. The very idea. She keeps her mouth shut.

As for Melena, this is her fine moment. For the briefest of instants she means what she says. Let them live, those appalling little mites, she thinks; even mites have a right to their squished lives.

"Take me," she says again, as if she's suddenly put together how her own actions helped bring to pass this moment on this riverbank on this warm winter morning in Quadling Country, southwest of Qhoyre. Though this is speculation; Melena has rarely bothered with cause and effect.

When Turtle Heart finally left the stone cottage in Rush Margins, Munchkinland, on the shores of Illswater, abandoning Melena and Frex, who had both been somewhat smitten with him, the simple Quadling prophet had taken up his quest again. True, after leaving Rush Margins, it had been some months before Turtle Heart ended up at Colwen Grounds. But he'd experienced his pilgrimage as part of the lesson. He had meandered and dragonsnaked with others as he had with Melena. Dust on the soup. While Melena's belly swelled and the days of her confinement neared an end.

The Quadling glassblower had continued north in Munchkinland, stumbling upon that despised highway of yellow brick. He'd been told Center Munch was the provincial capital but that the most senior of the province's Eminences, the Eminent Thropp, lived in a place more remote (the isolation of the privileged). A redoubt called Colwen Grounds. Which as it happens is right over that way. Cross three fields and a deer park and breast the ha-ha and there it is: That stodgy manor of stone facades and forecourts, arcades and symmetrical outbuildings. At last.

It must have been hard for the Quadling glassblower and self-appointed emissary to fathom, that his erstwhile lover Melena had been cultivated here—like a prize cabbage.

The hapless pilgrim hoped to get advice from a bigwig about how the Quadlings could best register a complaint against the Emerald City. He would knock on the wrong door, however. The Eminent Thropp had no influence upon the arriviste Wizard of Oz, that bounder who had deposed Pastorius, the Ozma Regent. The Eminent Thropp had no stake in what happened to mucky Quadlings. Despite Munchkinland and Quadling Country sharing a border. Not his bailiwick.

Turtle Heart, in the wrong place at the wrong time. An unlucky envoy of his people, anticipating an invasion yet foolishly trusting in diplomacy.

He had sallied in, bringing salutations from Melena and her minister husband. She says to tell you they intend to move from Rush Margins. I have complained of our plight and so they are intent on settling there, a presence for good among my people. They are taking up a position as missionaries to the Quadlings. You should be so proud of them.

The Eminent Thropp believed the Quadling's assertions. His second daughter Sophelia having died of the flu, leaving no issue, the continuation of the line of Eminences depended on Lady Partra's only child, Melena. That heiress granddaughter had already slipped her harness once; and out there in Wend Hardings tottered a small girl named Elphaba Thropp, in line to become Eminence. Growing up shoeless and untutored, probably. If Melena and her family chose to disappear even deeper into Muckland, the Peerless Thropp's ancestral title and lands could be lost, his legacy squandered. And for what? For this blinking, peaceable foreigner delivering unwelcome news? And for all his ill-luck kin and kind?

In rage the Eminent Thropp had had the innocent removed. When questioned by the local constabulary later about the unfortunate event that followed—pro forma enquiries at best—Peerless Thropp murmured that the Quadling tinker had offered himself to avenge the spirits of drought that had plagued the land. A sort of impromptu mob showed up to do the dirty, not so unusual. "Human sacrifice" was noted, in those ironic quotes, for the record, but that the drought actually lifted shortly thereafter gave the murder some aftershock of legitimacy. Unfortunate but there you go. And news of it spread, little by little. Including back to the prophet's home in the marshlands.

What the murdered man never learned was that the Eminent Thropp's granddaughter was actually in residence at Colwen Grounds at the very moment he presented himself—for the last time in her life.

As Melena approached the hour of her second delivery, her uncertain memories surrounding Elphie's birth had raised a sense of foreboding. She'd wanted the safety of medical expertise, not the gap-toothed leer of a Wend Hardings midwife. She'd persuaded Nanny to bring her back to her parents and her grandfather for the first time since her elopement. Naturally, she left Elphie with Frex—Melena wasn't ready to put her green child on display in the parlors of the Eminence. She still harbored hopes that the creature might grow into a more savory skin tone. (When back in Colwen Grounds, Nanny had remained mum on the subject, as required.)

To complete her lying-in at her childhood home, Melena had been sequestered in a back room overlooking the stables. With a physician and a pair of nurses in attendance, she gave birth to

Turtle Heart's daughter just as he was being slaughtered in the forecourt. She didn't know about it at the time. Being in labor does concentrate the mind. The roaring in her ears and from her throat drowned out sounds of the mob on the other side of the mansion.

So it is to avenge Turtle Heart's murder that the warring band has finally arrived in the morning mist, this very day a year or so later, and is now looking for either of the young daughters of the Munchkinlander missionaries, as hostage, or perhaps as victims of vengeance.

Still. Melena. Why is it hard to look at her? Is it that she is beautiful, and beauty is hard to concentrate on? Is it that she has only ever had a bum rap, being a cold and unnatural mother like the rest of us, and that this one moment of dignity and even courage doesn't conform with what else we know of her?

She will never be as brave again. As she is waiting for the chief to respond to Severin's stuttered proposal on her behalf, she's already sorry she spoke up. But her arms are still, her chin is high. She has more of her angry grandfather in her than she knows.

Elphaba will inherit some of this. But the green girl will not know it; she will believe she invented her own character for herself out of a lack of suitable guidance. But who cares whether she gets it right or not. Maybe it doesn't matter how we're made, in the end; it matters only who we are.

# 11

The chieftain's name hasn't been mentioned yet. This isn't the affront it might seem. A leader of a sortie would have been chosen, just that morning, out of a team of qualified volunteers. He'll retire from the position by nightfall (if he survives this encounter). In anonymity resides safety. In fact, this fellow's name is Oyi'iathi, but you don't need to hold on to it; you won't hear it again.

Picture him as taller than Melena and Severin, in every way their equal in backbone. Sweat brings his forehead and pectoral muscles into high, varnished relief. The others in his party are variations on the theme. Neither does any Quadling avenger look morally uncertain about this campaign, or irritated at having been volunteered by some parent.

But appearances rarely suggest the ambiguities that prove human behavior to be actually human.

Melena is certainly good-looking enough for martyrdom. Melena, born to a line near-enough royal to have its own livery design, and rich enough not to have noticed that lots of other families don't.

History lumbers on. It can't help itself. If such a moment were recorded in a marble tableau or a municipal mural, its meaning would evolve over the decades. Melena might come to be seen as arrogant, solipsistic. Nanny as oppressed. Severin and Snapper as opportunistic and venal. The chieftain and his backups as noble defenders of their land. The last stand of doomed animism, of Quadling independence. While Boozy—but no one would ever

make out how Boozy fits in. She's the one-off that makes the moment, static as it is, continue to fizz.

Memory and history codify perception, but in real life nobody
ever really knows what anyone else is thinking. Nothing stands
still. Here comes the moth in the tapestry, the hammer against
the marble entablature. The upset.

Pacing out of the reeds on her own two green feet, hardly three
green feet high.

# 12

The chief makes a wag of his left hand. It means: Those of you on the perimeter, scatter, comb the foliage. Beat out any lurkers.

Half the men fan out, their daggers now sheathed. The others come closer. With a *tch*'ing sound of his tongue the chief instructs them to keep the mission party corralled. He moves a few feet toward Elphie. Just close enough to suggest to his men he isn't frightened by her.

Elphie—neither Melena nor Nanny can guess what is in the child's head, if there's anything in her head, or if she's just a sponge living through this unforeseeable hour. Elphie knows nothing of unionism or animism, hegemony or marginality, sexual tension or spiritual need. She's a creature of wild reed and murky riverside, although she avoids immersion. (She won't even wade in the shallows.) Whatever she might perceive, she doesn't speak it—that skill is a few years out. Her language is slow in coming for a child her age.

But she's full of all the things there are no words for, the great inchoate passions that are reduced, as we grow up, to the smaller things language allows us to say.

— This is one of theirs. (A question. The chief.)
— You won't touch her. (Severin, and bravely; he could die for this. But:)
— I will not touch her. We do not want this one.

A moment ticks as the sun levers itself another degree above the mist. The chief scratches an itch on his hip and continues.

— We do not want this one.
— What is he saying? (Melena.)
— There are two, we are told there are two, where is the other one?

When Severin doesn't answer, the chief makes another click of his tongue. Two men draw dirks. Snapper flinches; he's the most dispensable one in the encircled pack, if it comes to that. He knows it.

"Where is Nessarose?" mutters Severin to his companions.

Melena swivels her head. From where they're huddled, the bassinet is out of sight, around the edge of a tent. "Nanny? Where is she?"

"In her hammock as always, I hadn't gotten to her yet. She was safer there," gabbles Nanny, "while you were purpling the air with your panic and we were pulling up stakes."

Melena starts to scream, a single ascending syllable. The Quadling marauders aren't amused but they keep their footing.

Elphie comes a little nearer. Her mother hasn't made a sound like this before and she's curious about it. An organic sound. Maybe it reminds the child of the wind over the fells of Wend Hardings, that desolation of shattered stone and stunted gnarly trees. Even though it's already two years ago since they left.

But the chief isn't going to touch Elphie. Fear of the child, respect for its unblinking integrity. Who knows. Maybe for its splendid aberrance. What child doesn't run to its mother's knees when an attack is underway? But Elphie stands there watching, listening, the least overwhelmed of the human beings there.

Nanny finally says, "Come to Nanny, child, there's a good Elphie," if a scrap insincerely. She isn't sure she wants Elphie nearer just now. But she's said it, and credit to her for that much.

Elphie, not for the first time in her life, behaves as if she doesn't hear Nanny's instruction. If this isn't quite disobedience, it's mighty near.

The chief is now being stared down by a four-year-old, which won't do his standing in the community any good. He begins to wonder if his reluctant warriors may need to kill him in order to save his honor. So he moves closer. His attitude isn't quite revulsion. He's just curious. Once he saw a marsh goat born with two tails, another time, a feral pig arrived in a clearing with another feral pig standing on its back. Such idiocies need to be slaughtered in order that their peculiarity not infect the world.

He won't murder her, but perhaps he'll let her loose in the wild, so the wild can do the job. The wild doesn't like competition, he's noticed.

The chief makes a few muttered remarks. Elphie, for her part, stands her ground. She's intrigued. As if she is making her first study of otherness. She likes the poise of the chief. Unlike Melena and Frex, who avoid their older child, and Nanny, who coddles her into submission, this chief is paying Elphie the greatest compliment she's ever received: keen attention from a human being.

She hears the noise behind her before the others do. It isn't the soft calls or softer footfalls of the warriors hunting for Nessarose. It isn't more drums on the water. The noise is a kind of dry sweeping. A smoothness with an under-rattle of grit.

Then the others catch it, and then the chief sees it. Elphie doesn't turn around to look at what is behind her. So no one knows what she perceives at this moment.

Melena's screams pause in the middle of her endless vowel —
— —. Nanny uses an outmoded countrywoman's curse that has
gone so far out of fashion it's not worth repeating. (Crude from
snout to stirrups, you can be sure.) Boozy drops her ladle. Snapper exhales for what feels like the first time in an hour and he
nearly passes out from the relief. And Severin audaciously reaches
to grab the chief's forearm. He simulates the throwing of a lance.
*There's your prey.*

The vile creature is low to the ground, familiar and deformed
at once. The Quadling term is perqu'unti, or some variant thereof.
Better known as a crocodrilos, or of the crocodrilos family. Croco-
dile in some vernaculars. But this a defective specimen. A thicket
of protuberances thrusts up from its spine, unlike anything ever
seen upon a crocodrilos. Biological bravado. Editorial objection to
the world, even before its nictitating eyelids can lift and its poxite
eyeballs focus. Its horny hide is mud green and mud brown, blis-
tered and battle-scarred.

The chief is agog. His associates grip their spears more tightly.
The kind of creature that could capably eat through several
Quadling canoes for supper. A mortal threat, and the worst one of
its sort ever spotted.

The animal has paused, too. About ten feet behind the child. As
if in Elphie's thrall, awaiting her word. It mutters, a glottal purr,
the grinding of broken glass. And it smells, it reeks of dried swamp
caught in its plates.

Not quite the puppy that follows a child home and begs to be
adopted. This creature looks as if expecting a command to kill.

And yet Elphie shows no sign of realizing that the crocodrilos
loiters behind her.

The beast snorts. Elphie has to have heard it. But maybe she
takes it for the sound of the universe groaning. Isn't *that* the fatu-

ous remark—what does she know of the universe at all, let alone of how it might express its opinions? Still, Elphie is a vigilant child. Maybe delayed in her development when it comes to speech, but attentive as a dog cocking its head to listen to something no human ear can pick up. So why doesn't she turn? Maybe the child is distracted by the mystery of her baby sister. Who knows.

The chief gives the sign. The men surrounding the missionary party fall back. They move beyond Elphie to encircle the deformed perqu'unti.

The old creature stares straight ahead. It has seen combat before breakfast more than once. The beast can move faster than they realize. But usually a display of might is all it takes. Its dorsal hedge becomes engorged, clacking as its thorns pitch and sway. The spears thrown by the Quadlings penetrate the thicket of appendages, but perqu'unti skin is tough as armor. The spearheads bounce off, while the spear-shafts get stuck. The chief barks at his band to stop wasting their weapons.

This old waterlogged hedgehog has been following Elphie placidly enough. It isn't snapping its jaws, nor does it advance when the child pauses. It has paused, too. Maybe it has its own take on the matter. So it smells bad and looks fierce. So it is a bizarre instance of its own kind. Does that justify judging it a mortal threat?

But perhaps the moment has been too keyed up for anything other than attack. Mob panic working out again.

A dumpy Quadling warrior, least physically fit of the lot, hurries past the missionary group to the cookfire, which Boozy hasn't yet extinguished. He lights the dry end of his canoe paddle. In no great hurry, he levels the torch into the beast's spineywork defense, locking the flame centrally, where the paddle can't be knocked off.

Only now does Elphie really clock on to what is going on. She whirls about and takes in the measure of the attack. She sees the lizardy creature. She shrieks, a little girl scream the world has known since before there were stars and sand. Perhaps not out of fright for her own safety, but as a message of warning.

Elphie's cry catches the creature's attention. It cocks its supple neck and opens its sedge-fringed mouth in outrage or surprise. Then the perqu'unti pivots with unnerving speed. A couple of Quadling mercenaries leap out of its way as it slithers toward the sandy verge in order to extinguish its burn in the river.

It doesn't make it in time. Its oily skin, even when wet, proves highly flammable. The crocodrilos contorts, the bottom half of a wheel, its thorny spokes meeting as if at a fiery hub. The flexing exposes its sensitive undercarriage, and two spears take advantage. Heart bleeds, spinal brush burns. Throat protests, a rent in the fabric of the morning. Its forelegs tremble, it reaches for the lip of the water only inches away.

The crocodrilos with the burden of a burning bush on its back. Just inches from the water that might have quenched the flames and preserved its share of moments. It has its ways, its slow-flickering mind, its woes. Whatever it perceives won't change what happens next. Still. Give it credit for noticing.

# 13

When its back compresses into a bow—driving its scorched spines against one another—one of its eyes lifts at a slant angle. It might be contemplating the heavens for the first time; a perqu'unti's attention is more often directed to the surface of a river than to the surface of the sky. But let's hypothesize that it has no more interest in heaven than the ordinary oyster or octopus.

Elphie is rapt. Alarm, or compassion, or cold clinical observation? No way of knowing. Still, she skitters forward in that marionette-twitch way she has. As if her limbs are being propelled and stilled simultaneously, by contradictory impulses.

Child and creature look at each other during the crocodrilos's last moment. Its limbs have stopped thrashing. The spears jabbed into its throat and heart have found their targets. Blood spurts and seeps through its abdominal wounds and its flared, gougey nostrils. It makes no noise.

It knows little of human beings except, up until now, how to avoid them. But it has spotted Elphie going about her morning campaign. Something has compelled it to follow her even, as it turns out, to its death.

Of the nature of that compulsion no sound thesis can be advanced. Why are we drawn one to another, whoever it is? The bee to the blossom, the lover to the bosom of another, the comet on its orbit around the sun and the seasons on their immortal tracks, ever approaching eternity? One creature will find another one. An intellect, a heart, a heavenly form, a capacity for charity, a look, an

attractive bouquet of organic odors. The perqu'unti, having happened upon Elphie, perhaps has seen something right in a world
that hasn't offered it evidence of rightness before.

Or maybe Elphie is broken enough, wicked enough, that the
perqu'unti has merely been suffused with fellow feeling, one rogue
for another.

That the child is green may only be incidental. Who knows if
the crocodrilos is color-blind?

Or maybe the only color perceivable is green, and Elphie is the
first human the perqu'unti has ever clearly seen.

It has died now. The Quadlings who killed it approach it with
tenderness and sorrow, still on alert in case it is shamming. But
it lies there, bleeding and smoking. They drag its carcass into the
water to extinguish the flames, then turn to the chief to see what
next.

# 14

The chief, this uncertain fellow, is undone by the execution of the creature, however monstrous it looked. He has a tenderness of heart belied by his killer musculature and expression. Sent, reluctantly, to slaughter a Munchkinlander missionary, he now finds he cannot. He had decided to abduct a child instead.

But the chief hasn't figured on the perqu'unti, a beast who features in some of the foundation myths of the Quadling nation. There's no love lost between perqu'untii and other natives sharing its habitat. A perqu'unti can rip the leg and buttocks off a wading citizen before the human can clear its throat. And the ugliness of this particular specimen, following along behind the frightful young girl! Why? Obeisance, appetite, sheer menace? Nothing is certain. It can't reveal its intentions now, either; already the chief's men are readying to knock back the spinal growths and slit the skin to get at the meat.

— Save the first portion for the mother of nations. (The chief, authoritative, referring to the clan matriarch.)
— What is he saying, why does he talk nonsense, they do it to annoy. (Nanny.)
— Shut up, and we may be clear of danger now. (Severin, sensibly.)
— I'll thank you to keep a civil tongue in your head, young man.
— Keep talking and you won't have any tongue in your own head.

Nanny purses her lips, and that is that.
The chief regards the green child once more. In light of this

transaction—the perqu'unti's life for a Quadling glassblower's life, as it were—he might backtrack on his decision to take a child. Compromise toward mercy. If so, would he lose stature in the eyes of his companions? By tomorrow's campaign someone else will be in charge, and he'll be a part of the squad. Who will even remember what he's said or not said?

If he abducts this child, in any case, what to do with it won't be his decision. Maybe some consensus will elect to rename the child *Turtle Heart* and raise it as a replacement for the murdered prophet. Or decide to take its life as compensation. Or maybe his people will return the child ten years later, with a souvenir pair of sandals fashioned from crocodrilos leather, a crown of water lilies on her brow. And a foreign tongue in her mouth and mind, a virus it will be impossible to shake.

Or maybe he'll be stuck with her. If he is forced to harbor her at home, his own boys and his sweet baby dumpling might begin to glow green, through contagion. Or a fatal affliction could bring down this lurid girl before she is ten, and his own children in the same frame of time.

The risk isn't to be tolerated.

He doesn't look at the child. He has the peculiar sensation that she might perceive his not kidnapping her as a slight. This child is already no stranger to rejection. He says:

— Leave the carcass. Let the birds and bugs and fish have it. An offering to the riverworld. Let the bones float away. Leave the thing, leave it. We are off. Spread out; find the other child if you can. In any case, we're not having this one. It is time to go.

The men back off, disguising their sense of relief. They don't want to touch the carcass. They abandon it where it is, a few feet into the water, rotating in the current until its head has swung around like the needle of a compass, hunting true north.

Nanny comes to her senses at last and opens her arms to Elphaba. The child pays no attention, but trains her eyes upon the crocodrilos. The eye that had caught Elphaba's is turned back to her now, staring blindly from the flood out of which it has first crawled. Elphie would wade in to touch its foreleg, its snout. But then: water: she can't.

# 15

The Quadling vigilantes lose interest in penning the missionary group. They begin to thrash the undergrowth with their spears, searching for the other child. Melena, dazed now beyond rationality, rushes forward. She drops to her knees in the marshgrass. She lifts the fallen Quadling bearer off the ground; so newly dead—this has been mere moments, all this—he is still limp and warm. His head falls back; he looks merely drunk; for a moment Melena has this rush of instinct to kiss him, as if in an old children's tale, and wake him up. But there is the odor of wound, attracting flies already feeding on the blood. She lays him back down, her eyes streaming for him. And this crying washes out her mind, somewhat, and she remembers herself.

Nanny has grabbed Elphie's hand and hauled her away from the edge of the water, not that there's any danger the child will splash in on purpose. Nanny's act is more a proof of her professional competence than anything else.

Boozy has gone back to packing up her kitchen, as if this has been an interesting diversion but lunch will still have to be served en route. Severin and Snapper dart away into the verges of the encampment. Melena realizes that they're looking to grab the baby first, to protect it. But rounding the corner of the tent, Melena finally sees that the hammock is empty and the baby is gone. While the invaders are dissolving into the greenery, some thrashing about, some recovering their canoes and making a noisy departure. The chieftain among them.

"Stop them, they've taken her!" bellows Melena, lunging toward the riverbank.

It's just now that Frex, finally, reappears, wading along the curve of the river from upstream, his clothes sodden, his hair streaming. He is followed by three water buffalo, two with curly horns and one with lateral lances, straight out on either side. They aren't following him as the perqu'unti followed Elphaba, but driving him.

"What the *hell* is going on here," he lashes out, as if everything were everyone else's fault but his. He stumbles ashore, his wet slippers in his hands.

"They've taken Nessa, they're going to kill her, stop the canoe—"

There's no stopping canoes that are launched thirty feet out from shore already, especially when you're cornered by water buffalo with lowered heads and fierce opinions. Though Frex flails with his hands as if dispersing mosquitoes, the heavy beasts only grunt. They aren't budging. They crowd Frex away from the water's edge and stand guard. Nearly falling over the corpse of the Quadling boy hidden in the marshgrass, Frex tumbles to his knees and his face contorts, and he mutters a prayer and throws up.

With Elphie in her armpit, Nanny hoists upon her own shoulders a sack of Nanny supplies—ointments, charms, a pack of cards, a romantic novel, strings and thread and Elphie's long-ignored dolly.

Severin and Snapper circle back to camp, calling that Nessa is nowhere. They've swung the empty hammock aside and kicked the grasses below, looking for her in the underbrush. She can't crawl away, they all know this already!—but they haven't seen anyone bundling her into a departing canoe, either.

When Frex can speak again, he berates them all for not defending themselves better, for failing to protect the poor murdered

Quadling bearer. "Where is the shield of Holy Faith, loaned me by the unionist bishop in Old Pastoria?" he demands to know. "Why didn't you get the gun and turn it on them?"

"Guns aren't for shooting, they're for brandishing," snaps Nanny, "and in any case for you to brandish, not Nanny. Where were *you* when trouble ran aground here?"

The story doesn't come out in its entirety right away, but they'll learn eventually that Frex had gone to a private spot downstream for his morning rinse and cleanse. In a moment of naked vulnerability he'd been startled by the water buffalo stalking the verge, who formed a ring and stood around him in the water, with their horns nearly touching. He'd been as penned waterside as his family and his entourage had been on the shore. When he tried to bully his way out of the ambush, the creature with the sharpest horns turned its head sidewise, as if ready to impale him. He'd never known water buffalo to be anything but docile, let alone to work in tandem hostility like this. They held him for half an hour while the morning gnats fed on his ears and his bum and his privates. The indignities suffered by men persuaded into missionary work! Surely these mammoth sentries had been corralled by the Quadling attackers. Hexed into service. Though at a certain moment the beasts slackened their guard, allowing him to scramble for his clothes. Then they bullied him back into the shallows as they ushered him to camp.

And they stand here still as he tries to grasp what has happened. He counts the party—everyone is present but the poor blighted Nessarose and the dead bearer, whose name they now remember is something like Sicapari. Scapari?

"We'll follow them and get her back," he promises, though he knows he may be lying. It is what needs to be said. Maybe this is Nessarose's path in life, after all. He isn't a prophet, just an agent of mystery in his faith, and this is mystery at its finest: the future of a child.

"They don't have the baby," insists Severin. "We'd have known it; she'd have been screaming." He continues blandly, "But in any case, we can't all follow them; they'd have to do us all in. I'll steal to their village tonight and sneak around, finding out if somehow they spirited her off without our noticing. And what they intend with her. The rest of you should head upstream. Boozy, collapse your tent; we have to hurry. Snapper, the canoes—have they been sunk, or stolen?" The canoes having been tied up in a cattail-choked inlet upstream, the marauders may not have noticed them. Snapper goes to check.

It's the dark-toothed Snapper who finds the baby's corpse. He doesn't lift it from its resting place, but comes back first to tell the family. They leave their baggage where it is and follow Snapper along the verge of the riverway. The water buffalo trudge behind, swaying like mourners at a state funeral. They might as well have thuribles swinging from their horns, such pomp and gravitas.

Here they all come, humans and creatures, through the tall scratchy marshgrass, sandstone and pale lilac, flecked through with butterflies and dragonflies. The sun having conquered the mist at last, the truth of the world is ready to stare them in the face.

They are all splashing except Nanny and Elphie, who keep to the drier patches. Elphie is reluctant and dragging her heels, contrary as usual. But she is still a child and Nanny is dragging her along. Nanny is not going to miss the saddest moment in the life of a family. Eventually Nanny may have to report this whole tragedy to the Eminent Thropp and Lady Partra. Such a frightful catastrophe, the death of Melena's second daughter; Nanny will need to witness the evidence. Anyway, it wasn't Nanny's fault. Will she be sacked for this? She can get a post with the Beckenhams over toward Center Munch if necessary. They're always popping out babies, that lot. Though Beckenham society is not as high as that of the Thropps, and a position in a Beckenham household would be seen as a comedown. Nanny straightens her shoulders and prepares for, well, whatever.

But the baby, there it is—it isn't even dead. How bizarre! Melena splashes forward and swoops upon it, lifting it from the burnished cradle to which it has been secreted. The pacifier plugging her mouth has delayed the inevitable wailing. Nessa now coos and shoots bright eyes about her, and tries without success to kick her little feet in their bunting.

Who dropped her in the shield and set it to float among the cattails? It must have been a tender-hearted Quadling who couldn't bear to see his fellow ambushers do it harm. But how had he gotten the shield? Was the assault upon the camp so overwhelming that nobody among them had noticed the shield being taken from where it had been laid in the sun that morning, the polish upon it to dry? Back before anyone knew this would become Encounter Day?

Then someone remembers having heard it fall on the ground, resoundingly, and that Elphie had been trying to see if she could lift it, if she could roll it like a hoop.

"Nonsense," says Frex. "She couldn't have foreseen the danger to Nessarose, and set her adrift to hide her from her abductors. Elphie can hardly put her arms through her own sleeves yet." They look at Elphie, who glares back at them, unrepentant, imperturbable.

"Who else," says Melena, "and does it matter now? We're safe. We're whole. We have Nessa. We can go."

They return to camp with the baby in their arms, the bronze

shield across Snapper's back. Nanny follows last, her hand stolidly clamped in Elphie's whether Elphie wants it or not.

The water buffalo must have spooked the war party, for those still left are rushing away. The massive bovines nudge the body of the fallen Quadling boy into the river, allowing it to float to its rest. As if following instructions, the creatures then wade out to where the perqu'unti has drifted and they slowly nose its remains back to the shore. Elphie picks up Boozy's ladle where it dropped. She pokes the perqu'unti's snout with it, helping to snag the creature and pull it forward.

"She wants to take it with her," says Snapper.

"She doesn't want a doll any more than she wants a baby sister," says Nanny, who gets Elphie better than her parents do. "No, she prefers the *corpse of a crocodrilos*. I worry about that one. I really do."

"We'll leave it for creatures to clean, and if the bones are here when we come back this way," says Frex to his brave and selfless daughter, "we'll collect them for you." Nothing of the sort will ever happen of course, he thinks, but a little lying to calm a fractious child is acceptable, and anyway, it's how children learn what lying is all about.

The morning rolls toward noon, and the encampment has been abandoned. The water buffalo stray off and are never seen again. The Quadling boy, looking baggy and relaxed, drifts downstream, soon out of sight. The canoes are snug enough, and the local guides and bearers, turning upstream, ply their paddles with nearly noiseless precision. As the temperature rises, sweat rolls down Melena's aired bosom. Frex's brow furrows at yet another failed attempt to establish a more permanent mission. Nessa babbles in relief at being rescued from her exile. Elphie glowers.

Someone in the party knows what has happened here, but there are many questions. Who, if indeed anyone did, had spoken to the

water buffalo and given them their standing orders? Why did Elphie return to camp, return from wherever she'd gone missing,
with a crocodrilos trailing her? The intensity of Elphie's interest in
the creature, its sacrificial slaughter having righted some imbal-
ance and saved herself and her family—could she have arranged
this somehow? She is only four, after all.

It makes for ridiculous conjecture. Maybe only Elphie considers
the sum and minus of the exchange, unintended but no less accurate: a life for a life. How could she see that, a crocodrilos's life for
her own, or that of her sister? When she hardly can say her own
name yet? A perqu'unti's heart is not a turtle heart. But still.

Of course she can't put any of this into words. Of course she
can't think like this. No one is even sure if she can think at all.
And no child at the age of four is capable of working out a moral
equation about wrong and right. Right? Right?

# PASSIM

The truth is, she won't remember much about that day, but the brined crocodrilos has to have come from somewhere, and it has been with her for the duration, and will be hanging from the rafters of her witch's aerie in Kiamo Ko on the day she evaporates from her own history. She will think of herself as having adored Nessarose and cared for her sister always. She will mourn Nessa's death without recognizing that guilt is part of the chemical composition of grief.

✦ ✦ ✦

It's raining now on the black water and on the green and brown lily pads. The surface of the water puckers, the sound rises all around, as noisy on the river as on the succulents that overhang both banks. If you're growing up in the wettest part of the world, by the time you're eight or nine you've heard this noise three thousand times already. It rains every day in this part of the world, at least a little. Sometimes more.

Elphie recoils even when a few drops splash off a sloppily handled canoe paddle. But her family works out accommodations for her. Alone of the mission party, Elphie wears boots rather than sandals. Nanny has rooted in the chest of Melena's castoff clothes and she has repurposed leggings for all four of Elphie's scrawny green limbs, cutting holes in the toes of stockings for fingerless gloving. Elphie lives under a shallow rattan hat, broad enough to guide rainwater off its eaves.

There's also her famous jungle bumbershoot, which gives young Elphie the air of a junior botanist in the field.

She gets by. Managing her own needs around the weather becomes second nature. It won't need to be mentioned again, but it's a condition of hers as real as her preternatural skin tone.

The lily pads circle and float on, in the rain. Some memories disappear around the bend and die while others link arms and make moments into episodes so firm it feels you could walk across the water, walk upon them across time itself.

PART TWO

# THE HEX

# 16

The sisters have survived; they grow; they grow apart.

"All sisters hate each other before they come around," says Nanny, with a bland lack of conviction, since she has no sisters, and is grateful for it.

Nessa's neediness siphons off attention previously paid to Elphie. In time, Elphie comes to realize a debt of gratitude—a gratitude she resents having to observe. But observe it she does, as Nessa turns into more of a person and less a scrap of accident.

The younger sister can't stand on her own feet because her balance is imperfect. That's the assumption, anyway. She's come into the world a defenseless babe—armless, in fact. (Nanny has tried tickling at the ends of the baby's shoulder blades, hoping she might tease the limbs into a late sprouting.)

Some back in Munchkinland, thanks to the gossip of attendant midwives, have fatalistically considered Nessa's deformity a collateral cost of the relief from the seven-year drought. A cost piled onto that shabby murder in the forecourt, that is: a top-up, a deal clincher. The drought is over, after all.

This second great-grandchild of the Eminence. Nessarose Thropp, was born at Colwen Grounds. No hiding her handicap, if that's not too cruel a word to use for her particular affliction. And as Frex is a self-important minister with presumed ties to the Unnamed God, this makes the punishment meted out upon his second daughter more pointed. More poignant. (More delicious— though the poor child!)

Nessa could eventually become the Eminent Thropp, were her

sister Elphaba to die first or abdicate the title. If so, Nessa's limitations would be on permanent display. *Two* children born with ir-
regularities! (Yes, word about Elphie has finally gotten out.) Could
Melena Thropp do *nothing* right in the birthing tent? If Melena as
the Thropp Second Descending tries one more time, and comes up
with an unblemished child, perhaps both of her older children can
quietly disappear from the line of succession, and from history,
and a third and more perfect candidate be designated to carry the
standard. Such a break from protocol has never been advanced,
but come on—a green Eminence? Or an Eminence without a
full complement of limbs? A little thinking outside the box here,
people. Third time's the charm. If only Melena is still fertile, can
carry another baby to term.

So Melena sets herself to the task, but her body is having none
of it.

Elphie is spared knowledge of her mother's failed pregnancies,
and of the parade of miscarriages. Weird poppet though she is,
Elphie is as myopic as any other kid. She doesn't grasp how her
parents are subsiding ever more deeply into Quadling Country
as she grows. The child knows little of life but tents and stakes,
cots and sleeping rolls, kitchen pots and sacks of rice, trunks of
tattered leather in which the family has hauled scraps of their past
and out of which they dress. Life is vitality, instability, curiosity.
Home is portable. Personnel come and go. Elphie doesn't remember
how and when and why Snapper disappears, or Severin. Boozy,
of all of them, proves the most reliable, or at any rate when the
cook skives off it is seldom for more than a few weeks. She always
returns before the family's temporary posting is nearing its end.
One year she comes back pregnant herself, but loses it. She says
she coughed the unviable baby up through her throat in the middle of the night. "That one is hexed," she says, pointing at Elphie.

"It's her fault." By now Boozy has learned enough of the common speech to be offensive. Nanny opines that Boozy points fingers where they hadn't ought be pointed. And she'll pay for it.

"What's hexed?" asks Elphaba, when Boozy has sauntered away.

"Touched with a little power of magic," says Nanny blandly.

"Don't put ideas in her head," says Melena.

"You thought so, too, when she was born," Nanny reminds Melena.

"Is Nessarose hexed?" asks Elphie, but as the subject is deemed improper, nobody will answer her. So Elphie decides that Nessa must be hexed, too. That night in the tent, or soon thereafter anyway—she may be about seven, and Nessa five—Elphie raises the matter solemnly.

"I'm going to blow out the snail-oil lamp and tell you a secret," says the big sister.

"A good one?"

"You can decide. It's about hexes."

"Don't like no hexes."

"You don't even know what they are."

"They bite."

Elphie thinks: Maybe Nessa is right about that. Then she says, "No, you're thinking about foxes. Hexes are little magicks, I think."

"Magic tricks?"

"Tricks for some. For others hexes are for *real*, not tricks."

"Hex hex hex." Nessa tries out the word. "Like what real tricks?" She is a skeptic.

"Like—" Elphie doesn't quite know what a hex is, either. She glances around. In the small basin of water sits a smooth black stone, which Boozy says absorbs enough of the water's sulfur smell that the little girls can bring themselves to sip if they are thirsty enough. (Another kind of magic?) Using a spoon, Elphie nudges out the thing, which when dried off, rolls in her palm, egg-shaped and opaque. "I'll hex this into a marsh plum for your breakfast." Elphie knows that Nessa is partial to marsh plums.

"You can't. Can you? Show me. Then show me how."

"I can't hex it in the *light*." Elphie puffs down the glass chimney of the oil lamp, extinguishing the flame. The swamp night is clouded and the darkness near total. She sets the stone down with a clunk upon the clothes trunk between them. "Abracanexus, abracahexus," she intones in a low voice, while her sister moans in fake terror.

"Did it work?" asks Nessa.

"It doesn't happen right away. It takes time. Like making a baby."

"How much time does it take to make a baby?"

"I don't know, but it's more than a minute."

"So when will you light the lamp and show me the marsh plum?"

"It has to wait till morning. Go to sleep."

"Will it be a green one?"

"Yes," said Elphie, and then, "and it won't have little arms, either."

Nessa works this out and concludes happily: "So it'll be like both of us."

"Shut up and close your eyes." Elphie lies down in her own cot. Usually Nessa drifts into sleep quickly. Tonight when she drops off, Elphie plans to get up and steal to the larder box and pinch a marsh plum from Boozy's supplies. She'll replace the stone with a plum. Nessa will think her big sister can do magicks. Elphie isn't sure what use she can make of such a truth swindle, but something will occur to her. The leverage is bound to come in handy.

Restless Nessa keeps muttering, "Is it morning yet?" While Elphie waits for her sister to nod off, she falls asleep herself. "Elphie,

Elphie," says Nessa, who today wakes up earlier, "it's morning, look and see!"

"Fiddleferns," says Elphie, the only swear word tolerated by the grown-ups. She rubs her eyes and begins to scrabble about in her mind for a plausible lie to explain why the stone is still a stone.

Only she doesn't need any such alibi. On the chest sits a small lumpy marsh plum with a leaf still attached to the stem. Almost too perfect to be true, like a painting of a plum. Like the most perfect idea of a plum that anyone who ever thought of such a thing could come up with. Every other plum in history anticipates this ideal specimen, every future marsh plum deviates from it.

"You're so good at hexing," whispers Nessa.

"I know that," says Elphie, afraid to get too close, afraid to touch it. But it just sits there, smelling faintly of its plummy life. She eventually kicks her legs off her cot and leans forward and touches it. She isn't sure about it. Maybe it's going to burn her, or explode. Or disappear. It does nothing, just rocks on its shadow a little and settles back. There's no black stone behind it. Nor has the stone magicked itself back into the water basin from where it has been plucked. It's just gone.

"What does it mean?" asks Nessa. "I mean, that you could do that?"

"It means I'm older than you."

"Can you teach me?"

"Teach you how to hex? No. It's just something you can *do*, if you can do it. Like whistle. Or walk." This is cruel of her to say, and she knows it.

"I can whistle," says Nessa, a short little lie. She can't do that yet, though maybe one day she'll grow into it. Will she ever develop enough strength in her back to walk on her own? "Put me in the cart and let's go tell Mama and Nanny and Father."

The cart is a wicker wheelbarrow that some Quadlings worked up for Nessarose a year or two back. She will outgrow it before long, but for now she is still small enough that Elphie can lift her from the cot and set her more or less in a sitting position. Pillows tucked on both sides of Nessa ensure that she won't fall over. Elphie isn't strong enough to do slopes, either uphill or down. Sometimes she wonders what would happen if she lost control of the cart at the top of a slope. She imagines it pitching forward. But sooner or later the back legs would settle onto the ground and the front wheel jolt to a stop, and the vehicle would park itself. Perhaps rather suddenly. Then there would be a terrific spill-out. But nothing worse than that.

"Bring the magic marsh plum," says Nessa. "We have to show everybody."

"They won't like it," says Elphie. "They don't like hexes. All lies and trickery."

"Then hold it up for me so I can take a bite."

Not sure exactly what kind of charm she might be administering to her sister, but curious about the effects, Elphie does as she is told. What if this magicked marsh plum grows Nessarose some arms at last? Good thing or bad news?

The juice runs down Nessa's chin, and Elphie wipes Nessa's face dry with the edge of her blanket. "How does it taste?"

"You try it, too."

But Elphie doesn't dare. "Don't say anything to them."

"Why not?"

Elphie pouts, but she is behind Nessa, at the handles of the cart, and realizes Nessa can't see her. "Father is a minister. That means he thinks magicks are bad."

Nessa screws her face up in concentration. "It's a good *plum*. You're a good cook."

"Thank you. But shut up about it."

Elphie has yet to work out when being bossy to Nessa is counterproductive. Nessa can get all stroppy and turncoat. But the younger child promises to hold her tongue about the matter, at least in front of Melena and Frex. There they are, in front of the marital tent. Melena stands with both palms flattened netherward upon her hips. Her stomach pushes out in front. On his campstool, Frex hunches with his pipe and his scholar's tracts, making notes in the margins. Boozy is gently scorching a breakfast porridge over the fire.

"Oh, look at the big sister being such a good big sister," says Nanny, threateningly, since she can read the temptation to overturn Nessa in Elphie's eyes.

"We got hexed," says Nessa brightly, not for the first time ignoring Elphie's counsel. "I got hexed."

"You and me both," says Melena.

"Oh, Mellie-belly," says Frex. "You know I don't like that kind of talk."

"And you know I don't like that nickname, especially when I'm in a condition. So guard your tongue better or I'll order up a hex designed especially for you."

Nessa tries again. "Elphie turned a stone into a plum."

"Now hush, you child, none of your nonsense." Nanny hurries in to salvage the moment, but Frex lifts his chin from his right fist and swivels his head.

"What are you prattling about, Nessa?"

She's started, she can't stop; it is hard for Nessa to get any attention other than food, medicine, or hygienic care. She takes her moment. "Elphie said that hexes are real and she knows how to hexy-hex something and she did it. She turned the water-stone into a marsh plum."

"She couldn't possibly." Frex's voice comes out less assured than he has intended to sound. "You're playing a game, or she's playing a game on you. Elphaba, admit to your sister you were lying. Tell her you're sorry. The truth is hard enough to come by in this life, and that's why we need ministers. Fooling around with make-believes is unkind. It's a cheat. And it can be, well, a little dangerous."

"I don't fool around," growls Elphie, looking at the ground.

"She gave me some of it, the magic plum. A bite. It was good."

Frex looks at his oldest daughter. "Are you teaching your sister to be tricksy? She's going to need sobriety and clarity in this life, Elphaba, not deceptions."

"She did it herself," says Elphie. "I thought up the idea but I think she wanted it so much that she made the hex happen."

"I did not!" cries Nessa. Still, a hint of happiness threads through her outrage. What if she did? The powerless have nothing but hope.

"Really, deal with all this, Nanny, earn your keep," says Melena. "But first, unlace my morning shoes. I can't bend down at this point, and they're choking my feet. I'm every inch a balloon. Even my hair feels tight on my head."

It falls to Boozy to wheel Nessa away, Elphie scuffing in the sandy grit of the clearing behind them. They settle far enough beyond that their voices won't carry. They talk in that patois of Qua'ati and Ozish particular to the family camp.

Boozy is the one who first mentioned hexes, so she's the right one to grill. Elphie reminds the cook that she said Elphie was hexed. What did she really mean? What does magicking a marsh plum out of a stone have to do with anything?

At first Boozy is reluctant to discuss the subject. She hums and mutters and allows that the way this family talks about stuff, as if everything is in a tin box of its own meaning and doesn't touch anything else or ever change, so weird and bizarre, she can't work with that. If Boozy says something in the morning and she says it again at sunset, it doesn't *have* to mean the same thing and she can't *make* it mean the same thing and sometimes she can't tell what it means anyway.

"So what are you saying," says Elphie, who still thinks concretely, in objects, not notions, "that nothing is"—she hunts for a word to mean *stable* but it isn't immediate to her—"that nothing is fixed?"

"Water come to ice, come to air, leave the pot on a hot morning and come down again on a rainy afternoon. It always moving even when it look stopped and still. That what hex is."

"So why did you say I was hexed?" asks Elphie.

"Why I say it yesterday and why I say it today, could be two different things," explains Boozy. "That the whole idea. Things change. You change."

"So do I," says Nessa, "so do you. Sometimes you wear that black skirt, sometimes the ugly stripey one."

"You don't change like your sister do. She the sly one. Green little girl on the outside, who know what on the inside. Maybe she a piece of green moon fell on the ground. You," says Boozy to Nessa, "you got the took-away arms that you can't see. She has the added something that you can't see. I don't know what it is because I can't see it either. But it's there. She hexed. She raw. It not a good thing it not a bad thing. Don't fret about it. Tomorrow if you ask me again I say something else, and it will be just as true. Or just as wrong. But I know one thing. I'm not hexed. I'm just me, as Boozy as Boozy can be, and no more. And never will be more."

She reaches in her apron pocket. "While we're waiting for them to settle down and call for their breakfast, you want a marsh plum to keep your stomach calm?" She pulls out a sour-looking fruit, nothing like the magnificent item that has appeared on the trunk in the girls' tent.

Elphie thinks: Maybe Boozy was pacing around outside the tent and heard me talking, and made a switch of the plum and the stone just to trick us. Have some fun.

When she goes back to the girls' tent, the magicked perfect marsh plum is gone. She doesn't remember what she did with it after holding it for Nessa to take a bite. Had she tossed it on the ground, or out the tent flap? She looks into the bowl of evening water. The black stone has returned. It sits unblinking and accusatory underneath the skin of water, as if it has never left its post to parade about as a marsh plum, on a sweet anonymous morning in the marsh country.

## 17

Nanny has an entirely opaque view of the subject. "There are too many breezes in the air to know why the seed of a tree falls and takes root here and not there," she said to Elphie. "Your father insists the Unnamed God has taken coordinates of every hillside known to geography, and has selected the precise spot for each germination. I am not so faithful. If someone sneaky pulls a trick, maybe a hex magicked the impulse into that sneaky someone." She pulls a face at Elphie. "I mind my p's and q's and I don't make blanket assertions like your father does. Praise Lurline for sensibility and sense."

This is too abstruse for Elphie. She is sharp, yes, and by now she's more verbal than her peers might be, if she were to have any; but she is only seven or eight years old. She makes wishes on falling stars still. She trusts the world that much.

# 18

As for how Nessarose thinks and feels, it's not as easy to guess as it is for some of the others in the mission. True, Nessa isn't locked into silence as a deaf-mute person might be. But something inscrutable wraps around her in a way it doesn't, quite, wrap around her sister. Elphie has interiority, to be sure, and this will swell inside her to the point of making her practically eligible for an asylum, but she will never be anything but entirely readable. Elphie will have little control over the way her unspoken opinions flash through her expressions, even her body language—the ways she walks, stomps, pushes, dashes off. Nessa, whose deformities are so apparent, inhabits her Nessarose-ness with the continence of porcelain. Smooth, no purchase.

Here she is at her weekly bath. Nanny and Boozy set her in the tin tub that doubles as a sink for soaking laundry. When balanced, Nessa can now squat upright. She closes her eyes as Boozy dribbles lukewarm water over her hair and shoulders. She doesn't mind being touched, perhaps because she can't touch herself, not with hands. Nanny uses an old sponge. A scent of vanilla in the water—vanilla is in rich supply here. Elphie is standing nearby, thinking—

— but this is Nessa's small moment. She closes her eyes. Where is she in there?

We can at least imagine what she is hearing. Birdsong, if you can call it birdsong. Not every utterance of a bird is melodic, or joyful. There are alarums, raking shrieks, coughs that stutter and finish in a falling tone, plangencies evoking regret or despair. The stands of reed conceal flocks who squabble, sex up, dispute territory, and try to ward off predators. A noisy operation, to live by water, both for fowl and for humans. Nessa has to have noticed such aural commotion. Is she ever tempted to shriek like the birds, yearning for liftoff? She who has no arms with which to swim may wish for wings. To get away, to get anywhere. The birds circle and gossip and settle. Nessa is among them, but is she of them—

But no, this is an experiment that isn't taking. Nessa is imperturbably confined in herself.

Elphie watches her, imagines the shawl of water cascading over the shoulders. For Elphie it is a nightmare. She can't look away though. Elphie's own ablutions are conducted by Nanny, too. For the older sister, the conscientious woman whisks up an unguent out of a few drops of palm oil and some gooey white froth she wrings from the inside of aloe leaves. She uses a stiff browned pod like a strigil to scrape the excess oil and dirt off Elphie's skin. It leaves the girl feeling scoured, but in a good way. Her hair gets shampooed in oil and egg white. Comes out glossy and smelling a little like lunch. But it is clean. Messy, but clean. Nessa's hair, however, is rinsed in water. In revulsion, Elphie shudders, and so does Nessa, but in another kind of mood—an appreciation of sensuality. "Enough," says Nessa, when she can't take another frisson of trickle. Then Nanny pulls out the softest of cloths from the famous trunk with which Melena eloped, and Nanny towels Nessa dry, up and down.

Here Elphie does look away. As she doesn't personally like people to touch her, she doesn't get a sisterly pleasure out of seeing Nessa lean back into the flannel with such abandon.

# 19

It's about this time that Elphie has a run-in with a poltergeist. How old is she, exactly? Counting birthdays in Oz is not an exact science. But the girl has reached the age when chronology starts to grip its teeth. Undisciplined memories begin to line up. Elphie starts to suss out the notion of cause and effect, the relativity of events. The infant Ozma, for instance, didn't disappear until the so-called Wizard of Oz arrived; otherwise he'd have had no one to overturn. First this, then that. The encounter at the riverbank happened when Nessa was small enough to be floated in an overturned warrior shield, not when she was big enough for Elphie to run her around in that wicker barrow.

If there was ever an actual poltergeist, it will remain in dispute. Nanny will insist she never saw hide nor hair of any interloper on the premises of the camp proper, and she and Boozy are the ones who paid attention.

There's a night guard, too, a scrap-haired local named Ti'imit. He patrols the camp and stokes the fire—it's the time of year when jungle cats pass through in migratory stealth from somewhere to otherwhere. Their presence quietens the jungle. Even the leaves and spiderwebs are on alert, or so it seems to Elphie. Things are beginning to *seem* to her. She isn't sure how real such impressions are. But she notes them with a kind of pleasure, in that they help her feel distinct from the others. Nanny says, "Imagining such fancies, and from the likes of *you*, Elphie? Some foggy figment there when it patently is not? Get along with you, I thank Lurline that I have no taste or talent for such a pudding of nonsense." On the other hand, Boozy nods affably at any outlandish assertion of Elphie's, contradicting nothing—it isn't worth the effort. Elphie's parents, throughout, remain distracted.

Poltergeist or not, someone is squirreling around on the edge of the family's long labored days, and only Elphie seems to notice.

First of all, things go missing. Nanny's needles and threads. Who could want that small wicker hand-basket? Nessa is always in the clear, of course, because she can't make off with anything. And Boozy is a woman of few personal items, the fewer the better. (Less to pack up when camp-breaking comes around again.) Can't be Melena—Melena doesn't know the business end of a needle from the Seven Lofty Sayings of the Bishop of Wend Hardings—which she also doesn't know. And Frex, bless his clumsy fingers, can darn his own socks and reattach a button, but as to thievery, he is guilty only of stealing his bride from her family estate, as some would tell it. The smaller the infraction, the more publicly Frex detests it. He won't even pick a wodge of clumpy rice from someone's dinner plate without leave.

So when Boozy's bamboo pincers disappear overnight, suspicion naturally falls upon Elphie. "She hexed 'em to the *moon*," says Nessa promptly, with curious conviction. Her slightly lisping delivery is suspected of being put on.

"What did I tell you about hexing?" Nanny scolds.

"*She* hexed them," says Elphie hotly, pointing at Nessa. "After all, isn't that what she wants—a way to pinch things? She's in sore need of a grasp."

In sore need, a Nanny phrase if ever there was one, and Nanny catches it. "Don't go putting on Nanny airs, you're too highborn and weird for that," she says. "If ever a false accusation was made to throw the constabulary off the scent, that sounds like one, Elphie. You ought to be ashamed of yourself."

"Maybe I ought to but I'm not." But Elphie is bewildered. The pincers are required to turn over marrow-bean shoots sizzling in the skillet. Boozy threatens to quit unless the implement is returned.

"As long as we're making claims against each other, Nanny, maybe *you* took them," says Elphie.

"I am above kitchen," says Nanny. "I sniffed at larder, snarled at laundry, I sailed past kitchen. I trained for parlor. If I only made it to nursery, more's the pity, but I still eat with the family."

Boozy snaps, "You eat no fried marrow-bean thingies till my pincers walk right back here. Or I quit. I quit good and hard, and when I'm ready, I quit for good. And for hard."

"That'll be the day," says Nanny to the cook. "You wouldn't leave her ladyship, not now, not in the state she's in. You don't have the moxie for it. And, I admit it, also you're too kind." She forces a wintry smile.

"I find my pincers and I clamp your scheming lying lips closed like they belong," says Boozy, "and then I sew them up with your needle and threadlings if they turn up again, too. Enough of you and your airs! And I don't *train* for kitchen, like the stupid girls you grow up next to. Kitchen is in my blood and it comes to me natural. Like hexing comes to her," she finishes, pointing the soup ladle at Elphie.

"Why is this always about me?" Elphie feels angry and also a little proud at being thought that capable.

But it isn't her, is it, doing the thieving. *Is* it? Might she be stealing things—in her sleep? Where would she put them? Why would she bother? To be noticed? Sure, Nessarose gets all the attention available, and always will—always will have to—but in most ways this suits Elphie just fine. She doesn't crave centrality, she prefers to skulk and slide. Elphie is coming to realize the only place in this world where she might be invisible would be naked and lost in the jungle, where her natural coloring would be protective. An asset for once.

But independence is nearly as good. She tries to button herself at the collarbone in an invisible cloak of stealth. She doesn't yet know that she has the kind of face that advertises her marketplace emotions, those sentiments legible from half a mile away. She isn't sure she even has emotions. She hardly ever cries, for instance. She's a secret unto herself. While this is bewildering, it's also a relief. If she doesn't understand who she is, she can't be blamed for stepping outside of her own bounds.

But this is true of all children, she will think later in life, when she comes to know a few children in Kiamo Ko, and rather detests them. That she can remember being flummoxed during her own childhood won't make her any more sympathetic to those still enmired there. Why don't they just grow up and get it over with already?

The pincers; the sewing basket. The matter of the hexed marsh plum. One morning the missionary party rouses itself to find that the old ceremonial shield upon which Elphie once tried to float her baby sister into the next world is overturned on the grass. Its slightly convex basin is piled high with a heap of maggoty bananas. "Why would I bother myself with rotting fruit?" shouts Elphie, as much to herself as to the others, before they have time to begin to blame her.

She stomps toward Ti'imit, who has concluded his night watch and is lolling in an over-easy way upon the blanket Boozy has set out for him. "You must have seen something, if you're up all night being the night watchman. Or do you snore your head off as soon as the rest of us go to bed?"

"Sleep is a demanding lady of the night, when she call I answer. I sleep with sleep," he answers, "she my bad habit. But the fire is here in the morning, and so are all of you. That's my job every night; to see you safe into tomorrow. So leave me in peace. And toss away those bananas, they are calling every pest in the neighborhood. You want answers, ask the next monkey you meet what a banana is for."

For once she does what she is told—jettisoning the rotten fruit—but not because she is told it. The bananas are an affront to her, somehow, a challenge. First a perfect marsh plum, then a heap of aging bananas. What next? The deliquescing corpse of a gigantic muskmelon?

Elphie decides to become a detective. She teaches her eyes to sidle sideways while her head is pointed front and center. She will catch whatever pair of hands is about to pilfer the next useless item. She stands stone-still to scan the campsite. A bird actually lands on her shoulder once and—magnificently—she manages not to flinch. The bird takes her as a limb of nature, nothing more or less. She doesn't know what kind of a bird it is, but realizes that it is more itself than any of the rest of them can be. Ever.

This is devastating to her and also exhilarating.

She decides to try an experiment. She takes the dolly from the place where Nanny tucks it into Nessa's cot, whose high edges are shaped to keep the younger girl from rolling out, since she thrashes in her sleep. The dolly is an old abandoned thing of Elphie's. She's always hated it, that cursed poppet. A gift of Nanny from Colwen Grounds. Maybe it had been Melena's. It once boasted of silly yellow locks made of wood shavings, but long ago Elphie pulled all the hair out. The creature is now bald and nearly featureless, its smug painted smile worn off with abuse. It has become Nessa's toy, her only toy, but of course the younger girl can't play with it, unless you count kicking a doll something of a game. The figure is as immobile as Nessa herself. They deserve each other, Elphie had thought when she finished hating it enough to pass it down to Nessa.

"Where you taking Ninnakins?" asks Nessa from the threshold of sleep.

"I'm putting her outside the tent to keep watch. You heard about those bananas. Some kind of joke, some kind of insult, I don't know what. Ninnakins can watch out for us."

"She can't tell us nothing, she don't talk," says Nessa.

"Yet," says Elphie, and then, more slyly, "perhaps one of us will hex her into a confession. Something is going on here. Maybe she'll open that clamped smile and say something useful. Like: *Nessa is the one behind these thefts.*"

"Need her here," says Nessa, but mawkishly; she doesn't care much for Ninnakins either. It's just the ritual of her.

"She'll make a great night guardian. *Somebody* has to pay attention, Ti'imit just snores the night away. The big cats probably come and dance around the campfire to make fun of him. If Ti'imit is too groggy to notice who is playing these tricks, maybe Ninnakins will."

Elphie hopes Ninnakins will be the next item to disappear. Nessa won't be *very* sorrowful, but she might cry a little, and that would be worth it.

Ninnakins is propped up on a cushion of stacked palmetto leaves. Her blond-wood face gleams in the fire's glow. Tired, unappealing, ripe for abduction. In the morning, however, she remains as alone and unmolested as before. Her expression is unchanged, as if this is what she has expected all along. A doll's life is exhausting.

"Well?" asks Nessa, and Elphie throws the doll into Nessa's cot, hitting her sister in the face. Nessa wails. "Oops," says Elphie.

Ninnakins and Nessa kiss each other's ouchies away as Nanny comes hobbling from her own tent next door to brook some pretense of peace between the sisters for the nine dozenth thousandth time since the marshlands first flooded with Lurline's tears.

# 20

As Elphie begins to command the world about her (even if that world doesn't obey, now or ever), the private lives of her family grow more obscure to her. Once what her mother thought or felt, or her father, might have seemed like an extension of Elphie's own inner state. But now most conditions of mutuality are severed. We become less porous, less fungible as we claim our own agency.

The girl doesn't articulate such things yet, even to herself. But she's beginning to consolidate some Elphie-ness into an eventual Elphaba. When she grows old enough to reflect on this period, she finds her parents distant, inscrutable.

A comfort, in some ways, this independence; but it sets the seal of loneliness upon her, too.

In time Elphie will build upon the clues of her memory to construct her theoretical parents—what they must have been like at this time, given available evidence.

So: Frex. At her age Elphie isn't able to identify the notions either of benign neglect or of loving affection. Her father's existence is beyond comment: it's the invisible aspic, the unacknowledged oxygen of her life. Yet she's in awe of her father's determination. On his own intuition Frex leads the family from post to post, from marsh to swamp to the occasional trading post on a hump of higher land. (At this point he's still rather hapless as a proselytizer.)

Elphie will later wonder how her father heard his marching orders. He never explains it to Elphie, and she never thinks to ask until he is gone. Gone to the Unnamed God, or to some hitherto unannounced destination.

Her father no longer runs to fat. Years of the Quadling diet (and, yes, deprivation) have trimmed him. His beard has settled into a nest of widely set coils. Each curl distinct, as if carven. His face seems burled. He's not a bad-looking man, though few children manage to apply any rubric of aesthetics to their own parents. He isn't yet at the height of his confidence—that much Elphie can guess, and she is right. If once long ago, looking over the shoulder of his wife, he'd felt a stirring of tendresse for Turtle Heart, that hasn't recurred. Frex may have decided that such an inconvenient affliction was part of the deity's subtle strategy to turn the minister's attention to the mucklands. To nudge Frex toward the conversion and consolation of the less fortunate, these misbegotten damp people. The damplings. About whose peril the hapless Turtle Heart has been first herald and finally martyr.

Year in and year out, the Quadlings fail to grasp the rationale behind Frex's mission. They've never invited him to convert them in the first place. But then, they're by nature a polite people.

It seems unchanging, the exercise of his calling. He reads and rereads the texts of the unionist fathers. He sermonizes and delivers advice, asked for or no. He smells like citrus peel and beeswax. He stalks about with presence, being one of those Munchkinlanders more ponderosa than dwarf pine. He isn't an exhibitionist like his wife, so Elphie doesn't learn from him how the male animal in the human species is kitted out with its master-joke of exposed plumbing. Indeed, Frex is reticent. He wears a frayed white shirt buttoned to the neck except when retiring to his tent. (He and Melena have twin tents, usually pitched adjacent unless Melena is feeling monthly, when her tent is relocated farther away.)

He's a good person, or good enough. Maybe he isn't good at

being an evangelist, though. Maybe his converts sign on more quickly to placate him, or to convince him that his work among them has been so effective that he really ought to move on to riper pickings, a readier heathenage. Shall we help you pack?

A single instance of his ministry, for what it's worth. A few Quadlings are approaching from a backwash loop of the river system. Upon a blanket between them they carry an older boy, maybe fifteen, whose limbs are wrecked with rickets or something. He looks as if he was sat upon at birth. His forehead is protuberant and his narrow chin ducks inward toward the gullet. He gibbers. What can Frexispar Togue Thropp, Frex the Godly, do for this unfortunate creature? Elphie remembers this bit, because from early on she is vexed by not knowing how much change is even possible in this world. If Frex can untangle this child, why can't he petition his boss, the Unnamed God, to heal Frex's own Nessa? Elphie inches closer. This family grouping is so intent on the suffering of their kin-child that they pay no heed to the green girl. Help us, they say to Frex. We beg you, we pray you, we trust you. Tell us what to do.

Frex chants his chants and rants his rants. The family hangs back, wary and hopeful. The boy moans and shuffles his torqued shins. His hands are bent inward like paw of a dog who has been taught to shake. His eyes don't focus on the company of the mission.

The language is Qua'ati. Elphie is conversant enough now to recognize most of the vocabulary, though not always the inferences. Frex is by turns cajoling and hectoring. He isn't applying his attention to the sore needs of the boy, however, but to the people who have thought to carry their invalid forward. If Elphie had been able to put it into words, she might have said that her father didn't exert himself to cure the invalid, the way a magical physician might, but rather he admonished the family for failing to see the beauty in their broken child. A swan on the water—she remembers this part, maybe the single most memorable statement her father ever speaks in her presence—a hobbled swan on the water may be unable to wheel aloft with her sisters. But she is no less beautiful, and she is doubled by her reflection in a way she can never be doubled in the air.

The small party weeps and shuffles, and probably pays for the privilege of being dismissed. They pick up their ailing relative and haul him away. But here's the thing. They seem genuinely grateful. Consoled. A change has been worked upon them.

Is that a kind of magic, thinks Elphie.

And if so, what good is it? To the crippled boy, anyway?

But maybe it is good, if his people love him more unrestrainedly.

Ah, but there's that thing, love, the secretest charm.

The whole mission camp has been watching. After the family has left, bearing the stretcher, Ti'imit and Boozy are wiping their eyes. Nanny coos some outmoded hymn to Lurline, that ancient goddess whose influence has been eclipsed by the rise of unionism except, as Nanny puts it, among the *truly* faithful. Whenever Frex goes whole-hog into ministerial mode, Nanny publicly appeals to a more maternal divinity. To annoy him, or perhaps to suggest to supplicants that this mission affords a full range of services. Frex tolerates this, mostly. He can't do without Nanny. She's always on the lip of packing it in and going back to civilization where a body can get a proper cup of tea with cow's milk and a bit of a chin-wag. She puts up with Frex, and he puts up with her. But it's a fragile contract.

Nanny will be with Elphaba her whole life, in and out. Of course, neither of them know this yet. The governess will become set in her ways, a threadbare grab bag of rural wives' wit, stale bromides, and a keener talent for observation than many. From humble origins—Cattery Spunge was born in a cow bier, of a milkmaid and a shepherd—she'll defy the demographics of poverty through her natural wiles and a preternatural patience. She paces herself. If she's ever had romance in her young life, nothing is known of it. A nanny's job is to keep her personal life away from the scrutiny of her employers. Cattery Spunge was pretty in her adolescence and will be dignified in old age, but now, in the swamp of midlife—and the swamp of Quadling Country—she's afflicted with a kind of mildew in the bones. Her movements are slow. She complains. A rheumatism born of the climate. It will lift when this period of her life is over. She doesn't know that yet. She thinks she is old. She has no idea. Elphie thinks Nanny is old. Elphie has no idea either.

Of Melena, then? But no. Melena has been exposing herself from page one, and her time of delivery is nearly upon her. There's nothing more to assert about Elphaba's mother.

# 21

And here, Elphie is alone, herself alone in the center of the camp, outside the tents. It's high noon, though the thick jungle canopy allows too little direct sunlight to prove the moment. Everyone is busy. She doesn't know why. Nessa has the rheumy chest and is resting in the girls' tent. Ti'imit and Boozy are conferring in Boozy's tent, and the flaps are tied shut and go away, don't bother us. Nanny is distracted in Melena's quarters. Melena hasn't gotten up for several days. All on his own, for once, Frex has taken a canoe a short distance upriver for some stores and to suss out the rice market exchange as a source of possible converts. For the first time Elphie feels—well, what is it she feels?

Is it loneliness or is it fear? She isn't sure. There's all this talk of the migration of jungle cats. They steal invisibly through the growth all around her, she can tell. Today the grown-ups have left Elphie alone. Probably in the hopes that she'll be eaten alive. It isn't fair. Nessa is safe in her cot. Only Elphie, standing in the middle of the circle of tents. Let the cats come and get me. It'll serve you right if I get devoured.

She starts to chant a little. When she was younger, Nanny had sung to her, lullabies and husha-husha songs, but it's been some time since music marked the silences of camp life. Elphie twists her fingers and makes up some nonsense words. *Seppada seppada meppada me, somebody somebody, twiddledy twee. He-body, who-body, me-body, you-body. Riddle-dee ree.* She hardly realizes that she is singing. The words come spring-loaded with a melodic intention so her voice just follows.

And this is when she makes the acquaintance of the polter-monkey.

She doesn't call it that at first. It's just a creature on the side-lines, crouching. It looks as if it is eating its own knuckles. More or less the size of Nessa—in fact, in the shade, Elphie has thought at first that it *is* Nessa, somehow hexed into greater mobility—though of course Nessa has no knuckles of her own to bite.

It turns sideways as if it is shy, but it doesn't back away when Elphie takes a half step forward.

"You're a nasty-looking little piece of monkey business," says the girl.

The monkey swivels its head a quarter-turn and bares its con-siderable burden of teeth. It isn't a smile, nor has Elphie been trolling for one.

But any monkey knows how to keep itself hidden if it wants to. So this nervy bundle of fuzzy shadow has come forward by its own design. Is it even really there, or is Elphie making it up out of boredom? In any case, the company is welcome. "What? What do you want?" The creature isn't going to help her figure it out, but still it doesn't flee. It opens its mouth again with a shocking hinged jaw. At first Elphie thinks it is yawning. Then she gets it, maybe, and replies with some more ribbony phrases. "Pumpernickel rock, snickerlicker snock," she sings. At this the creature drops its curled hands to the ground. It is carrying something in one of them. Its mouth closes and its eyelids lower, as if anticipating sleep. She has sung it out of hiding, that's what she's done.

Better ghost company than none at all. It sways a little and holds its own elbows, a gesture looking uncommonly like one of Nanny's. Out of green jungle air Elphie creates an aria to tease it forward. Having an audience spurs invention. She is forging a crescendo, and the polter-monkey is in a trance. And then—

"Elphie, for the love of Lurline, quit the caterwauling," hollers Nanny. She and Boozy have burst simultaneously from their respective tents because Melena is having a bad dream or something and is screaming. Maybe to drown Elphie out? In any case, before the girl can see how or where, the polter-monkey has disappeared.

She's furious. Leaving her alone all morning, and just when something decent is happening, messing it up.

"Boozy, some coconut oil or turtle butter, I have to get the rings off her, she's complaining of the pressure. Elphie, tend to your sister!"

Elphie will go try out her new gambit of singing on her sister, who has been awakened by Nanny's shouting and is braying for attention and service. But first Elphie skirts the grass where she thinks she's seen that creature. On the ground lies the small pair of tongs that has gone missing.

## 22

In the evening light, Nanny tells Elphie that she may bring her little sister around so they can visit with their mother, who is feeling poorly today.

"Today and every day," says Elphie, who doesn't understand the difference between poor and poorly—nor between poor and prosperous, for that matter.

Melena is in a state of dishabille, but this is normal for her. The girls might not have noticed except that there is so very much exposed belly. "*Somebody* eat a big lunch," says Nessa.

"Come to Mama," says Melena. Her hair is lank across her pillow. She's thrown up a little. Nessa wrinkles her nose when Elphie wheels her closer. Melena stretches out her arms.

"What happened to your rings, they ran away," says Nessa, peering at her mother's fingers. Having none of her own, Nessa always attends to her mother's.

"They just bounced right off didn't they," says Nanny. She is preparing a basin of warm water and soap and folding a stack of small flannels.

"I couldn't bear the chafing." Melena's face twists. Nanny mutters some coded instruction, Melena grits her teeth against the ailment but comes back to herself. "Elphie, are you filching things from here and there? Boozy and the others tell me objects are developing lives of their own and walking about to take the air."

"No."

"You'd say no in any case. Just cut it out, Elphie." Melena flags a hand limply at her older daughter as Nanny hoists Nessa onto the edge of the cot, where the girl lies, inert and cringing, in the lee of the tumulus that Melena has become. "Nessa, tell me," says their mother, "is Elphie being a good big sister to you?"

Nessa shrugs. One of the more expressive bodily gestures she can make.

"I want you to be good, Elphaba Thropp," says Melena. She says it twice more until Elphie finally lifts her chin and looks her mother in the eye. "I haven't said so before, but I'm saying so now. I want you to tell me that you hear me."

"Oh, I *hear* you," says Elphie, too young to have perfected the withering ennui of adolescence, but practicing.

"You hear me and you remember what I say."

"I found the missing tongs in the grass." Elphie takes them out of her pocket.

"I know you be'd the one to snitch them," says Boozy, who's arrived with some malodorous tea. "Give them here, you pinching thief."

"I never did, I never stole them or hexed them or anything'd them." Elphie, hot in the cause of justice for herself. "I think there's a lone monkey hanging around the camp. It's been taking things."

"The monkeys all fled, swum away through the trees, they don't like jungle cats no more than we do," says Boozy. "They smart and they keep to their own kind. No rogue monkey hanging around us, Elphie."

"Elphie, don't spout nonsense, you're making it worse," says Nanny. "Stop taking things, that's all. Now give your mother a kiss. She isn't feeling herself."

"Then who do you feel like?" asks Elphie.

Melena's face contorts. "I feel like a muskrat giving birth to a baby hippo. You girls better go." Full-body pain wrings her for a moment. When she can catch her breath: "We'll have a baby brother or sister for you soon. Elphie, *no more stealing.*"

"If I didn't steal anything yet, I can't do any more of it and I can't do any less."

"Mercy, the mouth on you. Go to law school, if they'll have a girl like you. If they even take girls. Good-bye, my darlings."

This is the only good-bye, casual, flung down like a damp kerchief. Good-bye.

They leave as Frex is arriving home in his punt. Ti'imit tells Frex he isn't welcome in the tent now because the hour has arrived. Frex doesn't hold with that peasant prohibition. He goes in to greet his wife and pray for her. Later, they largely agree this was the big mistake. Men visiting their wives in childbirth is not done.

# 23

Sometimes Elphie and Nessa scream in laughter together. Sometimes they just scream.

So they are improbable sisters. But are any two girls likely to be more consistent than they are? Even identical twins, underneath their matching gendered miens, often take stances in opposition to each other. And no one in the missionary camp has a benchmark to make a comparison about sibling sisters. Melena Thropp is an only child; Cattery Spunge had a stepsister and a pet goat, and neither of them made much of an impression on her. Frexispar Togue Thropp, the Godly, is the seventh son of a seventh son, but brotherliness isn't the issue here. Anyhow, comparisons are futile. As the ditty goes, Girls are monster humans and boys are human monsters. And for Boozy, she is so Dust on the Soup that she can't seem to remember if she has sisters or not. Kinship relationships among Quadlings being less crisply delineated than they are among Munchkinlanders.

They hate each other with affection, Nessa and Elphie; they tolerate each other with impatience; they love each other with scorn. When they play cards, Elphie manages both hands, and won't allow herself to cheat. If Nanny or Boozy are busy, Elphie feeds Nessa with a spoon sometimes. (Sometimes.) It will occur to those who come after these famous girls that while they shared a mother, their fathers were probably not the same man. So their differences might have an origin in lineage. But it's more than that: it's always more than that.

You plant two sunflower seeds in a pot of rich soil. You water them with the same can, at the same time, with the same portions. You rotate the pot daily so they get equal access to the sunlight. Yet on some early, pertinent day, perhaps there is a cloud across the sky, and the plant on the left doesn't get quite the strength of light that the one on the right does. Or there is a worm in the soil in one quadrant of the pot who eats through more of these roots here than those ones there. Who can say.

Sisters are not flowers. And parents can never, from the first day, give the same water and light and soil to one girl that they gave to her sister. Sisters grow, if they grow together at all, in adjacent sorrow.

So sometimes Nessa screams and Elphie screams, just because. They have no words for their spontaneous outbursts. It is a mutual sort of melismatic yodel, saying, more or less, *we're fucked*. They look at each other and shake their heads, scarcely believing the untoward luck of having been born adjacent—to *that*!—and like *this*!

But the screaming can turn into screaming with laughter a moment later. This is called spiritual health, and no one has ever known where it comes from, or why.

# 24

Elphie teases Nessa about what to hex next. "Maybe I'll toy with Nanny's pincushion," she says, "or that sack of medicinal tablets she keeps on a cord around her neck."

"You can't get close enough to hex Nanny's pills," says Nessa, mixing up hexing with petty larceny.

"You try it then, see if you can."

A noise outside. Frex comes in to kiss them good night. "It's going to be a long evening, and I don't want you to be frightened if you hear your mother, um, making noises," he says. "She's having a baby tonight, did you know that?"

"Well, obviously," replies Elphie, though she's only just putting it together.

"I'll tell you all about it in the morning. Having babies is hard work but it's worth it. Look at you two."

Nessa and Elphie glance at each other; the green one, the hampered one. They aren't the ones to say whether it has been worth it or not. No scale of judgment.

When Nessa has rocked herself to sleep in her hammock, Elphie steals outside. The supper things are cleared away, everyone else is in tents, and Ti'imit has already built up the fire against jungle cats. The blaze makes the air tremble. Elphie sings a little, again, to stifle the forces opposed to her. Out of shadows approaches the polter-monkey. It is blue in the blue moonlight but gold on the edge nearer the flame. It feels like a dream, so she speaks to it, why not. "Are you here to do a hex for me?"

"You sing me near, you are the hexing one."

In her isolated and rural life, Elphie has neither come across a talking Animal nor heard tell of a real one—only in nursery tales. In the jungle, Animals keep to themselves. So this *is* a dream; she's dreaming this night. Then she wonders if into this singular figure she herself might have magicked the gift—or the curse—of a tongue she can understand.

She stares at the creature. It seems more solid than it did that other time, or times, she has encountered it. Language does that.

"What do you mean, I sing you near? I do not." Already oppositional, our Elphie.

"I like your voice; it cuts through the blather of your family. I am alone, my own clan has been scattered by the cats. I have been hiding near your camp for safety and company. My name is—"

"You can't have a name, you're not a pet!"

"I am not a pet and I have a name. It is Oporos. You are—I know—you are Elphaba. The others I don't know and I don't care."

"Have you come to kidnap me? I'll need a moment or two to pack."

Oporos makes a pout that Elphie registers, correctly, as a smile. "I would not carry you into the path of cats. You're safer here. So am I."

"Why are you taking things and bringing them back?"

The monkey turns its head a quarter of the way around and puts its forefinger against its lips, as if thinking—or mocking the way it has seen humans appear to be thinking. At last it says, "I am trying to get you to notice me."

"You could just call my name."

"And be shot by your father's gun? He doesn't like Monkeys who talk."

"Does he know any? He doesn't! Are you sure?" Her father

couldn't have kept such a marvel from her for all these years. He just couldn't have.

"We're not open to—to persuasion. About the god thing. He *has* tried."

"He's come across your people and preached to you?"

"If that's what you call it. We like the stories where they have wings. The angel people. We asked if we could have some if we joined up his church. He said no."

"Why do you want wings?"

"Oh, don't you know?" Peering at Elphie, the creature looks tired. The girl doesn't know if Oporos is male or female, or maybe those distinctions don't happen in Monkeyland. It looks young and old at the same time—old from experience and young in aspiration. She won't be able to think out things like this until she's much older, but her practice of analysis—from observation—has already begun. For now, she just listens when it continues. "If we had wings, why, then, this business of cats, of losing our family members to the stalkers of the jungle—we could escape. If we had wings, we could be angels. We could see more, we could know more. But mostly—just—we could survive. That's all."

"If you think I am about to hex you up a pair of wings . . ." says Elphie, in a Nanny voice.

"I don't think that," says Oporos. "Not at all. But if you sing, two things will happen. You'll help the fire to keep the cats away. And you will lift me up."

"Lift you up?"

The creature smiles and hands over a marsh plum. "There's more than one way to cast a hex."

Unriddling a statement that can mean several things is not one of Elphie's strengths. She stares at the polter-Monkey, perhaps a little coldly, and then drops her gaze to the piece of fruit in her palm. The wind soughs in the palmettos, clacking the dried-out fronds. The air smells slightly rank. Her invigilator hulks there, waiting for her to say something, to react. No next thing to say occurring to her. But she's good at being still.

A groan from her mother's tent—a groan opening out into a teary cursing.

When Elphie has turned back from glancing tent-ward, the creature of the evening is gone. Skittish item, a polter-Monkey.

She inches back to her cot. On slightly damp groundcover, her bare feet sting. She ought to have put on her boots. She never realized dew begins to collect at midnight.

# 25

Screaming; silence; wailing. Another kind of silence. Finally another kind of wailing. A more laborious sound, pacing itself. Then the thready voice of an outraged infant. The absence—Elphie finally notices this, now she's been alerted—of nocturnal monkey screams. If there's another absence that she can hear, she doesn't know that for sure.

She stays in her bed, her hand reaching out to steady Nessa's swinging cot, as if in stabilizing her sister she might somehow keep the whole world from rocking out of its margins. Nessa sleeps through the commotion that besets the campsite. Should jungle cats sometimes be drawn to the sound of human activity, it will not be tonight.

Toward the morning, Elphie lets go of the rim of Nessa's basket. She pads to the entrance of their tent and undoes the ties of the flap. In her leather boots she steps out into the predawn. A sky of liquid cobalt above, shadow of black moss below. The mosquitoes haven't come awake yet. The fire has succumbed to embers. She already knows, somehow, that the new baby will need breakfast. So will everyone else, except for Melena. Little else to be sure of, Elphie stirs the embers, conjuring up sparks of white and scintillant red. Ti'imit has abandoned his post, as she always suspected him of doing.

She turns her back on them all, on all the sorrow and suffering yet to name itself. Perhaps that is the sound of her father crying very, very softly, as if to hide it from everyone. In small steps she circles the tents and lean-tos, the canoes and the campfire and the pitchy cudgels kept on hand in the event of a wildlife raid. She makes her way through the reeds—she can't tolerate water but, in her boots, she can pick her way through mud—as close to the edge of the river as she can get.

The overgrowth on the opposite bank, a single wall of foliage. The matted perplexity of green-black life. She'd hardly be able to tell it from the black surface of the river but for a line of light, reflected from who knows where, that underscores the shoreline. Like the underlining of a stretch of important text, she might think later. Saying to her: *Here, this is the important part. This is the part to remember.*

The line is pale white, and because it is etched on the edge of water, it wavers very slightly, delimiting here from there.

As the dawn inches closer, Elphie sees in the water the upside-down reflection of two figures distinguishing themselves from the background. They are moving from right to left on the other side of the water that she can never cross or she would die, too. She cannot see them above as their dark silhouettes are one with the jungle growth, but she sees their upside-down reflections some-how. The polter-Monkey with her mother. The Monkey is leading Melena by the hand.

"Oronos," she hisses, because she can't bear to call after her mother, it would be too terrible not to be acknowledged in return, she can't risk it.

The reflection of the polter-Monkey pauses and lifts a fore-arm. Elphie can't see any eyes or any facial expression. Only an upside-down silhouette upon water just slightly lighter in tone. Its gesture is a response to her cry. But the Monkey then continues its job of chaperoning Melena into the past.

The girl looks away from her disappearing mother. When she recovers this memory years later, after its banishment from her mind, this is what she wonders about—perhaps she looks away to avoid the possibility that her mother has already chosen to look away from *her*. Whoever wields the cudgel first has a momentary advantage.

The pair of them, there and then not. The sky goes a soft, resistant pink, bloodstains in the laundry water. Elphie makes her way back to the tent where her sister swings in midair. In the khaki gloom Elphie pauses upon the mat of stamped grass between their two beds. Nessa is stirring, she is nearly awake. In the lowest voice Elphie has ever governed in herself to date, she starts to sing to Nessa, a song to comfort her, before either one can guess how soundly consolation will be needed.

She begins with baby babble syllables, *tarra-ma bersy, tarra-ma bersy*, but in the closed air of the tent they sound more like *terrible mercy, terrible, terrible mercy*.

## 26

**B**oozy alone believes that Elphie has spoken to a ghost Monkey. "Is it only ghosts who can talk?" Elphie asks her.

"Usually ghosts don't bother, they're fed up with talking," says Boozy. "But of course some *Monkeys* can talk. You father never tell you this?"

The green girl never admits that she saw Melena leaving before dawn. The others would just complain that Elphie should have stopped her somehow. Still, the jungle river would have had to drain down to dry gravel before Elphie could have considered crossing it.

They bury the body in a graveyard used by the locals, thereby consecrating it in a new way. Weeping great ugly tears viscous as wax, Nanny ties some of Melena's jewelry, baubles and a few of the rings, to strings. She hangs them from a bough that stretches over the grave. The jungle grows so fast, thwarts itself and revives endlessly, that without some marker they'd never identify the spot again.

There's little else to disperse. Nanny's already light-fingered an item or two—that ivory brooch, a bottle of green medicine. What else is left? Some gorgeous gowns from Melena's girlhood, probably long out of style. Also an ornate mirror in an oval frame. Nanny crushes the dresses back into the trunk, cushioning the mirror, for dealing with another day. Maybe Frex can auction them for funds to build a shrine to Melena.

But Frex won't stick around to establish a mission church. No one can posit why not. Arguably there's just as much reason to memorialize this spot as to abandon it. But never question the visions of the wannabe mystic; you can't get a grip. Enlightenment seems to be selective. It rarely occurs to more than one deserving soul at a time.

So they pack up the foodstuff and dismantle the tents. Bundle the newborn in his swaddles. He is a dropped rose petal, an angry squawling snail in a cotton wrap. Nanny carries him, fussing over him until he screams for peace. Frex has named him Shelter-god, perhaps with the hope that the baby might be a homestead for the Unnamed God in this wicked place, or that the Unnamed God might provide the baby shelter that will not be supplied by a mother. They will come to call him Shell.

# PASSIM

Days of storm, days and days of it. The rice is often watery because it rains into the lidless cooking pot. Rats huddle on the riverbank, shivering. In a backwash cove, with orgiastic fervor river eels slip amongst one another just below the surface of the water. Elphie wears a coat made of waterproof canvas cut from an unneeded old tent. She watches them, she watches everything.

Days of hot light, too, sun-glare that you can barely see through the multiple veils of vegetation. Mere chinks of sky, like the many pieces of a blue clay plate, shattered and irreparable.

And nights of long, drawn-out yowls—the jungle cats. A parade of stripey-tailed lemurs floods into camp, bold as you please, trying to steal Boozy's cooking utensils to lick them. Jungle owls, with their high, haunted doxologies. Midges at dawn, flies at midday, mosquitoes at dusk, and at midnight, a persistent stinging insect like a microbial scorpion. By now the missionaries have taken to sleeping in white nets hung from a hook at the joist-pole of each tent. I'm in a cocoon, thinks Elphie, listening to the play of life and death that she can hear while lying in the dark with her eyes closed.

I'm in a cocoon, but I won't always be.

In the dark all cats are grey, goes the saying. In the dark, no children are green.

Asleep, all children appear innocent. But Elphie is often awake.

On some anonymous night when she cannot sleep, damp

with sweat in a white cone of muslin, she shuffles through her memories and collates them.

Which is to say that she begins to have a history, and it is always in the past. Writing about it in the present is merely a conceit. She will recall little of what has happened up in her life until now, only smudged impressions—an encounter by the river, the hexed night when her mother evaporated from her life. What she remembers from here slots more or less chronologically in the library of her mind. In the once upon a time, first this happened, then that. Melena has taught her that much: birth and death. Elphie is no longer immortal.

Whether this affords any relief it is not easy to know.

PART THREE

# THE VEGETABLE PEARL

## 27

Elphie starts to chart change in herself. Not manually: she's no budding diarist, and anyway there's hardly any paper. Furthermore, her thoughts don't come in sentences and paragraphs, but rather in gusts of noticing and guessing and forgetting. Whenever there is arresting novelty—let's say the day in which the eternity of jungle gives way to a small city—she will remember it.

And so one remarkable midmorning, she and her family make their riverside approach to the upland municipality of Ovvels, in the heart of Quadling Country. The southernmost city in all of Oz.

While sometimes they've broken camp and traveled cross-country on foot, more often they've taken to the water. An experience that locks Elphie in lip-clenched silence as she sits in the middlest middle of the vessel, and the boat boys try not to flick her with drops of water from their oars or poles. When the family group leaves the punt, Elphie ebbs back into herself, noting a cool flush of relief.

Their scrappy luggage shared out among hired handlers at the docks, the family straggles up from the quay. Above them rises a substantial town, maybe even a city, indistinct in clammy weather. A fog loiters in the dirt streets and among the groves and stilt-legged buildings. The missionary party can smell corn flatbread. Fish and shallots on the skillet. A hint of the local cuisine. Breakfast never seemed so urgent a need.

The sounds of industry and of small children. Goats on the tether, goats on the loose with bells around their necks. Some unknown musical instrument far off, zither-like, playing in an exotic modality.

Relative to the mountains where Elphaba will end her known days, this outcropping is hardly even a hillock. Still, there's more altitude here than she's experienced so far. While not large, the city lolls across rises and dips. A good many of the buildings are nestled in the trees themselves, or on posts.

Shell is about five years old at this point. Nessa, eleven. Elphie, therefore, thirteen. She is on the lip of the metamorphosis that she can nearly but not quite sense. Ah, adolescence, save us all. She tries to take everything in.

It is a more temperate world, for one thing. Ovvels, pitched on this stray bit of outcrop, is spared the swampy character of so much of Quadling Country. "They're still froggy folk, even if they're tree frogs now," mumbles Nanny, looking forward to being able to take off her stockings and air out her toes.

Compared to the capital city, Qhoyre, where they spent a year when Elphie was ten, and which she can still sort of picture these two or three years later—but imagination is a memory cheat—Ovvels proves more humble and more beautiful. It is tossed together haphazardly, a metastasis of a single architectural vernacular. Ovvels has never been prettied up or Oz-ified. Nothing like Qhoyre, which in trying to strut about like a younger sibling of the great Emerald City has squared itself off with columns and porticos and ceremonial carvings. (Becoming moss-covered in months and tumbled ruins within decades.) No, the humbler Ovvels is a city built entirely of square-hewn logs, assembled at right angles as much as possible, for the anchoring strength of the joins. Rooflines leaf out into gambrels and dormers. Cooking chimneys built of stone or of tin pipe. Countless gabled windows peer in all directions, allowing a hundred widows to snoop from their attics to see who is passing.

Frex points out that this part of Quadling Country, because higher and less damp, is home to colonies of marsh pine. When felled the trunks remain strict; they don't go spongey like their lowland cousins. An inexhaustible supply of square-cut logs, impervious to the rains, needing little by way of tarring or treatment.

So the city of Ovvels resembles an arithmetically precise beaver's dam, one constructed with a plumb line and a builder's square. Look, the buildings aren't just raw brown, but subtle shades of mauve, cherry, pale cedar, and chocolate. Ovvels seems coherent, even serene. No one in this family bothers with the word *charming*, but they might.

They are here to continue and maybe to complete the expiation that Frex began years earlier. Previously he'd considered it Melena's task as well as his own, for hadn't she been the first one to take in Turtle Heart and put that Quadling whistle-blower at such risk? But the minister accepts that as widower, he's the responsible party now. He doesn't know how much time he has left. He doesn't want to bequeath his three children a heritage of unserviceable moral debt.

"So we are here," he tells them, whether they are listening or not, "to make amends. Pay attention."

Shell is tossing stones at the tree rats, trying to knock them off their boughs. Elphie grabs his right arm and says, "I'll break your wrist if you keep this up, you little monster." To her father, she snaps, "I *am* paying attention."

"So am I," says Nessa, batting her eyelashes. At eleven, she's learned the power of eyelash punctuation. "Look at the creatures carved into the ends of the roof beams and the porch supports. Oh my, Elphie, there's you—a pouting little monkey."

"Ha," says Elphie, who has only mentioned her dream of seeing a polter-Monkey once or twice, but the notion is glued to her for all time. "And there's you, a snake."

"Why a snake?" asks Nessa. She slips her tongue out between her lips, quickly. Wittily.

"Because a snake is a venomous creature. And, like you, has no arms."

"Don't make personal remarks," says Nanny with leaden promptness. "There was a snake in Lurline's magic garden, no doubt, and it did the job snakes do, so mind your tongue, Elphie." Elphie is minding her tongue, slithering it back at Nessa, mimicking, collaborating, besting, all at once. Elphie almost regrets that her baby viper teeth are long gone. A daggermouth would have made the joke stronger.

They are a smaller contingent now. Boozy has left, and so has Ti'imit. Brother Frex can't afford to hire replacements. What with pressure being put on the bishoprics of Munchkinland by the Emerald City tax authorities, the parishes can no longer underwrite the expenses of a missionary diving ever deeper into Muck Nation. They've tried to recall Frex, but he's gone rogue. He's chosen to forge on, to drill ever more southerly. Atonement is a bitch. You do what you have to do, and he's not done yet.

Elphie has struggled to manage the family cooking. She isn't a whiz at the cooking pot, but Nanny refuses to do anything other than direct the operation. "I was hired to raise children, not to feed them," she says. "I'd intended to see the new baby into his training trousers and then go back and take my retirement in Munchkinland. But Melena slipped the gate and got to her retirement first, so now I'm yoked to this family till you children are of age or until I'm dead. But cooking is not in my sheaf of talents. If you prefer to eat, fire the Nanny and hire a cook."

"This is good enough," Frex growls at such an outburst. Warm undercooked rice, nearly nutty, flavored with herbs and sand. "Delicious. Thank you, Elphie. The Unnamed God provides."

"The Unnamed God should choose from a better menu of options," Nanny says, sniffing. "In the privacy of my tent I beseech the ancient goddess Lurline to show up with a nice pork roast and cracklings, and an apricot pudding with treacle sauce, but she seems to be otherwise engaged and has not answered my prayers. This only deepens my faith and I pray harder. I'll break her yet, just watch me."

"We'll find someplace to live, someplace maybe with a floor," says Frex. "I have some money put aside from camp meetings. Depending on cost, we might establish ourselves for a couple of weeks quietly, scope out the situation before I start stirring up faith-spending among the potentially devout of Ovvels."

They wander along a sloping track. Pine needles make the going slippery. Nessa now walks on her own two feet, though more confidently if someone follows with a balancing hand. Steps and ladders are still torturous, but the muscles supporting her spine have shown up for the job. Frex is her most frequent buttress, because Elphie can become distracted and turn suddenly, toppling Nessa onto her knees or face or side.

They amble, on the lookout for an opportunity. If the locals are curious, they are too polite to show interest in the odd party— this gaunt, bearded prelate; a stout tufted armchair of a bonneted woman; a green child approaching adolescence; a younger girl with perfect skin and no elbows or wrists or fingers; and a five-year-old boy kicking stones and looking bored. The Quadlings of Ovvels, proud of being worldly, are accustomed to visitors from the north.

While there's not much physical difference between the natives of Ovvels and their ruddy cousins in the marshy outback, the Ov-vels attitude is keener somehow. Their gaze is more confident. El-phie sees this most sharply in the face of a woman perched on a tree-hoisted balcony of sorts, who answers their question about lodgings without any attitude. "*I'm* a widow who has rooms to let," she admits, calling down her chins as she regards the group of five foreigners. "I don't take single men, for reasons of propriety, but a family group, why not."

"I am not married to Miss Spunge," says Frex, up front about it.

"No one need know the details. You're married as far as I'm concerned."

"Well, I never," says Nanny, wondering if ever.

"We'll need three rooms," insists Frex. "A larger one for the children, one for me, a third for the domestic. The big room can also be for prayer and lessons and family life."

"I am Leili Leila'ani," replied the landlady, "but call me Lei. My husband is dead and my grown boys are off harvesting vegetable pearls in the north. Good sons, they send back a portion of their salaries but not nearly enough. So I can't be choosy. For my repu-tation in this neighborhood, you're married, do you understand. I can't have it otherwise. How you disport yourselves among three rooms is your own affair. Come, look, and make me an offer." She watches as Frex and Elphie together maneuver Nessa up the stairs. "I can see she won't be the one sent running to the market for caper jelly or fresh manatee milk."

"I can be a comfort to you around the house," proposes Nessa, smiling like a saint.

"We'll see about that," replies Lei. "This way, please."

The rooms are small but airy, fitted out with louvered shutters that slant bars of sunlight on the floorboards. Scantly furnished. The family comes supplied with sleeping rolls and a purpose-built wicker chair with high box sides so Nessa can sit without falling over. It'll do. No wardrobes, but their meager supply of clothes still fits into Melena's trousseau trunks from Colwen Grounds—with enough room left over to store their mother's outmoded fancy-party gowns, too. A hint of lost luxury.

Nanny's room has a shelf perfect for arranging a framed icon of Lurline, a faded rotogravure torn out of a holy magazine Nanny once pilfered from the back of a chapel.

Elphie, Nessa, and Sheltergod can doss down in the bigger room. Only one mosquito net to cover all three of them. "If Elphie makes beans for supper, I'm going to die in here," says Shell.

Frex's room, narrow and stale, is served by one window too high to reach without a stool. He likes discomfort, so he is pleased at the prospects. He bargains a reduced rent. Lei Leila'ani looks smug, though, as if she's scored a win here. She offers to whip them up a welcome breakfast.

# 28

Before prospecting for a possible congregation, Frex and Elphie venture into the marketplace. Frex wants to see if they can find out if anyone here ever knew their Quadling martyr, dead now ten or eleven years. "We may never be able to tidy up our condolences with an actual family member," he says, "but in this crowded city we're more likely to run into someone who's heard of Turtle Heart than in most other places in the lowlands. We can only try."

"I don't really get the point," says Elphie, who has become contrary. "*You* didn't murder him. You didn't send him to the Eminent Thropp's house to be murdered, either. You might as well atone for the fact that village cats kill village rats every day of their lives. It has nothing to do with you. Taking all this responsibility for how the world just *works*—isn't that a kind of hubris?"

"I haven't yet taught you what hubris is," he snaps at her.

"I'm nearly a teenager, I know already. I'm smart for my age. Besides, you talk about hubris. All the time. You think I never listen to your sermons? I try not to but I forget, so sometimes what you say seeps in."

"Listen, Elphie. Pay attention. These city Quadlings seem nonchalant, but they have their guard up with me, unlike the more innocent river clans. They may be more comfortable with you. You're just a kid. Even with your ripe complexion, you're less threatening. I need your help. You can be the spy." But they're passing establishments into which it isn't smart to send a girl on the threshold of adolescence. A smithy, a kind of tavern, an apothecary with a

sweaty proprietor who seems toked up and over-jolly. On the edge
of a more residential quarter they come upon a set of wide wooden
steps, rusticated in an artificial way, that leads to a lookout porch
and a treehouse-shop of some sort. Between branches hangs a
strung line of wares, showing off color and design. "Look, a lady's
shop. That's safe enough. March up there and nose around. It looks
like an emporium for dressmaking material. Finger some goods,
and pretend you're interested. Don't buy an inch of it, of course. But
shop women love to gab, I remember that from Qhoyre. See if you
can get the mistress around to the subject of Turtle Heart, and if
she's ever heard of him."

"Turtle Heart probably had his own name in Qua'ati."

"He probably did, but Turtle Heart is all we know. Maybe someone can translate from the Ozish."

She does as she is told, glad to be let off her leash even for ten
minutes. Shell and Nessa are home with Nanny. Nanny is probably
brainwashing the two younger kids with antique legends of soft
Lurlina while their father and Elphie are out trawling for absolution. They won't linger; Shell will be twitching to explore this
place, and as Nessa can't be left on her own for long, Nanny will
have her hands full keeping Shell distracted.

Elphie hangs back on the broad elevated veranda, hoping the
doyenne of the fabric shop will come out. Instead, a frail man ap-
pears, his lozenge belly snug under panels of brocaded garment. He
gestures her with a finger. Elphie follows him through a doorway strung with long lines of buttons and beads and dried beans,
lintel to threshold. Her eyes adjust in the gloom—a rich gloom. A
broad salon with chairs and tea things arranged socially. For clients. Wow. At the far side of the room sweeps a broad varnished
counter where, presumably, bolts of fabric are unfolded. The goods
are rolled up around bamboo poles, and they stand more or less

upright. Some powdery incense that smells of caramelizing tomatoes coils from a copper bowl on the counter. A small lizard waits
next to it, untroubled by Elphie's approach.

The man—maybe the missing shop-lady's husband—comes
forward with an uncertain step. He is weak of chin and high of
forehead, with thinning hair. His is a sly and whetted expression,
though perhaps that's usual among shop stewards. Elphie has only
ever been in a few shops, back in Qhoyre, apron-tagging, and she's
never yet ventured into a store on her own. As a pretend customer no less. This is risk, this is adventure. She is about to pass
out with nerves.

The gentleman speaks to her in a courtly Ozish. She answers in
serviceable Qua'ati. His flinch is a kind of gesture of respect, she
guesses, though she's slow at understanding cues given by eyebrow
and upper lip. Every person is so different, and so is every moment.
Like a clock—she's seen one once—with an hour hand, a second
hand, a hand to mark the day, and a pedestal that turns to follow
the sun. Who can do all that addition at once? Sort out what people mean, not just what they say? Well, she *is* trying. People are
organic puzzles every minute hour day and year.

He advances upon her, resting his forearms on the countertop
and crossing his wrists, and tilting his head, a manticore just before pouncing. Docile and dangerous. He probably wonders if she
is one of a tribe of hitherto unknown green-skinned foreigners just
passing through. She's intrigued.

"So the young miss is perhaps looking for some rural token? A
souvenir of her holiday visiting the hovels in Ovvels?" he says in
Qua'ati. "You'll be on your way soon, no doubt."

Nothing to lose here, and it helps that Elphie is free of tact and
guile. "Did you ever know a man named Turtle Heart?"

He repeats the name in Ozish and then translates it into Qua'ati.

"Turtle Heart. Chelo'ona," he says turning the words over and over in his mouth. "Perhaps. You are buying some fabric?" He splays a hand toward his wares.

"Do people tromp around in such giddy clothes? I haven't noticed. All these jungle flowers and sunset gleam."

"And you won't. This isn't fabric for wearing."

Elphie tries, and fails, to raise an eyebrow to indicate *Oh no?* She succeeds only in looking as if a bug has flown in her ear.

"In the homes of those who care," he says, "and who can afford it," he admits, "these lots of fabric are cut into strips and displayed upon moveable screens. Or tacked behind dark varnished rods of mahogany, paneling a plain whitewashed room with patterns of color. We live simply in Ovvels. It's a place of mud and rice and fish, and we are generally modest in our street garb. Smart of you to pick up on that. Even kinder to mention it." (Is he being waspish? She can't work him out.) "But behind the shutters of home we cherish brass, which winks when polished, and we are devoted to fine fabric, which consoles differently in different angles of light. It is our aesthetic, and a refined one. But I am a merchant, not a cultural anthropologist, so if you haven't come to buy—"

"I'm a poor girl from a poor family. Obviously." Elphie splays a green hand along her formless burlap shift. "We don't have a home of our own to pretty up with stripes of gaudy color. I am looking for Chelo'ona, was that how you said it? Turtle Heart."

"Perhaps I've heard of such a person," says the vendor, "or of one or two others. Or maybe they're the same person from different circumstances. But I can't help you. I have a business to run and I'm not the neighborhood gossip. And I'm woefully behind on my orders. Good afternoon."

Elphie isn't good at this and she's run out of gambits already. She doesn't want to return to her father having achieved so little.

As she tries to come up with a different approach, a sharp crack rings out in the room. The iguana creature disappears more quickly than Elphie's eyes can follow. The merchant whips his head. One of the windows at the side of the room has been broken by a bird crashing into it, or—she sees it before he does—a dense, water-smoothed stone. She bends down. "Let me see it then," says the merchant.

"You have glass windows," says Elphie. "They're so clean I didn't notice. I haven't seen many glass windows before."

"Show me that weapon, you wicked thing."

"I am no such thing. I didn't do this." But she brings out the stone for his inspection if not for his touch. A purplish stone, no markings on it.

"He was a glass-maker," she says. "Turtle Heart. I just re-membered, they used to say that. He could blow glass. He made a mirror of a sort that we still have in Mama's trunk. Maybe his polter-self threw this stone to get your attention."

"What mischief are you playing at, girl? Do you have an accom-plice waiting outside? If you're trying to distract me, you've come up the wrong steps. I don't keep cash on the premises." The man is calm and irate at the same time, a combination Elphie hadn't known was possible.

"I'm not a robber or a robber's sidekick. Look, I think maybe I could pay you for finding Turtle Heart's kin, if you can."

The merchant rummages about for a broom. "Don't move, there's glass all around you. You're looking for his kin and not him?"

"He's dead, didn't I tell you already? We've come to express our condolences."

"We. Who is we?"

Elphie says, "My family. My father and me. And my sister, my brother, my nanny. Look, if you're so interested in cloth, we have some beautiful old skirts and cloaks from Munchkinland. In a trunk. I could bring you something as a trade. If you can find us the route to Turtle Heart's people. Chelo'ona."

The merchant purses his lips, as if having bitten into a sour rind. "There are some around here who would look askance at foreigners hunting for a Quadling native or his family. I'd restrict your enquiries to those who aren't so parochial—I mean, *I'm* fine with it, I've traveled and met other types. But we're a close community here, and my fellow citizens don't all have the largesse I do." His comment mostly champions his own urbanity, Elphie thinks. Yet she takes his caution at face value and decides she will murmur it to her father.

Another customer comes through the door then, scowling at the broken glass on the floor. With an uplift of his hands the vendor herds Elphie back onto the veranda cantilevered over the pebbly lane below. He doesn't accept her offer but he doesn't reject it either. She turns about with a small sense of accomplishment. Below, her father, waiting for a report.

She doesn't wave at him, not yet. She turns to look at Ovvels from this viewpoint. Almost her first experience of a horizon. In this case, not just rooftops and tree limbs, but the distant rice terraces of Ovvels. The lagoon with its floating gardens. How cunningly put together, all the different parts of a world, the near and far, the mammoth and the particular.

The merchant has followed her out through the rattling beads. He catches sight of Frex loitering below and gesturing to his green-skinned daughter. "You've sent in a girl to distract me while you break my window to steal my wares?" he yells. He has become the testiest Quadling Elphie can remember running into during her short life—louder and more fierce than those warriors from the mist, which she can barely conjure up any more. The proprietor shakes his fist at Frex.

"He's a minister, he wouldn't break your windows," says Elphie, wondering if a lie is only a lie if you're sure it's a lie. Maybe Frex did throw that stone.

# 29

Elphie will never remember if she and Nessa went down to the edge of the lagoon the next day, or perhaps a week or two later. Either way, it's early on in their stay in Ovvels, to be sure. One of those moments that stick, though not in sequence, exactly.

Frex and Nanny are on the prowl for a venue to hold an impromptu faith convocation. Told to stay home, the children light out. Lei Leila'ani can't stop them ("You're not our mother!"). They go wandering through Ovvels on their own. Elphie wants to inspect the wide lagoon that she spotted from the porch of the cloth merchant.

Whichever day it is, and it doesn't matter, they find themselves descending the slopes on the north side of Ovvels. A great brightness of water curves beyond the honeycombed city. A lagoon, a slab of blue sky that fell earthward and turned to water, wider than any breadth of river they've ever encountered.

To the left of the vast blue, rice terraces climb the slopes of the near hills. These hundreds of irregularly shaped pools, held back by low ramparts of stone and mud, make a start at lake-edge and step up nearly to the peak of the slope. Were you a salmon who knows how to leap the falls, in a series of five or six dozen lunges you might spring from the shore almost to the top of the mount. The terraces taper and bulge as the contours of the hill allow. In full sun they wink hundreds of metallic eyes. No inch of slope goes uncultivated. Some smaller paddies hold as few as three dozen rice plants. Some are broad enough to harbor thousands of stalks.

The hydraulics of this arrangement forever remain a mystery to

Elphie. In time, she will wonder if the mountain range called the Quadling Kells drains through an underground riparian system and somehow emerges at the crest of the terraced hilltop. The splash at the top of a fountain. A faucet that won't turn off. In fact, the vast dampness of the Marsh Nation may result from serving as a slip-pool for the mountains of Oz. As Munchkinland is Oz's breadbasket, Quadling Country perhaps is its footbath.

In the lagoon, locally known only as "the lake," half the distance between Ovvels and the rice terraces on the shore is taken up by floating gardens: open-top oval or rectangular boxes made of rot-resistant wood. A few are filled with soil for ground plants, but most are pools for the raising of fish, water lettuce, and other wet produce.

Though privately harvested—vegetables, fruits, and all kinds of rare flowers—the floating gardens of Ovvels are open to the public for strolling. Every allotment abuts another. The pairs of cedar timbers yoked together make a path wide enough for any wobbly granddad to navigate—except when they curve at the occasional spandrel, where care must be taken. At the juncture of ovals and rectangles, choices abound. A watery labyrinth.

"It's like a colony of lily pads, the way they crowd and don't overlap," says Nessarose. "That close."

The kids see creatures feasting in the outer gardens—water impalas and herons and, over there, a murder of crows. Trained swamp dogs with unerring footing race around the perimeters to scare predators away. The dogs sometimes plunge in the earthen gardens with recklessness, but they avoid the basins of water. In time Elphie will find out why, but on her first visit with her siblings, she merely watches and looks.

It is high noon, an hour when most of the water gardeners of Ovvels have gone home for the midday meal, or are quaffing a beer in a back room of a shop. Eventually even the dogs slope off. So the floating allotments are empty of humans but for the Thropp children. The relative quiet means it's a good time for animal foragers, to be sure. A pair of deer, a doe and a fawn, freeze into statues and watch the children as they maneuver along the braided wooden paths. A couple of mangy creatures, too far away to be identified, are moseying about on all fours, splashing and eating at the same time. They might be pigs? Elphie keeps an eye on them. She supposes lunchtime for humans at home means a safer hour for scavengers.

Not putting a high value on being cautious, the Thropp children might as well explore while there is no one around to shoo them away. And off they go, balancing and squealing, Shell racing ahead, Elphaba guiding and steadying her sister with a hand in the small of her back. "Good practice, this," says Elphie. "One day you're going to have to walk on your own, you know."

"One day you're going to have to stop bossing me around."

"I'm being *useful*. Somebody has to be useful in this family."

"And I'm what? Useless?"

"I wouldn't say that. Ornamental, maybe. Anyway, everything isn't about you, or haven't I let you know that yet?"

"Don't push so fast. I have to find the right footing or I'll make a fall."

Does Elphie pull her hand back too quickly, does she stutter its support to remind Nessa that she's not Nessa's staff, she's her sister? Unanswerable. Upon her slender porcelain ankles, Nessa teeters.

What follows is easiest told as Elphie remembers it later, though she'll question the sequencing of her understanding. Had she ever really encountered a talking Animal before? Had the subject even come up, except in a fable of some distant world that only Nanny ever mentions? Elphie can never say. She's had dreams, she remembers: an impossible item called a polter-Monkey. She thought she'd made that up.

What Elphie is sure of, what she can see nearly to her last day, is the sight of Nessarose in front of her, unbalanced, tilting. Maybe the lake has unsettled itself. Maybe a crocodrilos has humped its spine right under where they are walking, just to disturb their lives. Nessa pitches leftward, and then slides sideways into a penned segment of lake. A pool with only a few ropy tendrils and rondels of vegetation. Nessa can't flail; she has no arms with which to flail. The water is several feet deep at least.

Even if he hadn't run ahead, Shell couldn't jump in. He can't swim, and he is still small. The depth of the water, they can't guess it. But he pivots at his Nessa's offended little shriek, and he begins throw himself about, threatening to jettison himself into the drink and double the tragedy.

Tragedy it will be, because Elphie can't plunge into deep water any more than she could run face-first into a bonfire. Her body won't move itself. Paralysis. Nanny and the jungle physicians with their charms and potions have all been wrong: Elphie has no more outlived her skin's sensitivity to water than she's outgrown her green skin. She screams. Nessa sinks below the surface of the water, face up, eyes on Elphie, conveying *something something something*. Her mouth closes though, to keep from filling up with water.

The sound of children hollering over the lagoon of private water gardens, such a common occurrence. No one comes running. All nearby families will have their own brats home already, sitting cross-legged upon a lunch cloth, everyone safe and accounted for, and you eat that swamp beet because it's good for you. In any case, this is the worst possible hour to call for help—it's the hour that help takes its midday break.

But before Elphie can decide whether or not to hold on to Shell's ankles and drop him into the water so he might fishpole his sister to the surface, somehow, a commotion occurs nearby. That hump-shouldered pair of foraging creatures out there is galloping toward them.

A whiplash of furry muscle. Tearing along the walkways, arriving in a pulse of animal intention. And then plunging into the water on both sides of the drowning girl, hoisting her head and shoulders above the water. A commotion of splash and thrash. Elphie recoils from thrown coins of water; she can't help herself.

Shell catches on his sister's ears and pulls from above. The creatures push and roll the rest of Nessa up the edge of the sill until she is lying flat upon the teak margin.

Is it instinct or learned behavior? These animals know something about water rescue. The bulkier one thumps upon Nessa's upper chest and the smaller leans upon her stomach. Nessa gives up the water she's taken in and begins to heave and gasp for air. While her eyes remain closed, she sneezes a few times. Her eyelids twitch and her eyes run, lagoon water draining. Or maybe tears.

"She's not what you'd call a natural swimmer," observes the smaller of the rescuers, not a pig but a sort of dwarf bear. Her fur has segmented into points, as if combed with a fork.

But: no: so: these are Bears, not bears. Elphie's first waking experience of talking Animals. Arriving in time to save her from accidentally murdering her sister. Figures more solid than the dream-figments of a polter-Monkey. Something marvelously both rash and undeniable, witnessed by her brother and sister.

Elphie flushes with a rage that threatens to overwhelm her panic over Nessarose. She's been lied to by—by everyone. Her father primarily. He hadn't *bothered to tell her about Animals.*

She's been blind to half the world. She's been kept in a prison of her own ignorance.

Now, she's just thunderstruck. The Dwarf Bears speak in a patois part Qua'ati, part Ozish: these creatures seem to be better traveled than most Quadlings.

Shell backs away a few feet. Talking Animals lived in stories, not in the wild. His fingers look itchy for a stone he can use as a missile, even though these interlopers have come in the cause of rescue.

"She'll be all right," says the larger Bear. It—he?—is a bit squinty. He rubs the epaulets of his shoulders, squeezing water out of the charred-toast fur. Then he shakes like a wet dog. Elphie flinches and ducks.

The first experience of hearing a creature speaking can come as a kind of welcome assault. Akin to listening to water and trying to hear melody in it, or eavesdropping on a pair of squawking parrots and imagining what they might be on about. You have to try. A certain effort of translation is required, due to accent deafness, if nothing else. But in Elphie the need to figure it out overrides her skepticism and ignorance. Some of us face the mirage and find it true.

The smaller one snorts a brave curse or a nasty word.

These bears—Bears!—are the ones with language; Elphie is stuck with sputtering silence. But not for long. "They didn't tell us you could talk," she manages, not certain how to address an Animal. "It sort of never came up, exactly."

"In this part of this country, we Ski'ioti live with our own kind and we don't mix," says the smaller one. She repeats herself so Elphie can move along the syllables and pick out meaning. The Dwarf Bear—a Ski'ioti!—then speaks even more slowly. "What's. Wrong. With. Her. Arms?"

"Nothing," replies Elphie. "She doesn't have any. On the plus side, she never worries about hitting her funny bone. On the minus side, she doesn't have much of a sense of humor to begin with."

"So she's a lot like a fish. But she can't swim."

"Well, it was only her first try." Elphie's breeziness startles herself. It derives from a combination of panic and joy. She's going slightly out of her mind, that must be it. "Shell, you better run find Papa or Nanny, or someone." Though Nessa's dorsal muscles are now stronger, she still doesn't easily get up from a prone position without some help. Elphie doesn't want to touch her sister till she's dried off. But the Bears are already putting their shoulders into it. Nessa's head lolls as her torso lifts upright, but not in a dead way. Elphie grimaces. "Oh, come on, Nessa, don't milk this for drama."

"Wh—wh—where am I?" moans Nessa, then sticks her tongue out at her sister.

"Shut up." Elphie pivots to the Dwarf Bears. "Why would you help us? Who are you? Why can you talk? Is this some hex put on you, are you really human cousins imprisoned by a witch into some animal shape? What is a Ski'ioti?"

"You ask such nosy questions, Elphie," remarks Nessa, back from the dead with a vengeance. In a Nanny manner: "It's hardly polite."

The Bears don't seem to mind. They introduce themselves as Lollo-lollo and Neri-neri. Lollo-lollo, with one fixed and one unstable eye, is the bigger creature. Neri-neri proves the more loquacious one. She says, "We're not supposed to feed here, of course, so rescuing your sister puts us in harm's way. You Quadlings are so grabby."

"We're not Quadlings."

The Bears look at each other and then slide a glance toward Nessa. Elphie tries to ignore the implication. "Why would you help us if the Quadlings are so interfering?"

Neri-neri replies, "You might want to see to your friend's care before we discuss public policy."

"Friend? Um. I don't have any friends. She's, um, my sister."

"Ah, if you're sisters, why aren't you both—more like sisters?"

"Answer my question. Why did you help us? Why would you?"

"So you're the bossy one? All right, we're not allowed to be here. We're illegal. Someone will already have spotted us out on the edge of the floating allotments. If your armless thingy-person-sister drowned while we were around, we'd be blamed, somehow. Reason enough to go after us. That's how it works, and that's enough of that. We should scamper."

Elphie isn't sure they're telling the whole truth. Hanging around longer only gave them more chance to be implicated, should a tragedy have occurred. But the social question is more pressing. "I don't get it. Why can't you feed here?"

"The Quadling humans consider it their property. And outside the floating gardens can be too dangerous. Lagoon hippos, you know. The occasional rogue crocodrilos."

"Perqu'unti," intones Elphie, not knowing where the word has emerged from. But that's how language works.

"They plant the outside rim of this raft of allotments with trailing brindlevine," says the smaller Bear. "It gives off a stinging poison to most water creatures. Keeps them from breasting the ramparts and making a meal of the harvest. But birds can approach by air. And we can arrive by the shore if we feel lucky. So can those impalas there, see. If we're in the neighborhood, I admit that we're tempted by the convenience."

"And by the fun of the risk," says the larger Dwarf Bear.

"Does that cover the matter for you?" continues Neri-neri. "We're done here, leaving before there's trouble."

"You should get me home, I'm in need of tending," says Nessa to her sister.

"Will you bolt up for a moment? When are we going to meet a talking Animal again?" But Elphie realizes that Nessa is looking decidedly queasy—perhaps not from her terrifying bath but, maybe, from the experience of talking to Animals at all.

"Your sister is right, she needs dry clothes," says Lollo-lollo languidly, as if he doesn't much care if Nessa gets them or not as long as she hasn't drowned.

Elphie snaps, "They'll dry in this sun in thirty-eight seconds if she'd stop yapping."

"We can talk some other time," says Neri-neri. "Few Quadlings choose to pass the time of day with us. We spook them. And they spook us. But you seem different. Maybe you're deranged? Anyway, we won't loiter near Ovvels for too long—we're migratory feeders, and we have our little routines. You can find us—" Neri-neri surveys the tidy little city and its outlying reaches. "Over there, do you see, the cedars crowning that brow to the left?"

"Neri-neri," says her companion, "you're off your feed. That's insane. Too risky. No way—"

She continues calmly. "We'll hide out there for a day or two and wait to see if you show up. We'll be able to see if you're making your way without hunters and trappers and guns. If you try to be sly about that, we'll disappear. But we'll wait, and hope. And why? I can see it in your face, why would we want to talk to you? We have our own curiosities, as it happens. You seem a breed apart. We're rarely interested in human chatter—but if you're willing?"

"What could you be curious about that I could explain to *you*?"

"Well, why you're green, for one thing. That's a talking point right there."

"Yuh-*huh*," says Elphie. The deal is sealed. Nessa is brought to her feet. Shell is waiting some feet away, creeped out by the entire sequence of events, shaking with the sort of excitement and terror a five-year-old lives for.

on't be fanciful, Elphaba; you didn't talk to any animals."

"Papa, I did."

"She *did*, Papa. They got Nessa out of the big water," says Shell. "I was there. They were sort of scary, and smelly."

"Shell, don't speak of which you know nothing. Elphaba, look what notions you're planting in your brother's mind. You ought to be ashamed. You were conjuring things out of panic—you only imagined that some creatures were talking to you."

"And did they imagine that I was talking to them, too?"

"Who knows what they might imagine, if they even can."

Elphie, impatient. "How is that any different from what I imagine you are saying to me, and I am saying to you?"

"Don't be tricksy, Elphaba. It doesn't suit a young woman in any circumstances, and in one with your—makeup—it can only lead to isolation and suspicion."

"Have you *met* a talking Animal before? Father? I'm sure you have. And you never told us about it. A whole separate—aspect—of the known world—and it's just there, sideways, out of our sight? Look, if you don't believe me and you *won't* believe Shell, ask Nessa. She's not remotely tricksy. She's too good to lie. She'll tell you the truth."

Frex frowns. "Nessa is resting. Recovering from her scare. I won't trouble her by taking her deposition. She's more fragile than you know, Elphie."

"She's about as fragile as an iron anvil."

"Let's concentrate on keeping your sister safe, shall we, and put these gossamer whimsies aside. We have work to do here, and distraction is a curse. Nanny, talk some sense into Elphaba. I can't tolerate this kind of frotherall."

Elphie hunches at a window, her back to her scheming relatives and complicit Nanny. Elphie has been betrayed by lies. But she's saved from falling into tics and lather by trying to remember some instance in her past in which, on her own accord, she might have arrived at an understanding of biodiverse sentience.

She had a dream about a Monkey, once. But what is a dream?— more often aspirational than it is revelatory. Only a saint can rely on the validity of a dream. And Elphie is no saint. She nearly grasps the concept of a polter-Monkey, but it's no more coherent in her mind than the talking animals of nursery rhymes and skipping games. She shakes her head. In so doing perhaps she dislodges the most potent of the toxins of anger that have already begun to pool in her bloodstream. She can't hate her father; she hasn't the time. And she can't spare him from her life, either.

"Though I do wonder how Nessie came to fall in the pond in the first place," says Nanny, threading a needle.

# 31

ustn't mind your father," counsels Nanny, some other conversation. "You know he's never been the same since your mother died. Without her, he's lost a wheel off his cart, that one. He's a one-armed juggler, he's a tin bucket with a hole in it. He can't deal with the variables. Men are like that. Of *course* there are talking Animals. I can't believe you need to be told. Where are your eyes, girl? You're thirteen or thereabouts, aren't you? There were Animals in Munchkinland, back in the day. Though the larger ones were often impressed into farmwork as beasts of labor. More often they scarpered off into the backlands. If they could. While the smaller ones always tucked themselves away better, didn't they, and in plain sight sometimes. They can more easily pass, the littles. But the Emerald City, now! A great liberal togetherness. Some disapprove. Cheek by jowl, can you imagine it."

Elphie winces at her to continue.

"In this part of the world, of course, which is all you've really known, poor dear, the Animals have much more wilderness to be wild in. And they can be suspicious of humans. Who can blame them, as we haven't wholly lost our taste for roasts and chops. I seriously didn't ever consider that you were ignorant of Animals. Didn't you once mention about talking to a Monkey that wouldn't show up and talk to anyone else? Long ago?"

"I wasn't sure that had really happened. I'm still not sure. Anyway, no one believed me."

"You always had a sly way of seeing out of the corner of your eye. Don't fret, it might come in handy someday. Meanwhile, you don't need your father's permission to notice what you notice. There's liberty enough in owning your own eyes, girl." She picks at her sewing. "Your father had a wandering eye in his day, but that's as far as it went, I think. And not uncommon in the clergy. Your mother had a wandering kirtle, which as far as I know isn't all that uncommon in wives of the clergy, either. But that's neither here nor there. Your father is concerned for Shell's welfare. Shell is most *certainly* his father's son, and that's some consolation. I've said quite enough," she adds primly, pins between her lips. She's said more than enough, but Elphie doesn't have the arithmetic skills to add up the nuances of grown-up behavior yet, so this remark goes over her head.

"It's a great conspiracy of liars, isn't it." Elphie's voice is small now, bereaved, a rare-enough effect for Nanny to notice.

"Every child begins to grow up by recognizing the Great Lie that's been foisted upon them. It is a different lie in each instance, but no less potentially lethal. For me, it was that natural charm would put food on the table." She sighs and primps her somewhat listless loops of hair. "Watch me work hard for my living, won't you."

"But Papa—never mentioning it once, all this time. Maybe he doesn't *know*?"

"Don't be intentionally dull, please. It's a look you can't carry off convincingly. Of course your father *knows*." She pauses. "I don't suppose you remember much about that day that—well, we had a run-in with a crocodrilos?"

"No," says Elphie, lying a little, trying it out for herself.

"It's always been my suspicion that your dear father was trying to proselytize three innocent Water Buffalo who didn't care for it so much, and harried him to make a point until they released him safely back to camp. Of course that's just guesswork."

"That's so long ago it's like it never happened. I'm talking about the Bears, they're right in our lives, but they're—hiding in plain sight."

"Bother them with your questions, then, if you want!" explodes Nanny. "Those Dwarf Bears, whatever they are. Your father doesn't own you, Elphaba, though he loves you enough to lock you into his mind instead of freeing you into your own. I'll look the other way. Don't take Shell, though. Or Nessa. Come back and gossip to me about it but try not to whisper to the others, or your father will catch wind of it. He might insist we move back into the jungle, and I prefer it here. They have floors, have you noticed? Such agreeable things, floors. Make you steady. They make Nessa steadier, too; she is more confident. You won't have noticed. You're a thirteen-year-old girl swamped in your own stormy self. Now do you want me to go through the trunk of your mother's items so you can barter with that clothier or not? Let's keep our mind on our mission, shall we."

# 32

Like any other thirteen-year-old girl, and like no other, Elphie is swamped in her own self, Elphie. Impetuous. Rational and superstitious at the same time. Attuned to injustice if metered out against herself, but unlike many kids at the vulnerable moment of near adolescence, she is also alert to oppressions that others have to endure.

Perhaps the puzzle of Nessa is at the root of Elphie's inclination to—to *notice*. Elphie's awareness of suffering isn't quite compassion—maybe it has no name. Elphie can be selfish as the next kid, even if she's seldom had kids other than her siblings to measure herself against. Her father owns all the compassion in the family, if you can call his kindly superiority a sort of compassion. No. Elphie is no saint. Neither does she aspire to that position.

Not being able to tolerate the feel of water on her skin, Elphie is, it must be said, not the most sweet-smelling of children. Perhaps, with their more relaxed approach to personal hygiene, Animals will find her more trustworthy because she's indifferent to lotions and attars.

At nighttime, after she has sung Shell to sleep, she coils in her own sheets, twisted as a nautilus, in a birth clench, waiting to be real, to be something other than herself, waiting to be herself. No different from any thirteen-year-old human child. No different, and so different.

# 33

From a distance, the Dwarf Bears appear out of the underbrush like apparitions conjured up from a nursery story, amusing and cozy. Clearly, they've concluded Elphie is on her own, and not a decoy sent by some ambushing party to distract them. Still, a semblance to living toys—roles that Elphie has seen domesticated cats and dogs inhabit with relish—dissipates the closer she gets to them. The Ski'ioti are wary. Even Elphie can pick that up, and she's not clever at reading emotions on the faces of human beings.

Curious.

Elphie hasn't mastered the art of small talk or shown any indication of wanting to do so. She plunges right in. "I wasn't sure you'd keep your word."

"Words are shallow currency with us. But here we are." Nerineri is in charge. Lollo-lollo hangs back, his walleye giving him the impression of waiting for some more interesting guest to arrive.

"I want to know something," says Elphie. "Since I met you, I've picked up a little about talking Animals from our governess. I never knew about you. Any of you. I'm so stupid. Right here in plain sight, or nearly. And not a whole lot of friendly chitchat between us and you. So I never, never knew."

"The world isn't always an us-and-them proposition," says Nerineri. "That said, I trust you haven't told your tribe that we're here."

"Of course she has," snaps Lollo-lollo. "She's only human."

Elphie flinches. What an insult. "Well, my brother and sister blabbed what happened, of course. But I didn't tell anyone but my nanny I was coming to see you, and even to her, I didn't say where. I mean, not here. In this cedar grove."

"You're telling the truth," says Neri-neri. "You're too young to lie convincingly."

"Well, you said you keep yourself apart. Fair enough. I would, too, if I could. So I paid attention. But you do it so well that I never even guessed. And I'm not an idiot. So if you prefer to be unsociable, why really did you rush over to save my sister when she fell in the water? Not too many Quadlings would do the same for you, I'm guessing."

"Is this all we're going to do," interjects Lollo-lollo, "*talk*? For this we stuck around? Put ourselves at risk? She didn't even bring us anything to eat."

"Sorry about that," says Elphie. "I didn't know I should. Anyway, we don't have much to eat at home, so if I stole it there'd be questions. And you can't eat questions."

"No, we can't," agrees Lollo-lollo. "But you seem to have brought them anyway."

"I want to know why you bothered to rescue my sister."

Neri-neri replies, "It's a moment-by-moment choice, isn't it, to choke or to be charitable? But instinct counts for something. Life is life."

"That sounds, um . . . rehearsed."

"Oh, you're sharp. Fair enough. It's true, we had no precise interest in your sister's personal death or in her personal survival. It's just that Dwarf Bears are useful pawns for when human tempers rise and when fear overtakes reason. We thought we'd deter a human death near where we might have been seen. Truly, it's exhausting always fleeing a mob. Big cats can outrun moonlight. We lumber and we're small and noisy."

"Sitting targets for a mob, if a mob is so inclined," says Lollo-lollo.

"The peaceable Quadlings still get themselves worked up some-times. What fun."

"Suppose other humans had come running? They'd have known you were, um, foraging."

Neri-neri screws up her face into a whorl of fur and snout. "Even Lollo-lollo with his vagabond eye could tell that you were doing nothing useful to help her. And—"

"I would do everything to help her, of what I could; but I couldn't do that. The water, you know."

"Don't interrupt. I'm answering your questions. You seemed to us like a strange species of walking bamboo, shrieking. We'd never heard a caterwauling plant, nor one that could jump up and down. I suppose we were more curious than kind. And you were rambling out alone, you three, evidently children without the ap-propriate guardians. It seemed safe enough for us to risk. That's being honest."

"I'm not a plant," says Elphie, not certain if she should be of-fended or perhaps wistful. What would it be to be a plant?

"Are you sure?" asks Lollo-lollo. "Seem like a real chokervine to me."

"What even are you doing here? How do you live, are there, um, a colony of you?" asks Elphie. "Why do you pretend to be ani-mals without the power of speech?"

"Safer that way," says Neri-neri. "You see, *we* can pass. You, I don't think you have that much luck. Unless there are hundreds more of you, all that verdancy."

"She could pass as swamp muck," says Lollo-lollo. Neri-neri throws a cedar pinecone at him.

Elphie goes on. "Are you a tribe, a posse? A, a caravan? A na-tion? I don't get it. Can you talk to a talking Monkey, assuming such a creature exists? How does it all *work*?"

"You're too nosy," says Neri-neri. "We saved your sister, that's all you need to know about how we're organized."

"Oh, all right. We're runaways," says Lollo-lollo. Neri-neri butts him with her snout. "What?" he grumps. "*You're* the one who wanted to stick around and talk to her. Isn't this talking? Let's get the gassing over with."

Family strife, Elphie knows it well. "Ooh, that sounds interesting. Being a runaway. From where?"

"None of your need to know," growls Neri-neri, but Lollo-lollo smiles, if that smirk is a smile.

"If we tell it all at once, we can move on, get out of here," he says to his companion. "We risk too much to make nicey-nice with a sprog, however nonconformist she is. We'll get all the chat chattered out of us and then let's get going." To Elphie: "We tried to work with men from the Emerald City, though we hadn't been much use in the building of the big bossy highway. Our paws are the wrong size to handle those bricks. But when the rubies were discovered, whoa, we got noticed. We got hired. We got paid well. We're harnessable, you know. Wagonloads of corundum. We're reliable labor. We don't get mange like the mules they brought from the north."

"Lollo-lollo, are you done? Concentrate for once in your fool life. We were paid well in food and in comfort, but not in liberty," explains Neri-neri. "Most of our kin were happy enough. But not us."

"But not you," Lollo-lollo corrects her. "*I* was snug and well-fed. But I came away anyway because you made me."

"Go bite your tongue if you feel like having something so bitter in your mouth. I won't have it. We're free, we're here; today is the day."

"What day?" asks Elphie.

"Just, the day, the day we have," replies the boss Ski'ioti. "The day we can breathe, and follow the sun in the sky, and eat and crap and find shade for afternoon sleep, and steal the human food at high noon if we're lucky. The day to avoid arrows and hippos and poisonous snakes. The day to talk to an uncoiled vine of a human being, and learn something new! Not the day to be yoked to a cart and lug minerals about."

Lollo-lollo rolls his rollable eye and closes both of them, pretending to snore.

"I suppose I owe you something," says Elphie. "Look, if I'd killed my sister by accident yesterday, I'd be having a different sort of day today than the one you just describe. So what do *you* want to know?"

Neri-neri shoves a few bamboo shoots in her mouth and chews thoughtfully. "What are you really?" she says. "Are you a human person? Are you of some other breed we haven't yet come across? It's only you we're curious about. We find that humankind is not very. Kind, I mean. But who are you? What's your name? I never came across your sort before. I can't work out what you are. Call it being nosy. Who *are* you?"

What child of thirteen can answer a question like that, when being thirteen is the apex of isolation? "I'm a puzzle to myself," Elphie answers at last. "But maybe not any more than you are to yourselves."

"There's something inside us that makes us turn out this way," says Neri-neri. "The thing that was around waiting to house in us before we were born, and that will linger after we die. We don't know what to call it, and maybe it doesn't have a name. But it's different for all of us—it makes a Ski'ioti out of me, not a snail or an egret or a grasshopper. It makes a boy out of your brother. Out of you it makes a secret."

"My father's a minister, shall I ask him?" Elphie is feeling pushed about. "He's got the rule book for why things are the way they are, not me. I'm just a kid talking to Animals. I don't have the answer to what you're looking for. I don't know a thing."

"Maybe you don't," says Neri-neri, "and maybe you do. I can tell you're fed up with the question. Would you want a banana? We have a few around here somewhere."

"Limited supply," objects Lollo-lollo, awake from his pretend nap.

Elphie shakes her head. "You could ask anybody a question like this, it doesn't have to be weird old me, green from underneath my fingernails to the roots of my scraggly hair. Why not ask a banana why it's a banana?"

"Same reason you came to us—because you can talk, and so can we. Bananas have little to say."

"My father says you only think you're real."

Neri-neri shrugs. "So what? I think *you're* real, and that's more interesting to me."

"Why should I interest you?"

"You're an idea," says Neri-neri, "that I didn't have before I saw you. Ideas make us jump. They shift us from before to after. I don't know who or what you are, or why you look like a walking edge of the jungle, but my sense of who I am changes now because of you. You don't have to teach me anything—what's your name?—you don't have to be anything but yourself."

Elphie is about to tell Neri-neri her name but she catches in the Dwarf Bear's offhand remark a rare allowance to be still. Elphie opens her mouth and closes it again. It will not happen often in her life. She will rarely be able to ignore the urge to motor through any given moment with as much commotion as focus. Now she sits in the sun, looking at Bears who are looking back at her. Each is Zoo to the other. Such is human astonishment. It can break over you so softly that, unless you're being quiet, it can go unnoticed.

For this moment, too rare a moment in her life, Elphie is aware of patience. She has ringed her bare green knees with her thin green arms. The wind plays a few strands of unbrushed hair across her brow. She lets them tickle her. Beyond, down the slope of cedars, Ovvels waits in its hewn thicket of built geometry. The floating pools and gardens adjacent to the small city are spotted with pale blossoms. The wind disrupts the human noise of the small city into unintelligible ellipses. Everything is happening everywhere, and at the same time, nothing much is going on. It is just the old world.

"I've given you nothing," she says at last to the Dwarf Bears. "You stayed behind against your better judgment to interview me, and I'm not worth the risk. Where will you go when you leave here?"

"No one needs to know that, safer that way," replies Neri-neri.

"When we were working as laborers and being well-fed, we had safety in numbers," adds Lollo-lollo. "Now we're a pair of fugitives. Thanks to her notion of freedom. Free to be hungry and on the run. What joy."

"You have so many questions," says Neri-neri. "It's a rarity among your kind. You've given us an experience of human curiosity, so thank you for that much. You can't even name your questions yet, and maybe you never will. Doesn't matter. Sure, we're talking Animals, but we're not geniuses. We're rural rabble compared to others I could mention! We know nothing of the world beyond our little lives. But some Animals do. There are educated Animals out in the wider world. You'll find out. You have curiosity in your eyes about this. That's a present for us to see, we who rarely have spotted anything other than commercial interest in the eyes of our, our employers. If you will. But we are simple sorts. We're migrants on the run. Find someone else to answer your questions about Animals. We saved your sister but we can't save you. That you have to do for yourself."

"And now is the interview over?" asks Elphie.

The Ski'ioti don't answer. Parlor manners mean nothing to them. They get up and wander off and don't say good-bye and don't look back over their padded shoulders. They move along the ridge, under the cedars, like furry boulders out to take the air.

# 34

Elphie imagines the Ski'ioti will lie low for a while, abandoning her—because they've gotten from her all she has to give.
Which isn't much. She wouldn't really blame them. She
would do the same. It is Animal behavior, perhaps—and isn't she
an Animal too, of a sort? Conservation of resources. She will have
the same attitude toward party chatter not only in Shiz, but also
later in the Emerald City, and everywhere else, all her life. Waste
of time.

Elphie watches them until they are lost in the underbrush. She
gets up and heads downslope to Lei Leila'ani's, eager that her having slipped away from home should go unnoticed. She is protecting
herself and—she consoles herself later—protecting the Ski'ioti. She
hasn't learned the concept of consorting with the enemy, but her
instincts say: Beware. On their behalf if not on your own, beware.

When Elphie arrives back at the family's rooms in Lei's sprawling tree home, Nanny is pulling out of the trunks those lengths
of shawl and fancy gown saved as a souvenir of poor Melena. Now
she's holding them to the window, inspecting the seams. Here's the
charity ball gown, blue and mauve whorls, still bright and fresh
after spending its retirement in a closed casket.

"I don't know if I want to let this go, these scraps of my precious
poppet. Whom I raised from swaddles. I'll have nothing of her left
if I give these to you to bargain with that clothier, Elphie."

"Um, you have me, and Nessa, and Shell," Elphie points out.
"We can be your souvenirs of Mama."

"Somehow it's not the same thing. Souvenirs remind one quietly of blessed happiness in the past. They aren't expected to talk back. While you rarely shut up."

Elphie shrugs. So what.

"And this was the item worn by your mother the night she eloped. I was saving it for you to get married in."

"No harm done, then, because I'm not getting married."

"That's what every girl says when she's your age. Anyway, little use crying over the past. If Melena's old trousseau can buy us escape from mudland province, so be it. Maybe that's why I hauled them about all these years, because I sensed these fancy clothes would come in use." She begins to fold them up, like a sacred shroud, and Elphie grabs the top one.

"That old merchant, he'll like this. I can barter for information about Turtle Heart. What else have you found?"

"Don't give away the store, save something for emergencies," counsels Nanny. Then, slipping through the laces of a rolled-up stomacher, a small bottle of a viscous green fluid. "I just remembered, Melena gave that to me for my service to the family," gabbles Nanny, but Elphie snatches at it first.

"It's a cologne?" she asks.

Nanny slits her eyes and regards Elphie. "It's a sort of bromide. When you're feeling punkish. Your mother sipped it sparingly, gingerly. That's not yours to take, Elphie."

"Nor yours, either." And Elphie has her there.

Nanny sighs as Elphie pockets the bottle. "If we could finally finish up this thankless hunt for atonement, we might remove ourselves to drier climes. Maybe your prime problem is mildew—I don't know. Well, do your best trying to hawk this outdated glory for information. Your father won't notice that a gown is missing. He pays no attention to things of this world. Do us a favor and drive home a bargain, Elphie."

Elphie goes off to the merchant's shop in the tree boughs. The suspicious old geezer is wrapping up some merchandise in a loose sleeve of plaited reeds while a handsome, bored young man waits outside on the deck, dragging on a perguenay cigarette. Not all that much older than Elphie. Or maybe he is, who can tell with the males of the species. "Oh, so it's *not* just gossip, the fact of you," drawls the client, regarding Elphie. "An articulate asparagus fern."

"I'm here to talk to the boss," replies Elphie, thinking, Well, whatever happens, I'm not marrying *you*—you'd only make fun of me, and you've just proven it. She waits until the sale is completed and the client has sauntered off, and then she says to the merchant, "I have a trade to propose." She bashes the squared mound of fabric onto the mahogany counter and lays out her terms. There is a more like this at home, in equally good state.

"Figured silk," says the merchant, his fingers assessing the fine napery of the material. "Unfashionable. Probably worthless. Still, I can take it off your hands, I guess. As for your search, it could take some doing. I can try, but I can't promise to find you the Turtle Heart you want. This Chelo'ona."

"Um, he's dead, you're not going to find him. I've told you this before. It's his people we're hunting down. In exchange for this cloth."

"If the other items you mentioned are in as good repair, they might make a fair exchange for my efforts. But the contract would be binding even if any leads I uncover turn out to be dead ends. In other words, no backsies."

"I'll return with another dress later today or tomorrow. So we're square then?"

He pauses and tilts his finger against his pursed lips, considering. She can nearly hear the sound of his thinking. "Not quite. There's the matter of the broken window."

"I had nothing to do with that!"

"Look. I saw your bearded guardian waiting for you down there. I watched you hurry away with him. One of you has to make good on that damage. That's how we do it in Ovvels. You come work for me for a few weeks. Be my shop assistant. I haven't had any staff this year and I'm only getting older. You can pay off the cost of a new window by helping out through the holiday. It's about to be the busy season." He shrugs one shoulder toward the window opening. He has covered it with a cloth of palest aubergine, dried vegetable pearls sewn randomly upon it, snails in a mulberry tree. The light shows that the frame isn't the easy rectangle of most window openings, but a skewed oval of sorts, a large eye-opening tilted upward on one section. A few panels of clear glass fit in the corners of the box frame, to make it come out right. Only the central glass, the eye itself, has been shattered.

"I'll have to ask my father about working. He probably won't let me."

"It's a double-bind deal. I won't take the cloth, and I won't do your research about some Turtle Heart character, if you don't also agree to help me out a while. Staff is hard to come by, and I'm getting on."

"I know nothing about cloth and, um, I have no interest in learning."

"I don't remember that I asked you what you were interested in learning. Or if you even have the talent to learn. You clearly know nothing about fashion! Now take away your bribe and come back with an answer. I'll have the sheriff collect you if you shirk me. I know your family is staying at Old Widow Leila'ani's place. See, I do know how to find things out, there's the proof of it! I'll expect you tomorrow morning after breakfast, with another sample of fabric, and we'll seal the deal. Clause one: In exchange for cloth, I'll try to hunt down information on your Turtle Heart. Clause two: In exchange for the price of replacing my window, you start tomorrow. You'll be done at the hour of the noon meal. I'm not taking on the cost of feeding you lunch, so don't hang around hoping."

"If I agree," says Elphie, "it's under the condition that I'm doing it to help my father find Turtle Heart's kin. It's not an admission of guilt about your stupid broken window. My father is a man of faith. He wouldn't break an eggshell if he could avoid it."

"I'll agree to pretend I don't blame him for it. How's that?"

"I don't even know your name," she says.

"Do we need to go that far? If you think so, do your own research on that. I'm not setting up to become your surprise kindly old patron. Get out of here."

# 35

Back at the lodging, Elphie is only a bit startled to learn that her father is unfazed by the notion of a job. "You have to start learning some skill," he says. "A man of business might fiddle around with a young uneducated girl from the out-back. But not him. He's all right; Lei vouches for him. I checked it out."

"I still don't understand about that rock through the window," says Elphie, probingly. The most disingenuous statement she's ever made. "Who threw it, and why?"

"I wouldn't put it past Shell, the little scamp," says Nanny fondly, splaying her fingers upon her bosom and lowering her eyes in an unconvincing trance of adoration.

"Nanny, he was home with you at the time."

"It's of little interest to us," says Frex, dismissing the question. "Perhaps the merchant has competitors who want to drive him out of business." He turns back to his books, running a finger along a column of tightly printed prose.

Neither Nanny nor Elphie mentions they are trading Melena's wedding robe for information on Turtle Heart. Frex wouldn't care in any case, so no need to bother him with details.

"I bet it was one of those Dwarf Bears," says Shell. "The ones in the lagoon gardens. They were kind of creepy, really. They talked like those puppets we saw on the puppet-show boat once."

"Shut up, you're a stupid little boy," says his bigger big sister.

# 36

She starts the next day, carrying a packet with the second garment and a couple of marsh plums for a midmorning snack. The old fellow, named Unger Bi'ix, Elphie has learned from Lei, is waiting. He has poured a bowl of tea for his new employee and it is still hot. "Set that parcel in the back room and then have a moment with me."

Unger—he accedes to his own name and nods, and says Elphie may use it, but only respectfully—Unger hands Elphie the tea and puts her through some exercises in computing and then in reading. Nanny has taught Elphie numbers ("helpful for if you're pinching a little from the pot; you never want to take too much or they'll notice") and Melena, one bored summer long ago, her letters; Frex has supplied holy texts for Elphie to struggle through. Reading is not a strength, though Unger admits the girl seems to have an instinct for mathematics as well as an assertive curiosity.

They finish the tea, which is possibly the first social event Elphaba has ever navigated on her own, standing on her own green shadow instead of in the umber-purples of Nanny's or her father's. Unger then shows Elphie the storeroom. He won't let her touch his precious wares for fear of her staining them green. "A superstition I will grow out of, no doubt," he admits, "but not today." Carefully he unfolds the packet Elphie has brought, patting down its wrinkles. He intakes between his teeth in grudging appreciation. "A little my-old-auntie," he says, "not a patch on the first one you brought in, but it'll go in this market, yes indeed."

He explains the systems of measuring cloth, and Elphie can

watch, but not yet wield a scissors. He shows her a chart for cost. He tries to explain his system of bartering, lowering subtle taxations upon the socially ostentatious, while extending quiet allowances to those in distress, like the newly bereaved. "But a lot of people lie about losing their mothers," he warns her. "We lose double the population of Ovvels in mothers every holiday season. Don't be fooled by the grieving. The more ostentatious the display of mourning, the more dubious the loss."

"I won't do any talking at all."

"Probably wise. For now, go sweep the veranda." He gives her a broom.

She's never held a broom before. You don't need to sweep the dirt floor of a tent. To say that Elphie wields it awkwardly is an understatement. "In time it'll come to feel like part of your arm," says Unger, watching from the doorway. "But here comes a client; don't be a fool and sweep leaves onto her!" Too late. The customer protests as a cloud of yellowed seedpods falls upon her veiled head. "Stand in the corner and keep a straight face; your smile is anything but genuine and it looks scary," hisses Unger. "Good morning, friend Parwa'ani. A cup of tea?"

"Quite a monstrosity," said this Parwa'ani, upon reaching the top of the stairs. She shakes off her veil, scattering the dust and leaves about so Elphie needed to go back to her work with the broom. "At which stall in the marketplace did you pick her up, Unger Bi'ix?"

"Very well, we'll proceed directly to the display room," he says. Elphie senses a touch of kindness, that he's chosen not to gossip about how he met his new assistant. Or at least not in front of her. He is heard to mutter, however, in a dark aside, as the two adults disappear through the doorway, "One doesn't quite know what to think, curiosity or curse?"

So their tentative arrangement, Elphie's and Unger's. If it collapses, as it probably has to, Elphie will just flee. Like the Ski'ioti. She is doing this for the family, such as she conceives family to be. She has no basis of comparison about how other families behave, living as she's done in the wild, in the lone.

Her family isn't sure it is grateful, because they don't know if this Unger will make good on his promises. Maybe he's just taking advantage of hapless labor. Frex grills Lei on the third night of Elphie's tenure. "You're certain that Elphie is in no danger? It's not worth whatever information this Unger might turn up if he has unsavory designs on my daughter."

"I've told you. He's a married man," replies Lei, with a sigh, because she'd prefer to be married again herself, and points it out to her lodgers frequently. "He has several families, in fact, in the outmarsh. Wives and children. He likes to father them, but he is well known for preferring business to parenting."

"Perhaps *I* ought to have gone into business," mumbles Frex.

"I'll gouge his eyes out with a serrated grapefruit spoon if I hear of any funny business going on," swears Nanny. "Elphie, you're going to learn something with that Unger, but it better be decent. What is he having you do? I want the full day, moment by moment."

"Nothing much. I gather there's some holiday coming up, sort of like Lurlinemas but they call it by another name. Se'enth, or something like that. It has candles and special foods, and people give each other presents with wings on them. Weird. Unger says the custom probably comes from some old story about how the first Quadlings arrived here from far away across the deadly sands. The story says they must have flown because how else could they survive?"

"More superstitious nonsense, as sick and stuffy as the Lurline cycle," snorts Frex. "Pay no attention to it. *Se'enth.* The idle appetite of the ill-informed."

"Lurline is going to strike you dead for your snide commentaries," singsongs Nanny. "One of these days, when she gets around to it."

Elphie continues. "So Unger is teaching me how to sew. People show up with their little dollies made of dried vines and bones and whatnot, and it's our job to cut out wings and fix them on. The more dead and lifeless the doll looks at the start, the more magical it becomes when it has wings of soft patterned cloth. I have to admit it, even though I hate the whole idea of dolls and toys."

"I would like one," says Nessarose. "A winged toy. Winged Ninnakins!"

"Pagan nonsense, temptation and distraction," says her father.

"Let the little girl have her wish," says Lei, who hasn't yet commented about the Thropp family protocols. Frex winces at her but can't risk agitating the landlady. He heaves himself off for a walk around the town, stewing. So far his attempts to rally a thin congregation have proved fruitless.

"I want a doll, too," says Shell. "Then I could kill it over and over and it wouldn't die, because it was already dead."

"You're a sick bunch. I worry about the whole lot of you," says Nanny. "Elphie, if you're learning to cut out wings and sew them together, make me an extra-large pair, would you. Out of your mother's morning gown, that would be fitting, as it's her behavior that landed me here in the first place. I have half a mind to lift myself out of this muckland and take my retirement back at Colwen Grounds. Meaning no disrespect," she adds, nodding at Lei and pursing her lips in an attempt at a conciliatory moue. "A very nice muckland it is, too, none better."

# 37

wice Elphie climbs the knoll where she last met the Ski'ioti. She calls their names as she remembers them, though maybe her pronunciation is feeble. "Lollo-lollo? Neri-neri!" But she doesn't holler. It's a trick, trying cautiously to summon fugitives out of hiding. Using an aerated whisper-bellow. If she opened up her lungs she could command the attention of half the town below, you better believe it. But what good would that do the Ski'ioti?

So maybe they're here, still, but aren't persuaded to show themselves again. They've taken from Elphie all that they want to know. They have no obligation to her. What is she looking for? *Friendship?* What would she know of friendship? She hardly understands the word.

Both times she heads back to town. Both times she is late for work, and Unger has sharp words for her. Once more and the deal is off.

The Ski'ioti will find me when they feel like it, she concludes, turning her attention to her chores.

Elphie learns to manage scissors and she learns to handle a needle. She learns to stitch. She bloods her hands. Day by day something new, until after some days in a row she has a routine. Too much of a routine, maybe. She remains eager to conjure up the Ski'ioti and figure out more of—more of something. What is it? She doesn't know.

The not knowing what she needs to learn is part of the excitement.

But she masters punctuality, at least. Daily she's the first to arrive. She unlocks the door with a key stored under a stone idol of some sort, a kind of lady with a fish-tail in place of legs. She takes out the broom and sweeps the veranda. Yes, the broom has become more subservient, as Unger predicated. Then Elphie attends to the floors of the salon and the workroom.

For Unger's repair work, to which he turns his attentions when the salon is quiet, she lays out the threads in a color sequence of a rainbow, more or less, though the black and silver and gold and bronze confuse her. And so does pink—it seems unrelated to red no matter what Unger keeps telling her. White is always at the far left, so she doesn't have to think about it. Black doesn't seem like the opposite of white, but more like a cousin. Unger despairs of her.

The night before, Unger has pulled forward the fabrics he expects they will need the next day. In the mornings, Elphie hoists these bolts of self-confident color on her thin shoulder, one by one, and carries them from the back room to the front. She slots them into a set of rococo brackets built into the wall. Some people get drunk on proximity to prettiness—a roll of woven red roses sloping down over this sheer, saturated blue piqué!—but that sort of thrill is lost on Elphie. She listens to the birds in the trees outside the wide oval window frame, still waiting its replacement glass. Before Unger arrives, Elphie pulls up the sheer cloth drapery so she can see the birds, too. She hopes they will fly in. She's supposed to be approximating their wings, after all. Once in a while the birds oblige her, but they dirty the furniture as they flutter about, looking for escape, and Unger is cross at their droppings.

Elphie brings forward the scissors and the marking wheel and the tapes for measuring. She puts them on a brass tray in the right order. She retrieves the shallow bowl filled with bits of white chalk that Unger uses to mark lengths on the cloth. On a side table that rolls on little iron wheels she lays out upward of fifteen differently sized templates used for the cutting of wings. Woven from reeds, they fray easily. On some mornings she melts the bottom of a candle, and while it is still warm and malleable she drips the ivory beeswax along the wing-edges, sealing them. Extending the useful life of the patterns.

Her movements make her feel prissy, but she doesn't care. Unger is particular. She squares paper slips for billing, perching a small brass monkey atop them to keep them from blowing away. Readies the quill pen, plops down next to it a bottle of ruby ink with a ruby glass stopper. Everything is elegant, as if made for a palace, but this is a shop, that's all. She doesn't quite understand the atmospherics of business, but she realizes that tone is important, somehow.

Once the shop opens, she sticks to Unger's elbow, responding to his monosyllabic requirements. When clients come, she mostly keeps her mouth shut. Here in this built environment Elphie feels as if she stands out more. So she learns to train her eyes to her task, not out of propriety but because she really doesn't want to engage anyone who is busy ignoring her anyway.

When the shop is empty of customers, Unger brings her tea, supervises her output, criticizes her sloppy needle skills, and makes her rip out inept work, which he calls lazy. But she can't criticize him as taking advantage of her in any way. He's respectable and he keeps custody of his own curiosity, not asking her nosy questions the way Lei sometimes does. (Lei drinks a little in the evenings.)

Unger also snips and stitches as hard as Elphie does, or harder, sometimes sitting across the work bench from her. He's not a young man—older than her father, she guesses. His eyes aren't keen, and the close work is vexing, but he keeps to it. He teaches Elphie the necessary elegance of the tight stitch. He whoofs and sighs as he gets up to lumber to the front of the showroom whenever a client comes in. His customers buy or sell fabric, or they order wings or fittings or, once in a while, clothes—though that is infrequent. The citizens of Ovvels have little time for pretty outfits that will only get rained on and stained by mud and refuse.

Unger works his clients over with charm and a skill at salesmanship that Elphie admires without quite figuring out how it works. She can't say he's unctuous or insincere, but nor does he seem personable. The calibration of his attention upon a customer shifts by the sentence, by the moment, as the person hesitates before plunking down cash and making a deal.

One afternoon Elphie has pricked her fingers a bit too often. She sits sucking two of her fingers to avoid dropping blood on the sample before her, a stretch of creamy silk blotted with drowsy fuchsia flowers. Unger has fetched a small stone vial of salve. This helps seal the wound, but her fingers need binding in cotton so the grease of the ointment doesn't do damage to the fabric. Elphie lets him apply the unguent to her fingertips. She feels a sudden urge to weep, and she doesn't know why. His touch is so—so concerned. As soon as she can do so without being rude, she yanks her hand away and says to him, "Where are all the boys in this town?"

He's entirely unfazed by the question. "Surely Goodwidow Lei has told you all about that. As soon as boys reach the age of seven, they're brought out to the eastern marshes, two days journey from here, to harvest vegetable pearls. They can work for ten to fifteen years before developing the crud-lung. It's the foundation of our economy, not just in Ovvels but all over this part of Oz. The market is bottomless, but sometimes the marsh seems so, too. Only boys can drop that low in the water. Their body weight is optimal—less resistance because less bulk—and their athletic suppleness a natural advantage. So you're quite right. The town has its share of girls and young women, who after a certain age often live in residential lodges until marriage. But maidens have to wait until the boys age out of the vegetable pearl business. And those maidens take what they can get, snap up the next available boy quick as they can. The crud-lung sometimes means an early death, and young brides want as much married life as they can curry. You'll have realized that Goodwidow Lei is not the only single woman running a household on her own. It's more common than not."

"*You* avoided crud-lung."

"I avoid gossip in general, and so should you. But if you're looking for some green boy here to go around with, I'm afraid you're going to be sorely disappointed. We don't seem to carry much in the way of green boys."

"I'm not waiting for that. Look, I hear someone on the steps."

Unger gets up and walks out to be convivial. There's no one on the steps. He lets Elphie return to her work and allows the subject to sink into the afternoon languor. However, before closing, he takes from a locked drawer a few vegetable pearls and rolls them into the brass incense stand. They look like albino peas, one as large as a thumb tip, others with a nacreous pink blush, or ivory, or a faint lemon green. All of them subtle, pale, and reflective. Apparently vegetable pearls harden as they age, but when first harvested they can be pierced with a needle, which allows for stringing. Jewelry, fabric ornamentation, who knows what. Unger uses them for trim when clients bring out the right sort of wallet.

Elphie picks up a few and looks at them, to be polite. The appeal of beauty escapes her, mostly. He is careful to lock them away as soon as she is done. No word passes between them about it.

She's begun to stay through the noontime meal and on toward dusk. At home that night, she complains of her work, of her bloody thumbs. Nanny coos and her father ignores her and Shell ignores her, but Nessa says, "I wish I could work there, too. Elphie, will you bring me? I could do something useful, surely?"

"Like what? Bite the threads at the end of a patch job?"

"You're horrid. I could sit and be attractive and talk to customers while they're waiting for you to finish up. You can't be very engaging, with your tongue, and I doubt you're very deft."

"Maybe not, but I can pick up any thread that I drop."

Elphie's gone too far, out of exhaustion and maybe pride. Nessa mutters, "What I wouldn't give to thread a needle and blood my fingers." So Elphie doesn't complain again, or not in front of her sister, anyway.

# 38

Think about it. Elphie is responsible for entering into two contracts.

The first is the trading of her mother's steal-away frocks and gowns in exchange for Unger's looking into the identity of Turtle Heart and the location of his survivors, eleven years later. If they are even findable, if they are still alive. Unger is taking the job seriously, or seriously enough. Some days he goes out for an hour to make enquiries at some lodge or lobby somewhere. "Such an effort, delegating people to ask other people, and then waiting for the replies to cycle back through the chain of chat," he explains. "You can't rush these things. Watch what you're doing; this is supposed to be cut on the bias and you've lined it up all wrong. You keep wasting cloth and you'll be my indentured servant till the next jackal moon."

The second contract is Elphie's working as Unger's assistant to pay for replacing the broken window, even if the breakage wasn't Elphie's fault. She just happened to be standing there when some bird carrying a stone in its beak flew into the window. Or some kid playing a game became an accidental vandal and ran away before he could be spotted. But Elphie has stopped pointing this out to Unger. She's accepted the terms. It's not so much that she enjoys working for him—though she does—it's that she likes having something to do that doesn't involve her family.

One morning when Unger is out making a delivery for a housebound client, the young fellow who made a snarky comment about Elphie's complexion early on, that first day, comes back to pay an installment on a bill. He's slight, like most Quadlings, but has a brittle quality, too—something about the way he puts his foot down on the floor, nearly soundlessly. Now that she's conversant with the secrets of bookkeeping, Elphie takes his coins and notes and gives him a receipt, and she writes down a note about the cash taken in, though doesn't know to whom to ascribe the payment, and she can't bring herself to ask. All the while she imagines his eyes drilling into her—she keeps her own eyes lowered—as if to see if her scalp beneath her hair is green like the rest of her. "Have you any questions, sir?" she asks. She is parroting what she thinks Unger might say at this point, though she can't imitate her boss's manner, which manages to be both unctuous and sincere. She can only be brisk.

"I just wonder where you came from, and how long you're stay-ing," he replies, in an indefinite tone she can't read, but she doesn't much like whatever slant it is taking.

"Do you now," she replies. "And I wonder how long *you're* stay-ing. I have other chores to attend to." There, she has made *him* sound like a chore. Unintended cleverness on her part, but she's glad of it. She hands the receipt over and gives a half bow from the elbows, a gesture of dismissal.

He's unfazed. "You're certainly not from here."

"And you are not off in the lagoons of vegetable pearl, though you look young enough to be wet behind the ears. I wonder why you're excused that task."

"Do you wonder that, now," he says, mocking her a little. "If one is born to the chieftain's clan, there are certain allowances."

"If one is a shopgirl, one gets no allowance." She turns her back to him, opening a ledger on the other desk, and studying the pages for no good reason except to show him she's done with him.

She doesn't like him, not how he behaves nor even how he looks.

But he is wearing a vegetable pearl in one ear, and she likes *that*—
that alone. She's too inept to work out the algebra of aesthetics,
but she can and does notice the paradox of it.

He thinks he can outwait her, so to toy with her the more, but
he can't, and eventually he pads away. As soon as he's descended
the steps she rushes to the porch and begins to sweep with ferocity. The morning's harvest of fallen leaves showers upon him in a
golden flurry. He pretends not to notice, and she laughs out loud.
She can't remember laughing at anyone other than a family member before. It feels full, and it feels mean. Both of these sensations
are gratifying.

When Unger returns, she wants to find a nonchalant way to ask
about the client, but Unger brings news. He tells her, "I've had a
spot of luck at the home of my morning client, of all things. Wait till
you hear. I've learned that there was indeed a Turtle Heart, someone distantly related to a family in the glassblowing guild. As I need
to have this window replaced, I'll send you there to place the order. After the holiday, when I can spare you from the shop. You can
make your enquiries at last. So we'll kill two birds with one stone."

"One stone broke your window. Let's not throw any more. Um,
especially not to kill birds."

"It's a saying." He looks at her, alert.

"Someone stopped by to pay a bill, a nervy young man, I've seen
him before. Older than me but not that much."

She explains she didn't know his name, so she couldn't record
his payment on the right page in the book. But she remembers
it was for an order of striped turquoise morgandy. "Oh, yes, the
Pari'isii crowd," replies Unger. "They run the city council, sometimes a bit too much for their own benefit. But they're good people,
mostly. I forget the young one's name. Are you smitten?"

"Smitten?" She doesn't know the concept. Unger tries to explain, and she flushes some different shade of green. "I have no intention of being smitten, though I would consider smiting," she barks at him. "He is rude and forward."

"Oh, and you, you're the very soul of manners, docile and decorative. Aren't you. I know. I've picked up on that." He looks at the note she took and then at the ledger. "Well, their bill is now all paid, so unless you're still here when the festival of Se'enth comes around again next year, and people need to redo their salons and freshen up their holiday wings, you won't be seeing much of him. I wouldn't worry about it."

"He should worry if he crosses my path when I'm not at work. I'm not as docile and, um, decorative as I look."

Unger raises an eyebrow at this but stops himself from further comment. He goes into the back room. Elphie doesn't concern herself with what he might think about in there. Enmired in the narcissism of youth, she has largely lost the capacity of empathetic fungibility that quietly characterizes the younger child. She does think about the Pari'isi boy, that is, until she is taking her midday bite on the veranda. She's distracted by the view over the water gardens and the lagoon, and before she realizes it, her boss is pushing through the cords of the doorway with a curious expression on his face.

He is brushing dots of rice from his combed chin-hairs. "This is the hour of rest, all of Ovvels takes its quiet time now. Why are you shrieking an alarm? Is there a fire someplace? Are you trying to annoy my neighbors?"

She has raised her voice in a soprano register, throwing it some distance; she hasn't thought this through.

Unger mutters, "You're caterwauling to attract that young snoot? The Pari'isi boy? Is that it? Is he lurking around for your approval and notice?"

"You're deranged." Elphie sounds too much like Nanny—it's sort of chilling. But Unger is on to her. She's been trying to send out a note for attention—not to some wasted rich kid, but to the Ski'ioti, whom she's spotted at the far end of the floating gardens. Lollo-lollo and Neri-neri, humping along on all fours, making a smorgasbord for themselves. She's at least realized that if her voice is heard, people would turn toward its source and away from the lagoon, so she isn't endangering the Dwarf Bears. But the Bears might hear, too, and lift their snouts, and remember that they had accepted her as a—what is the word? Not friend, that hopeless concept. As a—a—a fellow outcast? A resident of the margins? She's here, she's here, she's here: That's what her one-note carol has tried to remind them.

She hopes they won't scarper off before she can question them again. She's been lining up questions—every night another one occurs to her. If there really are lots of talking Animals—do they all speak the language of humans? Are there other tongues besides the human ones? What about when Animals come across nonspeaking animals of their own species—or any other? Can a preverbal animal be taught to speak? Where is the dotted line between Soul and soul—and is that even the question?

Likely she doesn't form these thoughts as rational phrases, likely her mind is really just going: Animals? *Animals* or *animals*? Huh?

The Dwarf Bears have heard her, for sure; they stop their foraging and lift their heads. But she doesn't dare not wave at them. Anyone craning to look at her for her sung bell-tone would turn to see whom she was signaling. She doesn't want to lead eyes to them.

The silence after her sonata has a presence of its own, a meaning.

Unger is still looking at her, with something of a raised eyebrow, waiting. She isn't a skilled liar, an unusual deficit and a liability in someone her age. So she just stands there. She doesn't offer any explanation for her sweet *taran-tara*.

But he's still looking, still looking. She gets nervous.

"You just can't help it, can you," he says at last, "drawing attention to yourself?"

"I'm a nobody, I've a right to be a loud nobody if I need to be."

"Ozma help us all."

When he's gone back to his rice and basil leaves, she steals a glance at the lagoon. It is serene and empty, nothing but the breeze pulling a rippled skin on the surface of the water. Those sly Ski'ioti have vanished. A trick she wishes she could learn.

# 39

When Elphie gets home that evening, her father and Nanny are waiting for her. Nanny looks wary. Frex seems a little predatory, or hungry.

"Not enough that you're green as a spring cucumber," says her father, "but now you're tricking yourself out in *song*? I hoped your mother wouldn't bequeath her exhibitionist tendencies to any of you. Oh, Elphie, the gossip."

She pretends she doesn't know what he means, but of course she does, she does. "It wasn't song," she protests. "I had a tickle in my throat. I was just opening my lungs."

"Oh, little Fae-Fae can sing, for sure," says Nanny, using the name that Nessa invented for Elphie, back when Nessa was hardly verbal. "Hasn't she been singing lullabies and night songs for her sister and brother for years now. Too deep in your books to notice, Brother Frex-ispar?" Her use of his more formal name is cutting, somehow. A father ought to know such a thing about his oldest child. He flinches.

"Lei was all but ambushed by nosy parkers on her way back from market," he says to his daughter. "Elphie! Calling attention to yourself. Just when we're trying to settle down here and fit in among these Quadlings."

"No hope of *our* passing unnoticed." She all but sizzles at her father. "You a hulking Munchkinlander man with a beard, and the rest of us bizarre in one way or the other. Anyway, I thought you were *trying* to attract attention. For a congregation?" This is an unstable argument but she's in defensive mode.

He won't strike her, he would never do that. But his voice is both flat and strategic. "Well, you want to be a trumpet, give us what you got."

She hates him. What does he want from her? How miserable a parent can be, so full of shift.

"Go on, favor him with that singy-thingy you do for your brother, love-him-to-death," says Nanny, in a voice that means, Oh, get it over with and let us move on.

Mostly in order to protect the Ski'ioti—to distract her grown-ups from asking *why* she's been ululating across the rooftops at top volume—Elphie takes her cue from Nanny and stumbles into a common nursery ditty.

> *Little lamb, little lamb,*
> *Wanted for the evening meal,*
> *We never wonder how you feel,*
> *We only think of how you veal.*

Her father stares at her. "It's an old song, I didn't make it up, it's the first thing I could think up," she declares.

"Do you remember the anthem to the Unnamed God that we sang back in Quoyre?"

She says no, but when he begins, she's able to join in a little. At least he isn't yelling at her anymore.

> *Beloved and beshadowed*
> *You give us sweet permission.*
> *To heed your call and do our all*
> *To spend our lives in mission—*
> *(Something something, she forgets the last line.)*

It doesn't matter that she can't remember the tiresome words. Her father is looking at her as if she's scored it to the very syllable.

Lei is peering in through the open doorway. "Who knew the little asparagus had a voice like a soprano toucan." The landlady's hypocrisy is curdling, as the news about Elphie's performance has arrived here through Lei's own gossip. Still, the landlady's regard is genuine, at least.

"Don't, just don't," says Nanny, turning to Frex, "after all this time," and she wags her finger at him, which could get her sacked, and how will she ever find her own way back to civilization, but she can't stop herself, "don't tell me you never noticed that your oldest child can actually *carry* a *tune*?"

"She sang in Qhoyre, I remember that," protests Frex, a bit feebly. "It just wasn't very good singing. More of a curiosity, since few people in Qhoyre sing at spiritual rallies. And not for the public." Her father regards her with apprehension, summing something up behind his holy eyes.

# 40

Over a supper of brown rice served on a bed of green rice, accompanied by rice wine, Nanny tries to steer the subject away from Elphie's big-mouth behavior. "Nessa," she says, spooning rice into Nessa's maw, "you've done such a good job at growing stronger. You'll be dancing one day on your own two feet, and no one needed to escort *you* around the floor."

"I won't ever get anyone," says Nessa. "So I'll dance by myself or not at all." A few grains of rice slip onto her chin. Nanny wipes them away.

"Your balance is improving by the day," Nanny continues blithely. "I've never understood how you could trip and fall into that rice paddy. Of course you shouldn't have been walking out there at all, you naughty things."

"Elphie was right behind me," says Nessa in a curious delivery, noncommittal.

"You were taking all due care, I'm sure, Elphie," says Nanny. Her attempt to keep the conversation from reverting to hymn tunes, so blatant. But still.

"I did my best," says Elphie.

"Oh, no one is suggesting otherwise. You wouldn't try to drown her, you're her sister. Nessa, you're not casting wicked aspersions upon your sister!"

"I was in front," says Nessa. "I didn't see. There was a slip, a rocking of the beams. Of course, I'm not accusing Elphie of anything." But such flatness of tone.

Frex is looking up from his portion. Lei Leila'ani has paused with the serving spoon in midair. Elphie can't speak, neither to defend herself nor to confess that she herself doesn't understand what happened that twisted moment in the lagoon gardens. The longer the silence, the heavier the unstated possibilities.

It's Shell who can't bear it, little Shell. "It wasn't Elphie," he says. "You know it wasn't, Nessa."

"Of course, how could it be Elphie, she's my sister," says Nessa.

"It was those Dwarf Bears. They came running to sniff us all over and they rocked the beams. It wasn't Elphie's fault."

"Shell, you're out of your pea-brain," snaps Elphie.

"I'm not," says Shell calmly. "I was there. I saw 'em. They gone and bounced Nessa into the bathwater. Like it was some kind of game. Then they saw she might sink and they got scared and they tried to drag her out. But it was mostly me who saved her. Elphie didn't do nothing."

"I'll have some more rice," says Nanny. "So good, yummy."

"Sing us a little song," says Lei, "a song of thankfulness, that we're all here and no one got drowned." She glances around the table with emergency complacency.

# 41

Ovvels is rich in open spaces. But Lei tells her tenants that the town council forbids the co-opting of any commons for personal financial gain other than the licensed hawking of edible produce or homemade handiwork. And the few formal municipal venues are restricted to military training—parade marches and the like.

Frex argues with Lei that religious excitation isn't essentially a commercial enterprise, but the goodwidow raises her palm. It's scored with designs in henna, Elphie sees, and the pattern on Lei's palm is, of all things, a smaller palm. Effectively she is holding up a double wall of resistance to argument. "Not for me to grant an exception," says the landlady. "For that you'll have to go talk to the chief of the council."

Which person, it turns out, is the father or uncle of the Pari'isi kid who was snorting at Elphie's particular glamour. No thanks, is Elphie's take on the matter. Let's go back to the marshways and eat bugs again.

But the holiday is approaching, that festival called Se'enth. The local alternative to Lurlinemas. Ovvels boys from the fields of vegetable pearls show up in noisy clots, home for the festival. The city—it calls itself a city, so why not—is becoming more urgent. A bit more rice tipsicle being consumed, and during the daytime no less. It makes a nice change, an uptick in jollity.

Frex relies on Lei to bring home the intelligence. Oh, she's happy to oblige, even if she hasn't quite cottoned on to Frex's strategies. She mentions that because one of the lodges used for the

education of the girls of Ovvels is vacant over the holiday, the locals sometimes steal into its playing field to mount an impromptu
morning festival event. A Se'enth picnic of sorts, on the day before
observance. Frex comes up with a scheme. On the day of the big
gambol, he tells Elphie she isn't to go to the clothier's for work.

"It's the last day of trade for the season. He needs me," she protests, but Frex will brook no resistance.

"He's using you. He got along without you before you showed
up, and he's taking advantage. I just hope not too much advantage. No, you're coming with me. I need your help today."

"To do what?"

"All in good time. First you'd better find something less grue-
some to wear."

"Where shall I find it?"

"Look in that trunk of your mother's old things."

"We've given quite a few of them away to Unger already."

"If there's something left, trot it out and try it on. Nothing too
bosomy, mind—you haven't got the goods for that kind of thing."

"I'm *thirteen*." Elphie's tone neither contradicts nor supports her
father's observation.

She and Nanny root around among the few remaining items
that haven't yet been surrendered to Unger. There's a dull red
skirt with a feathery motif stitched upon it in black cord. If you
roll it under at the waistband, it doesn't drag on the ground too
much. Though it gives Elphie an ungainly rope of fabric about her
middle. She hides it with a fringed shawl of pink roses painted
upon a brick-pink surround. "I look like a carnival attraction," she
complains to Nanny, who is busy sorting her out.

"You take after your mother," says Nanny grimly, through a
clenched mouth of pins.

"I want to go, too, wherever you're going," says Nessa. "Is there anything in that chest for me?"

"Nothing would suit you, you're already too beautiful to gussy up," says Nanny. "Anyway, I've been informed that we're staying behind, Shell and you and me. They'll tell us about it when they get home."

"Quick," says Frex, "let's get going before Lei returns with the marketing and insists on being our chaperone."

"Can't we go by Unger's so I can at least tell him I'm called away today? He'll be cross otherwise. Last-minute custom-work!"

"I've asked Nanny to make your apologies. *Will* you keep up?"

They set out, taking a series of suspended walkways strung from tree to tree. Heads poke out to follow them as they pass. Elphie is a sight, she supposes, even discounting the ignominy of her skin color. "I feel like a walking tree trunk," she complains. "This column of broadcloth. It's so stiff and unnatural. How did our mother stand it?"

"She often went without," says Frex shortly, then clarifies. "I mean to say that there was little call for formal wear during our time as missionaries."

At the edge of the student lodge, a few musicians are amusing themselves with bizarre stringed instruments shaped like crossbows. This is augmented by a percussion of tambours, bells, and a bleating of reeds. The good people of Ovvels are arriving with flagons and posies, and baskets of food for a midday meal. There's an air of harsh merriment. Small circles of dancers began to revolve. Nothing orchestrated, everything impromptu.

Frex scopes out the venue and tells Elphie they will mount the steps on the side veranda of the lodge. Around the corner. This vantage point doesn't face the main gathering directly, but perches at an angle to it. Beyond the floorboards stretches a grassy verge broad enough for a crowd to gather. Frex then says to Elphie, "You're going to sing when I tell you to."

"You're mad." She smiles at him out of panic. "I can't possibly."

"You'll do as you're told. We've reached the end of our resources. We'll have to throw ourselves on the mercy of the public for their charity if we don't begin to make good. The Unnamed God expects no less than our utmost. Start with the hymn we used to sing in the canoes. 'Tender Us Tenderness.' I know you know it."

"But that's in Ozish; these people speak Qua'ati."

"Trust me and follow my lead, or you'll be sorry, my girl."

When, around the corner, the meadow music breaks off for a moment, and a bit of noisy chatter erupts in the interval, Frex nods at her. Elphie does as she is told. "Louder," he says. "You're summoning people." She flings out an arm at the empty sports meadow before the veranda, daring him to notice nobody there. "*Louder.*"

Then as the anthem climbs the bridge to the second chorus, which unfolds on a higher platform of melody, her voice flutes through somehow. It has found its altitude; it unspools from her throat more naturally. Her mother's stiff dress holds her in place and stops her from fleeing even while a few residents of Ovvels round the corner of the lodge to see what human creature is making this sort of sweet thunder out of her own mouth.

When she has finished, Frex delivers an invocation to the deity, failing to mention which specific deity he has in mind. He quickly rolls his hand for Elphie to plunge into something else. The first thing that comes to mind, to throat, is a sort of nonsense catalog of animals that Nanny croaked in the nursery tent for years, to Elphie and to Nessa and again much later to Shell.

It doesn't matter that the lyric is anything but devotional. The

syllables make pleasant nonsense in the air. The melody is jaun-
tily off-the-beat. More people approach. And then Frex has them
where he wants them. He begins to stake a claim in Ovvels at last,
with Elphie as a spiritual lure, a reward. That it has happened
over the festival of Se'enth is deemed not just fitting but almost
prophetic.

# 42

Within a week Frex has formally established his mission to the citizens of Ovvels. Maybe they're flattered at his attention, maybe they're just polite. In either case, he's clever enough to see what they are hungry for and to give it to them. He styles himself an ambassador of change.

He details the challenges out loud to them. Surely these canny Quadlings can see that the world is unsettling itself? The people of Ovvels can't deny the risk to their way of life.

The old ways threatened, the revered ancestors panicked into silence.

First, the miracle of corundum in calcite: the *Ruby Peril*! Too many plantations of vegetable pearls are being despoiled by the mining of corundum deposits buried in the earth beneath the flood.

Next, the grip of the Emerald City upon the province is tightening. There's that damned highway. It's a yellow brick noose, constructed to strangle the good old ways, Frex claims. The overlords from away finance their incursion into Quadling Country by flooding their home markets with rubies extracted at the expense of the old Quadling way of life.

No, he isn't one of the military men from the Wizard's government; he's in opposition somehow, as the Quadlings are. He's here to teach them a new approach to coping with the forces oppressing them from beyond their marshes. His own deity hides behind the screen of an impossible name—the Unnamed God—while the local spirits of the Quadlings, if they're even addressed as spirits, seem evanescent. Sadly ineffectual. The forebears gone before us have all absconded into the mist. The Surges and Surprises, as they're called, those ancestral overseers; shape-shifters by name and definition. As unreliable dead as they were living. Where are they now when we need them?

In short, Ovvels is a community ripe for conversion. The need to believe in something more steadfast has become pressing.

Brother Frexispar is not like the Quadlings. That's part of the attraction, Lei murmurs, once her kinspeople have overcome their native courtesy and reserve and actually taken a look at him. He's tall and pale in contrast to their ruddy, more leathery miens. While they wear woven hats with shallow peaks and broad brims, Frex goes bareheaded, or he sports a blocky toque ornamented with a tassel, something like a bell pull. And there's the beard, which seems a prophetic accoutrement to the mostly beardless Quadlings. It's grown long and pillowy compared to the manicured moustaches of Emerald City civil engineers. That it's also somewhat rank perhaps adds to its effectiveness, though in saying so Lei provokes in her tenant a formidable frown. He stalks off to a lather and pomade.

Frex's command of Qua'ati has improved over the years since he left Munchkinland with his wife and oldest child. He's also learned how better to engage his clientele. His rhetoric is by turns cajoling and lyrical, and certainly less accusatory than it once was. Despite their worries, the Quadlings of Ovvels are a complacent lot. They respond to approval more surely than they do to condemnation.

And of course, Elphie. She'll never really take the measure of how significant she is to her father's success, but no doubt about it—she's his instrument. Her voice is his. When she manages one morning to sing a hymn in carefully translated Qua'ati, the congregation sulks. The attendees prefer Elphie's to be a voice of mystical connection to the unknown, so when she uses their own familiar language, the magic is cheapened. She reverts to standard Ozish in short order—at Frex's curt command.

# 43

By the fourth day her father tells her she'll have to stop by Unger's shop and inform him that she can no longer work there. She's needed at the camp meeting site, which the officers of the girls' lodge have allowed Frex to continue to use—it gives their establishment a slight boost among the competition. A glamour. Elphie isn't delighted to be enchained in devotions, but what can she do? The Thropps have to eat, and eventually to pay some back rent to Lei, as they're already in arrears.

In the later afternoon, she makes her way to Unger's emporium, climbs the stairs in that ridiculous heavy skirt. She looks to see if the Dwarf Bears are visible, but then, they had told her they rarely approach the floating gardens except at high noon. She squares her shoulders and ducks her head through the baffle of buttons strung to keep flies out of the doorway. "I know you're here or the door would be closed."

Unger comes out from the back room. "What a monstrosity," he says, regarding her garb. "So after your unsanctioned holiday break you come crawling back. Or should I say 'swishing'?"

"My father tells me I have to break this off. We must be paid up by now, with three or four of mother's dresses handed over, and all my time spent measuring, and, um, cutting, and sweeping, and making all those wings."

Unger nods. "I knew it was too good to last. There's so much more I could teach you. I suppose, yes, the dresses with their novel patterns—we got a lot of holiday wings out of them. All the rage. Killed the competition. So, thank you. I agree: as to the cost of my

researching for that Turtle Heart, you're paid up. Much good may
it do you."

"So where are his people? You going to tell us?"

"Let me finish. As to underwriting the cost of replacing the
shattered glass, your hours spent here may just about cover that.
I haven't done the sums yet. Even if"—he raises his hand—"even
if you insist that I can't prove someone in your party did it. I can't
prove they did and you can't prove they didn't. We're square, or
near enough to make no difference. So consider any balance still
owed me as a gift from me to you. But, my girl, what a sorry figure you cut there, in that lumpy garment. Turn around. Dreadful.
Look at that roll of wodge at your waist. Inelegant. Regrettable. It
does you no good. It doesn't become you at all."

"It better not become me. It's a frock for—um, for a siren, I
guess." Elphie grimaces; what can she do?

"Take it off. To thank you for reviving my custom these past few
weeks, I'll run you up a revision. You've been quite the draw, you
know. Everyone wanted to come and have a look at you close up,
back before you decided to parade yourself as a—what would you
call it?—a summoner? A saint? A holy tease?"

"Please!" she says, knowing just enough to be offended on behalf of her father, though she hardly cares a whittle about what
Unger might be implying about her.

"Take it off, I said. I'll cut that heavy carpet-cloth into strips and
chevron them into a skirt of much lighter muslin. It'll be half the
weight, or less, and tailored to your actual hips instead of to those
of your poor mother. Take it off, I insist; give it over. It won't be
long. If I can't finish it this afternoon, you can pick it up tomorrow."

"But I'm not decent underneath!"

"Oh, preserve me, I'd thought you might have better sense.
You've always seemed a freer creature than your upright father.

But never mind, I suppose people would talk. Wait." He disappears, returning with a simple shift of bleached white linen, light as gauze, just thick enough to be mostly modest. "You've seen these. I keep them for clients who come in needing emergency repair on ceremonial robes they haven't looked at since the last funeral. Change behind the screen and hand over that suit of armor you call a devotional garment."

She does as she is bade, stepping out in her bare green feet to lay the heavy pleated gown of her mother's into Unger's arms. He accepts it as a father receives the corpse of his son, fallen in battle. But when his eyes travel up to Elphie, he flushes. "Oh, you," he says simply. "White suits you. I suppose you've never had reason to discover this."

She sticks her tongue out at him. "I'm not interested in being appealing."

"You make that very clear. Still, once in a rare while, you can't help it. Oh, my, Elphie, what are we going to do with you?"

That's all that passes between them on the subject. He returns to the back room and she hears the sound of scissors amputating her mother's dress. "As long as you're here, please tie up the remaining winged figments on the cord above the porch rail," he calls. "The season is over, but we might still move some product at a deep discount. Next year will require new designs. Fashion is fickle. As is proven by this heartache of a Munchkinlander gown. What *were* they thinking? Was your mother a lunatic by any chance?"

She strings up a dozen and a half pairs of bird wings and has ten more to go before she has a chance to look down. The Pari'isi boy is at the foot of the raked steps to the emporium, lounging about with a fatherly smirk on his face and a cigarette between his fingers. "Unger's occupied," says Elphie. "He's got a rush job. You'd better go away."

"Oh, I have no business with him," says the lad. "I was passing by and I spotted your silhouette, and now I'm wondering if you're going to sing the glories of Unger's overstock. The Skylark of Ovvels, they're calling you. I'd think the Vulture of Ovvels might be more to the point, but vultures don't sing."

Elphie is decent, but her robe is light and blows about her in buffets of white, and her green arms and shins and feet made her feel nakedly on display compared to her usual cloak of hooded drabbery, essential in the event of a sudden downpour. "Go strangle yourself with a pearl choker," she snaps. The boy laughs and slips a handful of something from his shoulder pouch and begins to lob small items, one at a time, in her direction. She has to duck, to dodge. Vegetable pearls, those precious items, and he's squandering them to make her lunge about! More fool him, she thinks, I'm not going to throw them back to him. He can come up here and get them if he wants them. Otherwise, I'm keeping them.

But she guesses that he is teasing her for a gain; he likes the way she moves in her loose white shift, angled and cavorting, her dark hair spinning. She isn't sure how she feels about this. "Stop or I'll call Unger Bi'ix," she says.

"I am glad you're here, because I'm not permitted to go to that camp revival meeting your father has launched. Can you sing for me, at least? Everyone says you're weirdly compelling."

"I'm just weird. It's my father who is compelling." She's nearly done, working hastily and sloppily. "Whatever do you want here? I have business to see to."

"Just you come down, and I'll whisper you what I want."

She makes a show of scooping up the pearls. She tosses precisely one down and hits him on the head, to show him she can, and then carries the rest back into the shop. She deposits them upon the cutting table. "There," she says to Unger. "That ought to cover the balance of whatever it is we still owe you for the window. I don't want to take any gifts from you, thank you all the same."

He looks up at her shrewdly. "Where did you come by these, if I may ask?"

"They're a kind of donation," she tells him. "I don't wear jewelry. And I don't wear pretty white gowns. I'm going to go wait behind the screen till you're done."

"I may not be done by dusk, if other clients come to interrupt the job."

"Business is slack, you said. And I'll shut the door. If someone knocks, I can call through that you're engaged."

"That would do my reputation no good, the door closed with a young maiden on this side of it, and me 'engaged.'"

"Then you better work fast."

And so he does. By trade a merchant and not a fabricateur, his skills are nonetheless sure after decades of emergency assistance. The concoction he assembles is simple. A charcoal grey-black muslin, featuring a high neck and mutton sleeves gathered below the elbow; the shift falls loosely from shoulder to calf. Without the roll of excess fabric around Elphie's waist, the line is simple and draws no attention to her nascent womanly attributes, or lack of them. From the hips down, just a little flare, and this comes from the five or six segments of her mother's russet gown inset like darts from hem to hip. No pleating, no furbelows. For the first time Elphie recognizes that while her mother's gowns had all *meant* something—they'd meant blossoms, they'd meant birds and patterns of leaves, they'd been a catalog of something other than skirt material—the taste of Quadlings doesn't favor representation. These severed panels from her mother's dress are now largely illegible. Just color and form, not flowers. "I like it better like this," she says, putting her face to it.

"It's not as attractive as the simple white—"

"It'll suit me fine," she says firmly. "So, are we tallied out now? Is this good-bye?"

"Not quite," he replies. "You and your father still need to make the arrangements about the replacement of the glass. I will pay for it, now you've made good on the family debt, but you'll have to place the order. Quadlings are deft at glassblowing, though a piece this size takes a real master of the craft. I'll use a piece of cloth to mark out the dimensions, and I'll tell you where to find the tradesman. I'm pretty certain that he can tell you what he knows about Turtle Heart. Both contracts fulfilled on one afternoon. Once you manage that, our business arrangement is terminated."

"You won't come with me?"

"Wouldn't be seemly. You need your father or another chaperone—perhaps that Nanny. And, Elphie?"

He has scarcely used her name before. "Yes—Unger?" She either, his.

"I don't know where your life will go from here. Maybe you will live it out here in Ovvels. But I hope not."

"Thank you, same to you." She is grinning at him. "Why not, though?"

"Ovvels has nothing to offer you. You're a sharp child. You ought to strengthen your reading. Your mind is curious and your attention is keen. You need something that hasn't been provided you yet. It's called an education."

"Ha," she says to that, "not bloody likely."

"I mean it," he tells her. "You're just like a vegetable pearl. Harvested in muck, just waiting for the gleam and polish. Listen, there are places in Oz that could give you something more than your father can, or I can. But to be ready, you need more math, more science. Some children do prep schools, but I think you—you can pick things up in a hiccup."

"In a hiccup."

"Meaning: As you go along. Now, I don't want to get your hopes up. But you have good breeding, if such a thing counts at all. You're a clever girl. Don't squander it."

"When I grow old enough, I want to go live with the Dwarf Bears," she says.

"Not our local brigands? No chance of that. They were chased off a few days ago."

Elphie stiffens. "I'll find them."

"You won't," he says with certainty. "They won't be back, Elphie."

"But—but why?"

He hesitates. "Oh, I can't say, what do I know of the mind of a Dwarf Bear? They were seen to be coming too near the city. Who knows why. They can be hell on the local agriculture, you know. They eat everything, and they have no respect for private property. There's some chatter that Lei Leila'ani was passing about that the Ski'ioti threatened your poor sister and tried to drown her."

Unger sees the stricken look on the face of his assistant. He softens his tone. "Or maybe the creatures heard tell that you were singing in the crowd, and they wanted to catch an earful, too. And came too close. Don't take me seriously, Elphie, I don't know what I'm talking about. But I do know that they're removed from the environs, securely and permanently. Where they've gone, no one from Ovvels can further threaten them."

She is afraid perhaps he does know exactly what he is talking about. Neri-neri. Lollo-lollo.

"Prepare the pattern for the window glass," she says crisply. "Can you have someone deliver it to Lei's house with instructions on how we can find your glassblower colleague? I'll do that much for you and no more."

"Well, don't forget. The glassblower's clan may be able to identify your Turtle Heart's particular origins. Chelo'ona, that's the name of origin, right? Your father mentioned that the wandering prophet had been a glassblower. I haven't been idle, you know. I've kept my part of the bargain. This may be the lead you are looking for."

Yes, beneath the last of her mother's dresses in that trunk lies that oval looking-glass of sorts, which Nanny said was blown by Turtle Heart and given to Melena as a present.

In her cut-down robe Elphie all but throws the white shift at Unger. "I'll say good-bye now. Perhaps our paths will cross in the trees or on the grounds. But I don't want to live in Ovvels if the people here are willing to abuse those Dwarf Bears. I want someplace better than this."

"Good luck at finding such a place," he says, hurt by her brusqueness. "Let me know if you manage to locate it. Or maybe you'll have to establish a preserve of your own for the protection of the hunted. Elphie, you're looking stony. Remember what I said. An education, Miss Elphaba Thropp. Get yourself an education, and use some of what you have going on inside that vital spirit of yours."

"I've never liked you," she says.

"The feeling has been exactly mutual. From the moment I saw you."

Their arms ring round each other, her green cheek against his shoulder blade, his breath upon her hair.

# PASSIM

The business of fixing cloth wings to shabby old dolls, indistinctly or humanoid dried corn husks, is an annual gesture of reverence to ancestors.

None of the Thropps, including Elphie, who made so many of them, ever take to this practice. And even some Quadlings have forgotten where the tradition comes from even as they adhere to custom.

The premise is that our forebears who brought us in, and left us here, can only remain with us during our own lifetimes if we revive their ability to travel with us. Otherwise, they fall behind. They may fail even to recognize us, their descendants. We supply them regularly with new wings so they can keep up with us as *we* fly forward. The periodic change of styles is symbolic of our own growth. We need their blessing; they need our occasional attention. Or their influence decays like leaf mold.

It's our job, right up until our own hours end, and someone launches *us* into memory. Renewing the faded fact of our existence with newly felt significance.

Toy wings are only toys, but ancestors are real, and escape time.

PART FOUR

# THE FLEDGLING

# 44

Frex is dubious about Elphie's gussied-up garment. So much less ponderous, it all but provokes Elphie to whisk and pivot.

"What's wrong with that? Damn near the first thing she's ever had that fits her," snaps Nanny. "Nearly frisky."

"That's what I don't like about it." Frex turns to his daughter. "Not a moment too soon, I see, remanding you to the service of the mission. Just in time. I've always had my doubts about that clothier."

"Oh really, Father? Did you? And yet you allowed me to work for him *to feed the family*." Ooh, how cold she can be, a new accomplishment! Disarmingly cutting.

"Don't be snarky. I asked around, I checked Unger out, to make sure you'd be safe. And you were, weren't you?"

She hates to give him the point, but she can't lie. She nods.

"Good. Though now I've seen him doll you up a little, I wonder if my earlier apprehensions were justified. Still, as long as there's been no harm done. Nick of time extraction from that den of glamour, but no matter. We'll move on, making ourselves better through devotion. As all right-thinking people do."

Wearing this renovated outfit to her job of mission hostess and precentor, Elphie finds herself less precisely under her father's command. Even as she does his bidding. He's uncertain of the frock—so she likes it. She practices whirling on the ball of one foot, to make it flair and sail.

"It's the get-up of someone who has some get-up-and-go," murmurs Nanny, in a tone of mixed approval, envy, and skepticism.

One day Lei comes back from her daily rounds with a parcel of rough-cut fabric under her arm. It's been given her by Unger, for delivery to Frex. She suspects that Frex ordered it for a vestment, hoping to solemnize Elphie with something less show-offy. "I can cut out a pattern and run up a more suitable shift, that's what mothers do," promises Lei. But upon examination of the piece, Elphie explains why Unger had sent it home. "We still have to place the order for the glass that got mysteriously shattered the day I approached Unger. That was part of the deal of my employment. It's the unfulfilled part of the job."

When Frex arrives home, he insists that Elphie need have nothing more to do with Unger and his operations. "We promised," insists Elphie. She reminds her father this may also be the way to locate Turtle Heart's tribe at last. He was a glassblower originally, too. "It's a simple exchange. We'll see what we can learn. And we gave our word, Father. Even if no one has yet claimed responsibility for that broken window."

"Glass can shatter under its own weight," her father insists.

"So can hearts," adds Lei. She's so off the subject, no one responds to her comment.

Lei reads aloud Unger's instructions on how to find the glassblower's foundry. A place called Samani, a morning's trek to the north, beyond the lazy hills where Elphie had rendezvoused with the Dwarf Bears. "Fine," says Elphie. "I'll go and come back in one day." Maybe Elphie will yet see the Ski'ioti, catch up with what has happened to them. Maybe they are all right—maybe they didn't—

"I forbid you to even think of it. I'll go." But her father needs to troubleshoot a challenge from the town elders about his gathering a congregation in a public area. Frex has to argue the defense and win permission. It could take several days of meetings with different committees and jurisdictive officials.

Nonetheless, he won't let Elphie wander off to Samani on her own. Out of the question.

Nanny can't chaperone. She daren't leave Shell to run wild in Ovvels. The stroppy kid is enjoying a stage of being ungovernable.

Not to mention Nessa—never to mention Nessa.

Elphie wants only to strike out. At once. She isn't sure why. Looking for Turtle Heart is the least of it; that's her father's obsession. She's going itchy in the limbs. The world of Ovvels has become cramped. Parochial. She can tolerate mission singing but she feels a fraud; real devotion escapes her. She misses Unger's shop, but there's no going back. And she still hopes to find out what has happened to Neri-neri and Lollo-lollo. If she can.

So Elphie strategizes. She doesn't give her father any rest. She declares a headache. She is unsteady, she is unable to sing in public— Maybe if she gets a change of scenery? Some exercise? They could come up with a plan?

"A headache?" Nanny strokes her jaw. "How time flies. I'll get the cloths ready."

Since Frex won't think of allowing any other male to escort Elphie out of town, the matter remains at an impasse until, improbably, their landlady steps up. Lei Leila'ani, a helpful hand to the nation. "I know Samani," she says gamely, "I once had a cousin there. I'll bring Elphie to finish the deal. Happy to."

"Why doesn't Unger just go and order his glass for himself?" grouses Frex.

"That's where one of his wives lives, and their children," replies Lei, shrugging. "Families. You can't live with them, and you can't live without them. But you can try. I have been trying for some time. I prefer living with a family." Nanny rolls her eyes.

"Besides," says Elphie, "Unger has no business with Turtle Heart's people. That's our project, not his."

So the landlady and Elphie set out the next morning with the cloth template. Nessa, sore at being left behind, starts to shriek. It takes Elphie a moment to realize Nessa is mocking her sister's singing. A voice can be such a weapon.

"Mercy," says Lei Leila'ani, "what a widow of slender means has to put up with. Has your sister always been combative?"

"She'd much rather be the one to advertise for the Unnamed God," replies Elphie. "And she can have the job as far as I'm concerned."

"Not ready, to hear her have go at it. She wouldn't attract converts; she'd drive them away."

Quickly enough they've escaped the miracle of Ovvels, that timbered human beehive. The world of fresh breeze, of cedar trees and higher, drier ground, seems of a different nation entirely. Rarely on her own with Lei, Elphie has been readying for this. She wants to sniff out the truth about her landlady's possible part in spreading a rumor against the Ski'ioti. But she can't risk setting Lei against her this early in the trip. Maybe Elphie will find evidence that Lollo-lollo and Neri-neri are still nearby. If so, she can stop fretting about their having been run off. Retire suspicions about Lei.

She tries to keep an open mind. Lei doesn't seem malevolent, just—just malcontent. Elphie needs to step gingerly. Though she wants to ask Lei if she's ever had any congress with talking Animals, Elphie can't think of a way to frame the question without sounding nosy or suggestive. Lei may be a vicious gossip, but she's a humble woman and a proud one. Also, her pace heading uphill belies her confessions of female frailty. She's one hearty old hen.

When they've reached the crown of the hill, and Elphie is glancing about for the Dwarf Bears— for food detritus or scat, for crushed undergrowth that might suggest a sleeping den—Lei is the one to leap with advantage into the silence. Point-blank she asks Elphie about her mother. "Do you remember her at all?"

"Of course I do," says Elphie so abruptly that Lei is halted for a moment or two, giving Elphie a moment to gather her thoughts.

They trudge on among the noble cedars. No Dwarf Bears in evidence, or any creature more substantial than an overweight squirrel. Only bugs and birds and hidden creatures scurrying left and right into the underbrush. Nothing to distract Elphie from the ambush of memory. They start down the other side of the bluff, leaving Ovvels out of sight or sound.

It's been five years since her mother passed away. More than a third of Elphie's life so far.

The mother in her mind is unreliable, an occasional twist of vowel sounds, spoken as if from another tent in the dark. She's impossible to picture. Is this normal, to forget how your mother looked?

But should Elphie blame herself for this vacancy? Melena had had little time for her older daughter. She'd had to take care of Nessarose because the need was so complete, the situation so desperate. Why should Elphie feel uneasy about anything? She was only a little kid when Nessa was born. It was none of Elphie's affair. But she wonders now if she herself might be partly responsible for Nessa's sadnesses. Somehow. Despite the offense of having been born green, Elphie is capable in ways Nessa isn't. Both girls know it.

Elphie: a constant sliver in Nessa's own foot that Nessa herself could never reach to extract.

For a while now, Elphie's believed that her sister may have stolen her parents' attention, but she also concedes that Nessa has also diverted scrutiny from Elphie. Allowed Elphie some liberty from her father's abstracted calling and her mother's too-casual oversight. So Elphie owes Nessa something, much as she hates to admit it. It comes into focus because now that Elphie's voice has matured, she's slid back in her father's good book. And under his thumb.

To be fair to Melena, though, how could a mother have been expected to care for two damaged children at once? Nessa is a bottomless pit of need that no amount of shoveling can fill in. To use that word—*love*—which Elphie isn't sure she really grasps— how could Melena have *loved* two daughters at once? How could anyone?

Oh, love. Even innocent and ignorant Elphie knows that at age thirteen she ought to be starting to apprehend the concept. Maybe her mother would have been able to teach her. Maybe Melena would have come into her own when Elphie reached the yucky age and needed to know. But Elphie comprehends little of the matter. As Nanny tells it, love is something silly, lacy, a charm made of spun sugar and vegetable pearls. Useful for nothing but diversion. While to her father, love is a mandate shackling the devout to their cloudy creator, the Unnamed God. More an obligation, like a debt to be repaid, than a felt experience.

No, love has little to do with what Elphie grasps of family life. A different term is needed for that household dynamic. Not love but—obligatory accommodation?

Elphie doesn't harbor these thoughts in anything resembling sentences, propositions, ripostes. She merely thinks: Melena— love—mothering—family—*huh*? But something seeps and stings through Elphie's thinking as she and Lei trudge on. Quiet minutes lengthen, and lengthen further.

Melena. Elphie can't even picture her. Still, for the sliveriest of instants Elphie remembers the warm odor of her mother's clean hair. A smell of lavender and the faintest bite of sweat, with a tang of warm cabbage to it. Elphie's eyes start to sting. She knows from previous experiences that tears will burn her skin, so she fists them away and begins to swear softly, in anger, at her mother. If only to keep tender thoughts at bay.

"I guess you probably don't remember much about her," says Lei.

"No, why should I, she's dead."

"But during the year of obsequy, others will have shared their memories, and built up your own, even if they are secondhand. Do they not help?"

Elphie doesn't know what Lei means. The older woman explains that tradition requires the community to gather with the bereaved once a week until the first-year anniversary of the death. Together, family and neighbors recount memories and pose questions and—it seems—even air grudges and take umbrages. "Don't you see? Otherwise the dead become inert. Stamped in tin or carved in hard mahogany," says Lei. "To hold a person as she was in the final week or month of death, that isn't fair—not to the spirit of the person, not to you. Didn't your father follow the usual practice?"

"I don't think that's his tradition," says Elphie.

"Well, I wasn't sure if it was my place to order a pair of wings for the holiday, but it didn't escape me that no one has brought out a spirit totem for her. You don't carry her with you." The tone was sad. "Where is her resting place?"

"I don't remember what happened to—to the remains. I think we tidied up and we moved out of there, fast. Leaving the sense of it behind. The sadness."

Leaving behind even the look of the woman. The unseeable mother.

"Also leaving behind the healing," says Lei. She seems to be

mulling something over. Maybe Frex is losing ground as a poten-
tial second husband, if only because, should Lei predecease him, he
might consign her to a fate of neglect in afterlife.

What happens if you refuse to live in sadness, Elphie wonders—
and this is actually a full question, asked of herself in her mind,
grammatically. The only problem is she doesn't really know to
whom the "you" refers. Is she thinking of Quadlings, whose concepts of mortality are riddles and secrets to her? Or of her father,
who has three motherless children to see to? Or even herself? What
happens if *I* refuse to live in sadness?

Before she can worry this out any further, they are descending
a rocky slope into the settlement that Lei confirms is the camp of
the glassblowers.

# 45

Samani is nearly a glass village, rigged up for convenience, not elegance. A shabby workshop and a display of wares. Lei murmurs, "It's all so beautiful," but Elphie is clueless about all that.

Though she tries to imagine what it might be like to be seen through great flat panes of color. Would she look less green if spied through a green-tinted window?

She and Lei pause among five or six open-air buildings roofed with rattan. Around the work yard stand U-shaped cedar frames where large sheets of glass can be slotted in upright. For cleaning, for inspection, for selection. Here and there, workers with callused fingers pick through scrap piles of broken glass, clinkingly, looking for bits they might use.

Half the stock is clear, if bubbled, rippled, glaucous, and watery. Of the rest, an encyclopedia of color options. Greens and golds, on this side. The token shades of Lurlinemas festivities, according to Nanny. And over here, purplish blacks and bruising blues. Now the yellows: acid, citron, bad teeth, flax, lion-skin. Curious, not many reds. Since so much of Quadling Country stews on its bed of buried corundum, perhaps the local market for crimson glass is intentionally suppressed. Who wants to further advertise the presence of rubies?

Elphie is afraid she'll have to do the talking. This clan of tradespeople speaks a dialect of Qua'ati Elphie has some trouble following. But Lei Leila'ani surprises Elphie by shaking off her retiring manner. She throws her shoulders back, her no-nonsense capacities called into service. She identifies the yard chief by instinct and the keen reading of cues. Over here, Glass-master. I require your attention.

He's a shrunken, sclerotic, bleached-out man of a complexion Elphie has never seen, and which she will learn is called albino. A skin like milk thinned with water, and red-rimmed eyes of silvery ice. His reedy hair is pulled back in a knot of scarf. He walks with a permanent hunch, his hands gripped behind his back. Elphie wonders if he maintains that posture for balance, since his chin hovers below the level of his gullet. The others call him Ta'abi, though this may be an honorific, like boss.

Lei starts to explain about Unger's order, but Ta'abi cuts her off. He paces about Elphie and studies the girl with a scientific skepticism. He mutters. Elphie guesses it might amount to something like: "You get all the original color, and I get none. Which of us is more unlucky." Maybe that was *unlikely*. Elphie has no riposte at the ready. She merely brings out the oval panel of brown muslin to whose curving dimensions the new glass needs to be cut.

Seeing this, Ta'abi seems to remember the original job—he supplied the glass when Unger first opened his emporium—and the glass merchant tries to talk Lei into a line of pricier product. But Lei isn't authorized to bargain. She holds her ground. Ta'abi complains about being overwhelmed with back orders. He says he has all he can do to fulfill existing contracts. Lei holds firm. For the House of Unger, Ta'abi should see if he can push himself.

He rubs his protuberant eyes and seems to be reluctant to clinch the deal. Tea is brought out—tea, or some sort of foaming cold drink that looks like whipped algae. Ta'abi is curious about Elphie; she senses it with reserve and caution. But her being on display seems part of the process. She doesn't really trust Lei to ask the question about Turtle Heart, but her own grasp of the dialect is too weak to bring up the subject herself.

As if to prove how difficult it is to shape a single large oval of glass, Ta'abi takes them around the yard. With gestures and pidgin muttering he walks them through the creation of crown glass. A sweaty laborer, naked to the waist, blows a large bubble through a pipe. When it reaches the correct size, something called a pontil rod is attached on the opposite end, and the blowpipe is snapped off. The bubble is spun and reheated several times, and in the process flattens out. For a large piece, Ta'abi tells them, several glassblowers work in tandem to maneuver a larger pontil, keeping it level, thrusting the cooling material back into a massive oven. Lei make suitably awed noises in her throat. Elphie keeps her own mouth shut. Water may be Elphie's chief enemy, but fire is no friend, either.

"Lei, ask about Turtle Heart," mumbles Elphie.

"Let's get the contract inked first," replies the landlady.

Once Ta'abi and Lei sign a paper of agreement, the glass-master relaxes a little. He points out various bits of glass exotica to his clients. The colored glass tortured into the shapes of pitchers or totems or who knows what, it all seems vain and foolish. Elphie's attention is arrested, though, by an oddment on a stone plinth parked to one side in a glut of creeper. "Ask him what *that* is," she says. "It looks like a glass soap bubble."

Ta'abi whisks a sharp look at Elphie before he answers. How accurate is Lei's translation, Elphie wonders. "He says," the land-lady states, "this item is a gazing globe. Everything in the world is reflected in it because it has no edges and no corners. There can be no secrets kept from it. No one can sneak up to it undetected. It's considered useful for sorcery for that reason—"

"Oh, is that all," says Elphie, and shrugs.

"No, listen." Lei sounds put-upon, but continues. "He insists I tell you that some can see within its depths what others can't. For some, that is, it's a reflecting ball. For others, a window. I'm not sure I'm getting this right."

"Like, for seeing the future?"

"I wouldn't be able to ask a thing like that." But actually Lei likes the idea. "Can I see if I shall ever be married again?" she asks Ta'abi, using enough common words that Elphie can decipher her message.

He doesn't bother to answer her but turns to Elphie and bids her come look. Reluctantly she leans forward. He mumbles syllables that Lei portentously translates: *Can you see into it, and what do you see?*

It's like looking into one of Boozy's rank broths, long ago, concoctions that manage to be both transparent and opaque. Water and oil, probably, not emulsified. Boozy had been an indifferent chef. Elphie hasn't thought about her in years.

She doesn't want to touch the glass globe, but neither does she want to turn away. She sees her own face contorted by the curve. She looks monstrous—but then, so do the landlady and the glass-blower behind her, parentheses wavering around her prominent nose. She's never cared to study her own face in any reflection but she can't avoid it now. It looms, stupid and unrestrainedly verdant.

If she could, she'd pick up the glass ball and shatter it, but she has no funds of her own to pay for such damage. So she closes her eyes, shakes her head as if to clear sour reality from her thoughts. When she opens her eyes again, the glass has taken on a different aspect. A deeper viscosity, an atmosphere more of cloud than of mirror.

Somewhere below the reflective surface, an impression is sorting itself out. "Well, this *has* been a treat. Still, I think—" begins Lei, but Elphie holds up her hand and slices it sideways, to silence her. The apparition is trying to organize itself. A kind of infused, bleached color is registering shapes, rounding them.

Sometimes you look in a campfire and you can almost see a face, a dancing flame with a grin or a leer. It ducks and hides and pops up again. The same can happen in the formation of clouds. Once Elphie saw two white horses galloping in front of a grey mountain range, up there in the sky. That was an accident of wit, light as played by clouds, but this globe is a trick of a different order.

There they are, unmistakable, a hunched-over monkey-type figure leading some woman by the hand. The monkey—the word *polter-Monkey* comes floating up in Elphie's mind—dissolves in curvetted fragments as her mother's face seems to bob forward, expanding into the dimensions of the glass universe. Unrecoverable earlier today, Melena's face seems complacent, somehow more than a drawing or a marble bust. It has the shimmery feel of activity about it.

Say something, thinks Elphie. Call for me. Look for me. I can tell you we're all right.

Then the word they had so rarely used at home: *Mama*. I'm here.

The figment of Melena keeps its own counsel. Is it really her, is it a sleight of malevolence somehow? Is it only a memory floating up, arriving tardily because summoned, using this shaped glass as a conduit? The vision nears and enlarges in slow time, with an arrested quality. Movement decelerated beyond the rules of reality. Elphie has never had the chance to study her mother's face this closely, her mother may never have given her such access. Melena's face is neither beautiful nor harsh, her expression neither tortured nor beatific. It's merely human. Human, abstracted, aloof, unreachable. The forehead turns, the chin pivots, Melena's nose anchors forward, and her eyes focus, looking at something at last. But not at Elphie.

"What did you see?" Lei asks, at the glassblower's insistence.

"Not much." Elphie turns to the man. "Does this thing tell the future? What does it cost? I want it."

Lei does the translation, which takes quite a few exchanges, and seems to spin off into arguments and concessions. Finally she replies, on behalf of Ta'abi, "Maybe *he* can tell the future. Because he says you will have one of these one day—he can see it in your greedy eyes. But not this one. Go away, he says, and don't come back. And so we shall. And we can, because I've asked him for the details about the family of that old Turtle Heart. The young glassblower served an apprenticeship right here, long ago. Ta'abi says he's going to write down whatever he remembers on the back of the order form so we can bring it back to your father. Stop looking so ill, Elphie. You're nearly pink. What in a normal person would look like perfect health in you looks bilious. Are you quite all right?"

The albino glassblower and the green girl glance at each other. He is making small motions with his white wormy fingers, hexes to cast away from himself any danger this green girl has introduced into his yard. Yet he smiles thinly at her, no hard feelings. She nearly smiles back, but can't; she's not sure about hard feelings yet.

As Lei and Elphie turn away from Samani and climb the sandy escarpment, Elphie pivots to look once again. This Ta'abi has directed himself back to his work, and has shucked off his overshirt so he can help rotate one of the larger pieces. Upon the paper-white skin of his back, diagonally across his spine, she sees that he has a blood-browned scar. An industrial accident; a whip wound, maybe; a mark of disaster but also of survival. There he is, made more himself by life. She takes more comfort from this clinical observation than she does from any memory provoked by the crystal gazing ball.

Or so she tells herself.

Yet how vibrant, that simulacrum of her mother, her scarce-remembered mother. It had presence. Even if only a trick of glass. Summoned not by Elphie but by the muttered encouragements of a peasant artisan. Now, as Lei and Elphie crest the hill with the cedar grove, and look down upon Ovvels, she feels that the little city below is more inert than the shady tricks of a gazing globe were. And the hilltop itself—she can sense, like a drop in temperature, the absence of Dwarf Bears. The appearance, however artificial, of her disappeared mother highlights this further disappearance.

There's no reason to wait. "Someone said you've been talking around the town about the Dwarf Bears at the lagoon, who seem to have vanished," says Elphie. "If it's even true that you did, I don't know why you would do that."

Lei is unruffled. Perhaps she doesn't pick up the note of accusation in Elphie's question. "Your brother said they pushed Nessarose into the water. I had to let it be known so other parents could protect their own precious children."

"What's with this 'other parents'? We're not *your* precious children. You had no right. And you believe *Shell*? He's a punky little troublemaker. Why would you even bother to get involved?"

"Don't play the fool. You know it can't hurt for me to prove to your father that I, who raised three boys, can take care of girls, even two humbled and hobbled creatures. It is my duty to him."

"As his landlady? You'd set town vigilantes against harmless Ski'ioti to prove a point to your tenant?"

Lei looks levelly at Elphie though the sides of her eyes. "You're not as smart as you think. You don't know anything about Animals. Neither what they are capable of or what they aren't capable of. And you can't pin what may have happened to those Dwarf Bears on me. I merely sounded a murmur of a concern. For the good of the vicinity."

"For *someone's* good," says Elphie, hopelessly, darkly. Then: "So what has happened to them? Were they chased off by a mob?"

"I couldn't possibly say. I, myself, don't run with a mob."

# 46

Some days later, when Ta'abi's replacement pane has been delivered and installed in Unger's oval window frame, Elphie and Nanny are clearing up after dinner. Lei Leila'ani has finally persuaded Frex to go for an evening stroll. Shell has been dragged along by Frex—perhaps to provide a prophylactic against a marriage proposal. It's an hour before sunset, which seems to slam down upon the marshlands so hard it might as well make a sound. In the boardinghouse, the others busy themselves in Lei's buttery. Elphie can't wash plates—the water—so she scrapes them. Nanny rinses. Nessa moons about nearby, mewingly.

"What I still don't understand," says Elphie, "is why that window shattered when I was having my first interview with Unger. Are you sure Shell didn't sneak out, Nanny, and follow us, and pitch that stone through the window? It sounds like him. And you sometimes fall asleep during the day, don't pretend otherwise."

"Shell is a dab hand at destruction, like all small boys fore and since," says Nanny. Neither confirming nor denying Elphie's theory.

"He lobs stones at cats and such. I once saw him bring down a hummingbird with a meatball. Knock it clean dead out of the air." Elphie looks at Nanny. "It seems just like him. What, what's that expression mean? *You* didn't throw that rock through Unger Bi'ix's window."

"Certainly not," said Nanny, offended. "I have no arm."

"And," says Nessa, shrugging as much as she can manage, "you can be pretty sure I didn't throw it. So don't blame me."

"It's not blame," says Elphie. "Just a question."

"Well," says Nanny, "the answer is purely obvious, and I can weigh in on it if you like." The girls both nod. Nanny plunges her hands back into the soapy water and talks over her shoulder. "It must have been your father, of course, Elphie. Who else could throw a rock with such force as to break that glass?"

"No," says Elphie. "Really? But why?"

Nanny turns to them, a rub of suds on one cheek. "I don't understand men, never did never will. But I can venture a guess. You say your father sent you up to the porch of that fabric shop to begin to get a foothold in this town. But he thought the manager would be a woman. He didn't expect a man to usher you inside, did he. And he didn't like to see you being alone with a single man and no chaperone accompanying you. I'm guessing he regretted his decision at once—but he needed too desperately whatever you might find out about Turtle Heart. So the shattering of the glass was his way to interrupt whatever was going on, to get you out of there unharmed. That's my theory."

"*So* wrong. He doesn't think I'm capable of being in any danger. I'm too—" She makes a flapping gesture from wrists to fingertips. "Well, look at me."

"You will do that," observes Nessa, "drawing attention to your arms at the slightest possibility. I've learned not to take it personally." Her smile is sanctimonious and perhaps just a little lethal, but also, it has to be said, pained.

"But why didn't Papa just come up and get me, if he was worried on my behalf?"

"Oh, who knows," says Nanny.

"I do," says Nessa. She who has no stones to throw, no arms to punch out with, deploys her elliptic, apologetic, aggressive wince of a smile. "He's scared of you, Elphie."

# 47

Having come so far, and after such a long wait having at last received a clue about the whereabouts of Turtle Heart's family, Brother Frexispar Togue Thropp is stricken with a kind of paralysis. The minister seems in no hurry to complete the pilgrimage toward personal atonement that he'd begun after Nessa was born.

It's a temptation, this hesitation, but who can blame him? Nobody in his household makes a noise about it. They're okay to be installed here for a while longer. For all its airs and idiocies, Ovvels is less saturated with jungle and marshland splash than where they've lived before; even the climate is somewhat drier. And Ovvels is finally proving the fertile ground for converts that Frex has been seeking his whole career. He grows in stature—really, seems to swell in actual inches. He stands up straighter. His beard bushes ever outward. It makes Frex seem more crucial to the world, somehow. More authoritative, he suggests to Lei Leila'ani, who is lying when she says she admires it, so, *so* much.

It isn't as if the rent at Lei's rooming house is punitive. But the family has lived on scraps for so long that when the plate passed around and actually returns with some coin, Frex is happy to pocket it.

The board at Lei Leila'ani's improves. Nanny still has hopes of returning alive to Munchkinland, but every now and then there's a roast quail with quince jelly for a weekend luncheon, and Lei has replaced the tatty bed linens with fresh. So life is sweeter. They settle in.

Elphie misses going to Unger Bi'ix's. Perhaps the clothier misses her, too. Their paths rarely cross upon the beaten dirt tracks or slung treadways of Ovvels. Maybe he's veering away from her on purpose. She'd probably do the same. In any case, the moment never arrives in which to test her inclinations, to find out if she might change her mind and run toward him with a bitten but unswallowed smile.

She attends to her sister with as little feeling as she can manage. Nessa is learning to simper, and though Elphie can't blame her—what other tools does Nessa have beyond a practiced smile?—Elphie doesn't need to play along. She feeds Nessa soup with a spoon. Shell sticks out his tongue and hides the spoons. Lei pretends not to notice Shell's misbehavior, because to be disapproving might mean her valued tenants will get shirty and pick up and move out. Lei's stock in the town has risen along with Frex's, now the mission is more or less established. She's a figure of some stature herself now. She doesn't want to queer the arrangement.

So it falls mostly to Nanny to try to govern the children. Shell laughs in Nanny's face with a kind of innocent scorn it is still possible to forgive, he's that young, but Nanny can summon up a backhand if things get beyond a certain point. And Nanny keeps Nessa company when Elphie heads off to services. Nanny is quite indispensable, as she points out, loudly, most often in Lei's presence.

Frex hasn't been booted off the lodge premises. He's successfully negotiated a license to congregate. And as his ministry becomes popular, the lodge finds itself preferred among its several competitors. The school being a business concern, too, it insists on a cut. For the botheration.

Elphie does what she's told. She stands where directed. She sings when bade, often with her eyes closed, because to see congregants swaying in rapture gives her an awkward feeling, as if she's lying to them. She isn't a devotee of her father's faith, quite, but nor is she a hypocrite—she's uncertain of everything. No denying she's complicit at ushering others toward a greater sense of—of *belonging*, she guesses it is. Whatever that state is which music so mysteriously accomplishes.

Once she spies the Pari'isi scion on the margin of the crowd, listening. Oh, so her eyes aren't closed tightly enough, then. She corrects the situation. He is gone when she finishes the final chorus and sits down on a stool to pretend to listen to her father's sermons. She needs to look interested, Frex insists. She's grudgingly grateful that he doesn't insist she has to believe the dogma. Maybe he knows better. She's only thirteen, and can't begin to name whatever philosophy might be within her reach.

And why is that Pari'isi boy prowling about?

So Elphie trains her eyes on the floorboards of the porch, trying to plumb the meaning of her father's sermons. She rarely looks at her father. It's too shaming somehow, though she has no words for how.

The popularity of Frex's mission grows. The camp meetings need to start earlier. The young girls arriving for lessons at the lodge make a circuit around the sprawling congregation as they tramp up on the porch to their classrooms. Elphie has seen so few children other than her siblings that these girls seem exotic and peculiar, unfinished perhaps.

But Elphie can no longer hold her pose of devotion for as long as her father expects. She'll start yawning, not a good look. She raises the matter with Nanny.

"Unger told me I needed some education," she says one evening, when her father and Lei are out for another constitutional, this time meandering along the walkways of the floating gardens. A suspiciously romantic place to promenade. She hopes mosquitoes drive them insane and back from the brink. "Can you ask Father if I might attend some sessions at the lodge?"

"Oh, it's Father now, is it, I've noticed," says Nanny. "Not Papa. We're becoming ever so lah-de-Ozzing-dah, aren't we?"

"I suppose it's Father in public, and at this point he's hardly more to me than a public figure. Don't change the subject. I'm bored. Now that the lodge is in session while we're in residence, maybe I could attend to lessons there myself? When the girls are released for the midday meal, I could return to my post?"

Nanny doesn't approve, but she carries Elphie's petition to her father, and comes back with the answer a few days later. "I'm shocked," says Elphie.

"Truth to tell, I'm somewhat surprised," admits Nanny. "But don't sell him short, Elphie. I think he recognizes you are both an asset and a liability in the mission. And he thinks you're canny enough. He wants the best for you under the circumstances. And you'd be safer studying with girls than beginning to walk the lanes of Ovvels looking both bored and available. Still, I'm a little miffed. As if what *I'm* teaching you is indecent or inadequate. I have half a mind to pick up and flounce out of here."

"But? I hear a reservation in your tone."

"Well, nothing is all good or all bad, is it? The problem is that the lodge doesn't want you any closer than you already are. You're all right out on the porch, but you'd be a distraction in the classroom. The other students would be inclined to point and giggle and you would disrupt their attention to their tasks. Stop scowling, you can't blame them. They're silly Quadling children, and the head proctor of the lodge is no better, really. They've come up with a solution, and you can take it or leave it. Your father is agreeable if you want to try."

Nanny explains that the lector will set a stool outside a classroom of younger girls. After delivering a gathering song for the devout, Elphie can sidle around the corner of the porch and perch outside the window—always keeping out of sight, her back to the wall and her eyes to the yard. She can listen in silence. She might pick up something useful. When she's ready, she can let the proctor know, and he'll shift her stool to the next window, for girls one level up. Elphie is not to speak, not to go peeking over the sill, and not to draw attention to herself. But she *can* listen. From that position she can easily be summoned back to inspire her father's revival meeting if things start to flag. When the morning sessions let out, she'll wander around to the side of the lodge where her father is still tending to his flock. She'll deliver a closing anthem, singing with heart and simulating deep conviction. Then she and Frex will walk home together for the midday meal and siesta.

"I wish I could be there," said Nessa. "It's not fair. Elphie gets everything."

"If Elphie can pull this off without upsetting this, this *academy*, maybe you can follow in due course." Nanny is affable. "They must have two spare stools, and you could trail your sister around the edge of the building. Of course, you'd have to be sure you can sit up straight and not fall over. For I certainly won't be there to help, and they won't want you calling out for Elphie. I'll have Shell to care for at home. A royal handful, *that's* quite clear by now. But we're getting ahead of ourselves. Let's see how we get on."

# 48

What to wear, what to wear. What to wear to lessons when you're not allowed to be seen going to them.

What to wear when you have to slip away from your job to audit a course and then hurry back and take your position again.

"It's not as if you have a lot of choice," says Nanny. "You're outgrowing your old rags. And you fobbed off most of your mother's old garments to greedy-grubbing old Unger Bi'ix. So I think that item you've been wearing to sing in, with the pleats paneled in strips from your mother's elopement garb, it'll have to do. Perhaps a might saucy for a schoolgirl, but no one is going to see you, remember. You could weave yourself a cloak of straw and coat it with dung, and no one would notice. I mean that affectionately."

So Elphie strides up to the lodge, dressed only as herself. Maybe that's for the best. New clothes suggest new opportunities and— she's not ready.

It will take a few days before her mind steadies itself into a receptive mode. She waits. She's patient because she wants it so much. Wants what? Something. (Anything.)

In time, while listening to lessons, which means trying to understand what is being said without watching gestures and examining diagrams provided by the teacher, Elphie finds out something new about herself. Two new things, actually.

The first thing she learns is something said by a docent leaning out the window. A scrap-headed fellow with a patch over one eye, carried away by curiosity. He turns his head to take her in. He asks her a few questions, and at her answers he replies, "You're a quick sketch then, aren't you. Tomorrow morning, move your stool up to the next window. You've already gotten most of what I'm teaching. I'll let the next-door tutor know to expect your hovering." So, what do you think about that, Elphie *can* learn. Up till now, her limited grasp of reading and numbers has been picked up more by osmosis than by effort. Now, just by listening, she finds she can see more openly. She can spell by looking at the letters shaping in her mind and reading them. She can do sums in her head and arrive at something new. It's like conjuring. She can conjure up an answer—not by guesswork, quite, but by the nimble scaling of the framework of recently acquired information.

She advances along the windows of knowledge by listening, never even by looking in (except a sneaky peek as she comes and goes each morning). The girls in their exotic otherness. Remote, puzzling.

The other thing Elphie finds out, perhaps as important, is that knowledge comes to her without it needing to know what she looks like. Knowledge doesn't care about that. And in erecting for herself this tentative scaffolding of new skills, she discovers that she's losing her ability, or her need, to squirm with that awkward sense of not-rightness, not-enoughness. She might struggle to spell a complicated word, to remember the sketchy points of Ozian events that pass for history, to compute in her head without benefit of a slate and a chalk. Hard work, but still, she's freed of the burden of doing so as *the green oddity*, the minister's aberrant daughter.

The answer establishes itself despite her.

So learning becomes a holiday from herself, she who has hardly yet learned the concept of a holiday. It's better than sleep, for in dreams she sometimes meets herself again, and she can be even more ashamed and angry and desolate while sleeping than she sometimes feels while awake. But in schoolwork she steps out of herself into some other world of meaning.

Put another way: for the first time, she sees that the world exists beyond her, despite her. It will abide indefinitely, even if she steps on a poisonous marsh tarantula and dies the next moment. Reality has apparatus, and consequence. And maybe *apparatus* and *consequence* add up to something, too: significance. She isn't sure. Still, learning brings her out of her head, giddy and unmoored. Tearing through possibility.

Within a few months, when Elphie has reached the fourth window, Nessa begins to agitate that it's time for *her* to start her *own* schooling. Elphie has no interest in sharing her new sense of escape with her sister. However, Elphie's rounded the corner of the building, so if Nessa gets to come to school, too, at least she'll be stationed out of sight on the first veranda, set at ninety degrees to the second. (Oh, ninety *degrees*, to think Elphie hasn't known about degrees before, and all the time they've been quietly holding up tabletops! Holding them up against *gravity*, that greedy beggar, that killjoy.)

Elphie does her best to squash the notion. She insists that Nessa could never manage education on her own, and of course Nanny can't spend all day as a helpmeet. While Elphie, Elphie has plunged so far ahead in her learning, she can't possibly be dragged back to baby school.

Nanny is inclined to agree, at least about not having to sit on a veranda for hours listening to lessons she didn't grasp when she was Nessa's age, and isn't about to start now. Look, our Shell is becoming more unruly by the day! It's all Nanny can do to keep him in line as it is. Healthy of limb and boasting a normal complexion, Shell is starting to run around with boys his own age on Ovvels, boys too young yet to be sent off to the marshes of vegetable pearl. But he's getting a reputation as a bad influence. Parents show up to suggest the need to keep him under stricter supervision. Nanny can't possibly abandon her post now. Unthinkable. Shell needs governance, and Frex is busy with his work. Nanny's very sorry indeed, but Nessa's education will have to wait.

"Isn't it a shame." Elphie sighs, relieved.

Then Lei volunteers to give Nessa the support she needs—helping her walk up the steps with a supportive arm, supplying her with sips of water. Assist with personal hygiene, even. "You're not *family*," snaps Elphie. "Father, really!"

Frex looks up from the table where he's working over notes for tomorrow's schedule of hectoring, worship, and funds-harvesting. He says mildly, "Why not? It might do Nessa some good."

"Mother would never have allowed it. She'd be shocked."

"Don't be flip about your mother." Frex uses an unexpectedly strict tone. "Melena had more schooling than I did. In lots of ways I relied on her, when I could get her attention. What cleverness you have comes from the Thropp line. If you're enjoying this experiment in schooling, you have her to thank."

So Nessa begins at the lodge, too. She doesn't advance as quickly as Elphie has done. Elphie is secretly pleased at this. But Nessa is no slouch, either.

One day Nessa says to Elphie, "Do you think our mother was a woman of easy virtue?"

"I don't know what that means."

"A slut." The word is angry in Nessa's mouth, which purses in propriety after having let it slip out.

"I don't know what that means either, and don't tell me."

Meanwhile, Lei stitches herself into the fabric of the family even more tightly. Everyone but Frex notices. But Nanny's spool of white thread dropping on the floor, he doesn't notice that, either. Nor the increasing vehemence of little Shell's misbehaviors.

# 49

One morning Nanny is suffering from a fit of vapors, so Elphie is roped in to help Nessa dress for lessons. In pawing about Nessa's small sisal sack of private items, looking for a brush to scrape through Nessa's hair, Elphie spies a glint of something at the bottom of the bag. She pulls it out.

"What are you doing with this?" she demands of her sister, holding it up. A ring of dull brass.

"Oh, it was Mama's," says Nessa. "A wedding band, maybe."

"How do *you* come by it?"

"I am not sure. I think Nanny told me Mama took it off the night she was delivering Shell. In fact I'm sure of it. I was there. I remember. Her fingers were swollen and it hurt."

"Why are you keeping it?"

"Don't look at me like a hyena at a banquet. I'm keeping it because I want it."

"That's no answer." Elphie was full of rage for reasons she couldn't name. "Why should you have it? You have no fingers to put it upon."

"Maybe that's exactly why I should have it," Nessa lashes back. But she softens. "When Nanny was finally able to tug it off, I saw the mark it left on Mama's finger."

"So? What mark?"

"Elphie," says Nessa, "it left a green ring on her finger. Her skin was green underneath the brass. It makes me feel closer to you to have it."

"You are such a liar." Yet this is classic repartee; Elphie doesn't know if she believes Nessa or not. "You still think you're going to grow arms?"

"If I do, and if I get fingers, one part of me can turn green, and we can be better sisters."

"Huh." Elphie is stumped by that. "Fat chance," she says at last. Then: "And how really does it come to be in your possession instead of Nanny's?"

"How do you think?" says Nessa, retreating from the mistake of sisterliness. "I hexed it there. You taught me all about hexing, didn't you? And you don't even remember." A wreath of winking lies and feints in her expression. "Put it back, now, before I get to work and give you some trouble you won't appreciate."

Elphie does as she is told. Her hand is shaking as their mother's ring drops into the darkness.

# 50

Elphie is promoted to the next station. Her fifth in as many months. She's now a comet looping outside a star cluster of girls closer to her own age. At this classroom, no window, just a pair of double doors through which the girls come and go. So Elphie doesn't draw near until after the other students are assembled at their chairs. Easier to avoid the shame of being ignored if she's slipping in and out on her own timetable.

It's an education separate from the approved academic curriculum, to study these girls. Their cunning laughter, the unintelligible jokes, the implied allegiances and outrages, the reluctance, from time to time, to tend to their lessons. Elphie can't help eavesdropping upon the puzzle of conviviality. She's as mystified by this as she is by whatever subject is at hand, though mostly she'd rather the students settle down and let the teacher get on with it. Society is tiring.

One day when she approaches her post, she's surprised to find a small rattan tray on the floor next to the stool. She thinks for a searingly happy moment that someone has left her a present— perhaps a bit of snack, or some tool for learning that has previously been denied her. But when she looks at the tray more closely, and overhears some carping remarks among girls in the classroom, she figures out otherwise.

The item is a porcelain tea set. Elphie has rarely seen porcelain before. Food in the badlands is eaten raw, or prepared in iron pots and served in wooden bowls alongside bamboo splinters for forks, or balsa wood spoons. This is an object of idolatry, the whole ensemble of items on a tray.

Elphie picks up the clues. Some girl has gotten this exotic treasure for a birthday present and brought it to school for boasting
privileges. But, finding it a distraction, the teacher has set it outside until lessons are over.

A round-headed pot with a curlicued fish for a knob—you could
run your fingers over its scales, counting the imbrications by feel,
and so Elphie does. The pot gleams an aqueous blue-grey, shot
through with charcoal pink that means, perhaps, to suggest the
glimpsed movements of fish. Then, four small teacups of unbear-
ably cunning design. Each one set into its own socket of wires
whose filaments twist into leaf-shaped fins on either side. Each
teacup is a different color—corundum red, purple-brown, a viscous bile yellow, and the softest of greens, morning light through
jungle mist. A pucker of miser's gold is etched on the rims of the
cups. Glazing makes the colors shine as if they've just been washed
and set out to dry in the sun.

"Where on earth?" asks Nanny that evening, when she discovers the treasure under a scarf that Elphie has draped over it.

"A friend gave it to me. As a present. Friends give presents,"
says Elphie.

"You have no friends," says Nessa. "You wouldn't know what to
do with them."

"Friends have tea parties. Pretending. With this set of stuff. We
could do that."

"I'm your sister, not your friend." Nessa glances greedily at the
trove. "Still, I suppose I could pretend to be your friend. I mean, if
we're pretending."

Neither of the girls is good at pretending, but they've heard of
it from Nanny when she tells tales of Melena's wild youth, back
when Melena pretended to be a harlot so earnestly that sometimes
she forgot and behaved like one. Not knowing what a harlot is, the

girls guess it is some kind of robber. They've never asked, though, because during any such commentary by Nanny, Father lowers those dark looks to cancel the topic.

After the supper of fishbone broth is done and the dishes wiped and put away, Lei and Frex wander off in the gloaming to exchange whatever tedious remarks they can think up. Nanny sits Shell down to drill him on the alphabet while Elphie arranges the tea party on a square of toweling in the middle of the floor. Like a picnic. The toweling is a better shape (a *quadrilateral!*) than the larger parabolic (*parabolic!*) table, because a towel's proportions don't dwarf the set so much. The four cups in their woven wire baskets wait, one to each side. Elphie uses the saucers as plates. "What is our imaginary food?" asks Nessa.

"Marsh plums? Sweet, with honey sauce? Or cheese temptos?"

"Are those other two places for me and Nanny?" asks Shell.

"We're expecting two friends," says Elphie. "You do your homework."

"How quickly is born a snobby snob-snob," snorts Nanny. "Shell, how *do* you do it. Look there at that middle letter, it's both backwards *and* upside down."

"You don't have no friends, not even any made-up ones," says Shell.

"Some of the Dwarf Bears might stop by. You never know."

"Oh, they're all dead," says Shell, yawning. Elphie shoots him a look. "What?" he replies with mock surprise. "I'm only saying what the other boys say."

Earlier than usual, Frex and Lei return. Lei looks smug and Frex fretful. "Why don't I make some real tea for the teapot," suggests Lei brightly, and hurries to get started. About some subjects Elphie is beginning to have a reputation for temper; while Shell's remark about the Ski'ioti is probably a joke, it's a risky one.

Without having heard the exchange, Lei senses trouble and wants out of the room.

So does Nanny. She leads Shell out onto the narrow porch to finish up the lesson. Shell aims a kick at the teapot as he passes, but Elphie reaches out and grabs his ankle and nearly overturns him before he breaks free. From outside, he wails, which doesn't set the right mood for a tea party. His sisters do their best to ignore him.

"Strange weather we're having," says Nessa. "Listen to that wind howl."

"I do like a good strong wind," says Elphie, as adrift at the practice of party blandishments as her sister. She adds, "It strengthens the spine, somehow."

"Doesn't it just," says Nessa, and here they run out of fuel for the social fire.

When Lei returns with some mint tea in a tin scoop, she pours it delicately into the pot and then stands expectantly, as if she hopes to be asked to join them. The Thropp sisters extend no such invitation, so Lei repairs to her room and slams the door. Their father, meanwhile, has disappeared into his mumbling again. The household is out of tune with itself, unhappy.

"Well," says Elphie, trying to imagine how this is done. "I guess I'll pour out the tea. You want some, I suppose?"

"Well, it *is* a tea party. What's supposed to be on these plates?"

"Lemon temptos, I think. Or cheese."

Nessa says, "Pretend ones."

"That's all we've got."

"Well, I'll take two cheese temptos, then."

"Sorry, I ate the cheese ones. Only lemon temptos left. Yum, this tea is good." It is, too; hot and spicy; Lei has splurged and added a few drops of rash of gingerroot. The clever metal basketry allows Elphie to pick up the cup with both hands and put it down again without burning her fingertips. She has the green one, Nessa the yellow.

"It's quite simply the best tea in the world. Don't you agree." Bored tones of stating the obvious.

Nessa stares at her portion. "As you know, I can't pick mine up," she says at last, somewhat breaking the mood of the game.

"This is a pretend tea party with pretend lemon temptos. So pretend." Elphie takes another sip. "Oh, I just can't get enough of this."

"Elphie."

"Why don't you just hex the cup to your lips?" Elphie is in a scarier mode now. "You *know* you have some power. It's given you as a compensation, I think. Or just pretend you have the power to hex. See what happens. Go on. I dare you."

"I'll play some games but not that one. For one thing, Papa doesn't approve. He says sorcery is a, a gimmick of *public relations*, and where it does exist, it's risky. It goes up against the rules of the Unnamed God. I won't do it."

They look at each other over the grotty little square of toweling. They are little girls at their first play tea party and they are growing, growing up, at the same moment, and both of them feel it, and can't go so far as to admit it out loud. Heady, and dangerous; collaborative and antagonistic. So much at stake at a tea party.

"Oh, all right." Elphie serves her sister tea, sloshing a generous portion between Nessa's lips in the hopes it might burn her tongue. Just a little.

In the morning they find that some other malevolent sprite has climbed up to the high shelf where the tea set was stored for safety, and has thrown every piece—four plates, four cups, four metal

holders, the pot and the lid—down to the ground. All the porcelain lies in colored shards. The metal holders are bent but unbro-
ken. Still, there is nothing left to hold.

When word gets around that the tea set has gone missing without permission, and been destroyed, the family of the spoiled brat
child follows the clues and presses for damages. Elphie's privileges
for auditing at school are revoked. Frex is required to stump up for
a replacement tea set. That child's precious toy had come all the
way *from the Emerald City* and it had cost a month's wages. Nessa is
allowed to remain at school, as she clearly can't have been responsible for hauling away a treasure like a porcelain tea set in nacreous tones of envy, venom, despair, and fury, all rimmed in gold.

"I never did," says Shell, and then with an innocence too wide-
eyed to be convincing, "Maybe it was those Dwarf Bears, come for
revenge. Don't you think?"

"I thought you said they were dead," says Elphie in a voice like
drollery, but menacingly low.

"I went up to that hill place looking for them and I bet I saw
them growling in the bushes and stuff, but they wouldn't come out.
So I think they're dead but maybe not."

"You never went up there. You're five years old, you can't even
go to the outhouse by yourself."

"I went with my big boys who wanted to—wanted to find them.
Nanny falls asleep every morning after you go to mission, so you
don't know nothing."

Elphie is too despondent to beat him up. She can't bring herself even to keep the broken pieces of the tea set. Everything has
broken, everything. She falls into a funk of silence, reviewing what
school lessons she's learned so far, and wondering why they haven't
been enough to stop her from being tempted by the artificiality of
a toy. Wondering what she might do next.

To blame the victim, that weepy student, is a sore temptation. Such a pampered brat shouldn't have brought her stupid tea party set to school in the first place. It's all her stupid fault. Still.

To flush out the Ski'ioti, if they're there, would heal something, somehow.

Though banned from school, Elphie isn't relieved from her duties as the cantor of anthems at the morning meeting. The lodge still takes rent from Frex's mission, and Elphie is needed to keep the congregation showing up. She's caged into that chore. Exiled from the world of lessons bubbling just over there. Without her. Her singing strengthens as her mood darkens.

The wound represents itself as "No one ever gave us toys. How could we learn to be sisters when we had nothing to play with together?" Perhaps an irrational conclusion to draw, but hurt can distend rationality.

# 51

But someone who needs to be healthy sometimes can find a way. Without yet admitting that there's been much deprivation in her life, except in the realm of porcelain tea sets, Elphie inches forward to supply for herself what she requires.

One afternoon a few weeks later, Elphie tells her father she's going to slip away from the service after the first anthem. He'll have to close out the program without music. Why, he asks her. She makes a face meaning to imply: female moments we don't generally discuss with our father. He catches her drift and pats her hand, and that's that.

When the gathering song is done, the congregation plunks itself upon the ground, readying for mild admonishment, which is oddly thrilling to this peaceable people. Elphie steals off, intending to circle around the lodge so the congregation doesn't see her leaving. She passes the classrooms of the younger children. Before one of the windows now sits Nessarose with a scarily keen expression on her face, listening. Lei, bored out of her skull, lurks to one side, doing cunning little handicrafts with reeds. Elphie ignores them both, and hums to block out the sound of instruction threading across windowsills and thresholds.

Forensic curiosity about human behavior doesn't come naturally to Elphie. She's far more interested in Animals and what they know that she doesn't, or can't. It rarely occurs to her that she could pose the same questions about the nature of her sister or brother. Nessa and Shell are mere appurtenances, growths in the fabric of her life, so common as to be invisible. Yet stalking up the slope to the cedar grove, Elphie almost wonders about who squirmy little Shell really is, and whether he can even tell the difference between lying or not. Maybe nobody can. Maybe she can't either.

It doesn't go far, this line of enquiry, but here she is, scrambling up the knoll a third time—on the hopes that, whether he intended to or not, Shell is telling the truth about the Dwarf Bears maybe still lurking about. Is she being appalling, a busybody, a plague to the fugitive creatures? Perhaps they prefer to be disappeared. Or maybe they have fled from taunting boys or threatened men. Or maybe indeed they have been killed. She may never know. (She will never know.)

However, under a stand of cedars not far from where she had her one treasured interview with Lollo-lollo and Neri-neri, she finds not the pair of Ski'ioti but that Pari'isi boy, the one with the vegetable pearl hanging from an earlobe. He is sitting on a blanket of some sort and he has a book open on the ground in front of him. He has heard her approach before she has seen him. His gaze upon her is open, amused, and defensive.

"What do you think you're doing here?" she says, her hands on her hips, as if this is her hill.

"I didn't think I was waiting for you, but perhaps I was."

"I'm Elphie."

"I know who you are. Why are you bothering me when I've stolen away to be able to read in peace?"

"I said, 'I'm Elphie.' Aren't you supposed to tell me who you are next? Isn't that how it goes?"

He laughs. "If we're following the script. Wasn't sure you were that sort. All right. I'm Pari'isi To'or. What are you doing away from your holy post?"

She doesn't bother to answer. She doesn't want to share her concerns about the Dwarf Bears, nor to give away to this unknown threat of a lad the possibility, however slim, that the Bears are dug in somewhere. She won't blow their cover. This goofy fellow is here by coincidence, that destiny manager. "What are you reading?" she asks, to change the subject.

"A polemic on class and status, if you must know."

"Well, I have no class and no status, so I can't comment. What is a polemic?"

"An overheated argument that might have some merit anyway, if you can bear to read through the fire of its feeling."

She would like him to go away so she can stand and holler a hullo into the foliage. "Do Animals have class and status?" she asks, despite herself.

"Excuse me. I am reading here. Quietly. Not convening a discussion group."

"Too bad." Just to be horrid, just for some reason she can't identify, she sits down on the ground. Not on his blanket, but near enough. "Here you are. I've seen you lurking around the back of the congregation sometimes. Are you seeking a conversion?"

"No. I don't want that. Nor am I allowed. My uncle wouldn't hear of it. Class and status. He is the chancellor, Pari'isi Menga'al."

"Big deal. The minister is my father. If you're not ripe for swaying toward unionism, why do you keep showing up?"

"I like to hear you sing." He looks directly at her as he says this, unblinkered and brave; she nearly flinches at the rude honesty of it. She can't think of a snappy reply. Maybe he takes pity. He continues, "You were doing more of it at first, but then you seemed to disappear for large segments of the morning."

"I was, um, auditing some lessons. Until that fell apart."

"You miss it. You have a hungry look on your face."

"You seem to have been studying *me*. That's a bit creepy, did you know that?"

He shrugs. "I'm hungry, too. That's why I'm reading about class and status rather than following my uncle around on council business, which is boring."

He is her age or maybe older. It's hard to tell. He knows things she doesn't, and he isn't timid around her. Maybe he's only casual and openminded when he's escaped his kind. The class and status of it all. He lights a cigarette.

She makes an analogy with her father who, in the damp outback all his working life, is perhaps more liberated than if he had a country parish back in Munchkinland. Something to be said for making one's self a place apart. This is a conceptual leap for her, comparing one person's experience with another's. She feels dizzy.

"Tell me something about what you're reading, and something more about what you think about it."

They linger in the shade of cedars for half the morning. By the time she stands up, she has abandoned the hope of scaring the Ski'ioti out of hiding. Her mind has moved on to an arrangement she's cobbled together with this boy-man.

A kind of clumsy, tentative contract in which neither knows quite who is paying what and who is receiving what. Nor even why, except to talk it through is the first exercise, and they have both passed it.

If Elphie can insist on having independent hours between the start of morning meeting and its conclusion, a seminar of two people will convene here, in the cedar grove, on the hill overlooking the lagoon and its watery allotments, with the rice terraces rising to one side and the puzzlepiece town of Ovvels below. If one of them can't make it, the other won't take offense or worry. That's the only condition. They will see what is what.

And they do see, though whether either of them can name what they are seeing is uncertain. For the next season or two, though seasons in the marshworld scarcely change from month to month, Elphie Thropp and Pari'isi To'or sequester themselves here. They work on anything that he can teach and she can learn. He has had his own tutor at home, sometimes. He has a good keen mind and isn't bad at explaining stuff. She soaks it up.

She doesn't think of him as a person, quite, but more as a willing spigot. She's bullied him into helping her because he's ashamed of his prurience about her. But very quickly all that falls away. She hardly notices him as a form, as a male, as a boy verging toward manhood. He's a convenience.

Only later in her life, when she thinks back to this time (and such reflections don't happen often, she hasn't time for reflection), does she wonder why Pari'isi To'or had helped her at all. When at first, at Unger Bi'ix's, he had seemed to mock her, even to be disgusted. Of course, from time to time, curiosity can overwhelm revulsion, and maybe that's his game. There's certainly no sense of a flicker of interest romantically, not that she can read at the time, nor discern later on, looking back. She hasn't been especially enticing. (Ha!) Bewitching? Forget it. She's only a rubbishy thing, a scalawag scholar if she can even call herself a scholar, grasping for what he can teach her.

But when she comes into a more adult apprehension about mortality—say, when Nessarose dies—Elphaba sees that in the law of magnifying probability, death becomes more inevitable with every passing day lived. The fewer days you have left, the more crucial it is you spend them usefully. Blow something up before you get blown up. Even if it is just ignorance—blow up ignorance, blow it up in its own face.

So finally she assembles the few things she knows about that kid (he isn't all that much older than she is, after all), Pari'isi To'or.

She hasn't been interested in him per se. She's greedy for learning, a motherless wolf cub who goes for the milk someone has left out, but who will never become a pet. When you're dying of thirst, it's the milk that calls you forward, not the hand that pours it.

Unlike his male peers, Pari'isi To'or is excused from the job of diving for vegetable pearls. It isn't actually because he's a few notches above, socially—connected to the people in power. (Though that probably doesn't hurt.) The rotten part is that he suffers from some kind of lung ailment. The physician in Ovvels can detect no sound of air in To'or's left lung, and in the right lung, too little. The consensus is that To'or doesn't have a long life ahead of him. He's excused from diving because he doesn't sustain enough air in him to be competent at it. He's excused most things because he's nearer the end of his life, and he knows it, than people twice his age.

And so, Elphaba concludes when, later, she finally adds it up, To'or's meeting her in the cedar grove and sharing the benefits of his better education isn't puppy love or some sideways lunge at seduction. He's too well-bred to demonstrate any attraction or, more likely, any sense of revulsion he might feel toward her. No—Pari'isi To'or wants to teach Elphaba something so that his short life will have delivered some compensation to the world when the time comes for him to leave it.

She doesn't look at him. Maybe she's been shy, maybe there's been a little tension of affection between them. Later, she can't be certain. What is he like? She will not be able to remember much. She will recall in keener detail a bobcat once spied in a mangrove swamp than she will this boy-cub. Is his hair of the more spongey, loose-curled type, or lank and straight? Is he thinner than the average Quadling boy? There are too few others of his age hanging about Ovvels, no one with which to compare him. He's physically a little awkward, as if some belt of muscles around his rib cage isn't flexible; he turns from the waist, not the shoulders. That's about all she can admit to noticing.

Unger has taught Elphie to focus, with scissors and a ruler and with a precision of language that outlines the world more keenly that her father's dogma ever could. The teachers at that school have filled in the background, dispelling the fog of ignorance with exercises in proper language usage, supplying names for the concepts of mathematics. Building the architecture.

Pari'isi To'or diverts from those approaches. For a young person, he manages somehow to teach her about stance—about considering that *how* you think of something colors what you are free to know about it.

Eventually they do talk about the Dwarf Bears. He has picked up that she is curious about Animal life, since it's been hiding in plain sight from her all her days so far. He lets drop that there have been rumors about the Dwarf Bears, that someone said they'd pushed Nessa in the water in order to drown her, but that really the Ski'ioti were despised for plundering the floating gardens. Which are private. Or considered private by the humans who built them and tend them.

Rumors only. Maybe the Ski'ioti are safe. Elphie clams up at some of the implications of To'or's analysis, but once the possible deed of murder is spoken in the open between Elphie and To'or, she drops the topic. It is unbearable to think about it. The Ski'ioti were here and now they're not. She accepts this. She will live with a sense of bereavement about this for the rest of her childhood, and probably beyond. Though a curiosity to sort out the variables between Animal and human behavior—character—the absolute quality of being one thing or the other—is an appetite that has taken hold, and it will not quit her, ever.

She hasn't registered whether or not To'or himself is offended about the supposed attack on the Animals. She sees only that he's pointing out that because her stance of curiosity about the Dwarf Bears has gotten the better of her, she's learned more about them than anyone else in Ovvels. Class and status! Perhaps he regrets having said those words. They would have become a joke, were Elphie capable of anything as casual as banter.

None of this is as crisply perceived as is summarized here. She picks up more than she knows by his easygoing, dialogic style. It's only long after he is dead and she has herself abandoned Ovvels that she begins to admire his technique, and so to be grateful for his influence in her education.

# 52

Perhaps because of Elphie's expulsion from the lodge, Nessa begins to style herself as more deserving than her big sister. That regrettable thief, Elphie of the stolen porcelain tea set so mysteriously and wickedly ruined. A shame, really. The younger sister, pale and reproachful, purses her lips in a manner unsettlingly like the landlady's. Nessa makes no comment when the subject of Elphie's disgrace comes up, but her position on the matter can be in no doubt.

And the subject does come up, because now there's a hint of social notice, for Nessa anyway. Out in the world, even with Lei as a chaperone, Nessa keeps her place and increasingly, her balance, advancing along the corridor from room to room as her mastery of the material allows. Nessa is learning balance.

She's become a pet of the Quadling girls who arrive at dawn and flounce home in time for the afternoon meal. They take turns caring for her. Whether Nessa is a class project in public charity or simply a lumpkin of handicap that makes everyone else feel better about themselves, Elphie doesn't try to guess. She doesn't care. Maybe, sooner or later, Elphie will be free to pursue her own interests and not be obliged to serve as Nessa's arms all the time. Elphie notes that while she's envious of Nessa's advancement in Ovvels, she's relieved that her sister is showing signs of being able to operate, occasionally, without a prop.

Let Nessa curry favor with sycophants. Isn't she just the picture of piety, there with her shawl wrapped around her shoulders, her invisible hands folded in her lap. Her eyes lowered in modesty and allure. Sometimes Elphie wants to hit her sister just to make a real expression flare up.

Lei Leila'ani is cowed by Nessa's social advancement. Since being accepted into a course of studies, the girl is sort of managing on her own. Nessa even tries dismissing the landlady for an hour or so at a time from serving as her armature. Lei's campaign to make Frex her second husband, and to accept the baggage of his children as her own, consequently stumbles. She becomes by turns sweeter and more acid, a sign of desperation.

Frex hardly notices. He's digging ever deeper into his understanding of unionism. He exhumes from his trunk the tomes he dragged from Munchkinland all those years ago. He sets musty books out in the sun, brushes off mold spores, and peels the pages apart. Arguments on faith and dogma fascinate him. He hopes to dredge up material useful to his unoffendable flock. By now it numbers in the hundreds—well, a hundred and a half, anyway. Enough in contributions to cover the small family's expenses. Not to mention that a few converts often swing by the cantilevered home of Lei Leila'ani to drop off a platter of cooked fish and green fruit, or a twice-baked celery tart.

Lei finds a way to be insulted by gifts of food—brought mostly by leering widows, she observes—but she benefits from such largesse, too. The widow's reserve isn't vast. She's banked on becoming an indispensable adjunct to the Thropp family, graduating to wife sooner or later. So what that Nessa is learning to stand on her own two feet; there's still Shell to worry about. Lei styles herself a stabilizing maternal force. A minister can't be expected to attend to his own son, not when he's being Father to a considerable segment of the town.

Oh, Lei. Not everyone has a principal role. But the members of the family don't squander conjecture on what her inner life might be like, and we don't have the time. Life begins to rush, doesn't it? Lei is off to one side, rubbing her dry wrists with an unguent, wondering how she manages to be a widow of property and somehow a second-class citizen in her own home. That's all we're going to get of her. She means no harm; she does little good.

While those girls, the green aberration and the other, the more-becoming oddity, they are sliding through Ovvels life with as much seemliness as they can muster, given the givens.

The nanny, she might keep a better eye on the boy, surely, but she has her own aches and ailments and publishes them to any-one who will listen. The nanny's knees, these knees that the poor dead Melena dandled from in her day, these are already old knees. Nanny can't get out of a chair swiftly enough to stop Shell from running out of the room and off to some other caper.

As a result, Shell revels in delinquency in ever more public ways. The incidents of his hooliganism start to reflect unfairly on the landlady. Lei Leila'ani, it's suggested, ought to step in. Really, it's her duty, if she's going to open her doors to foreigners and aber-rations. Neighborhood regard for Lei begins to stutter and then to plunge. Nothing fair in this, of course. It's often the most reliable public servant who is best positioned to be the scapegoat, and this time it's Lei.

Think of it from Shell's perspective, though. There's no school for him, really. At this age, Quadling boys usually follow their father into the fields or the floating gardens. Or the trades. It's harder to follow a father into the dubious trade of being devout. Especially if as a high-spirited boy you have no idea of divinity, or of the obligations divinity imposes upon you about how to live your sorry life.

Shell begs to be allowed to go to the fields of vegetable pearls with the bigger boys. Frex's reply is curt: those boys are four years older than Shell, and he'd be out of his depth in more ways than watery. Lei tries to put it in more honeyed words, cozening up to the boy with a cube of sugared coconut, and Shell spits at her, literally spits.

With nothing to do, and faster on his feet than Nanny, the boy takes to vandalism. Earlier Elphie had wondered if, on the first day in Ovvels, Shell had escaped Nanny's clutches, had stolen after his father and big sister, and had been the one to throw the rock through Unger's window. She wouldn't have put it past Shell, but she's retired that curiosity. However, she suspects Shell of destroying the purloined tea set, which she'd intended to return early the next morning before the lodge opened for business. In that instance, her own initial crime of the theft of the delightful objects eclipsed the subsequent scandal of their destruction. If she hadn't brought the set home to Lei Leila'ani's, there'd have been nothing for Shell to break.

In any event, Shell has escaped punishment. Since no one had blamed him for the wreck of the tea set, he's become emboldened. All those bright scraps of colored glaze. All those naked pink bisque seams exposed on the edges of the shards. He's gone on the prowl to find other things to bring down, to muck up, to shatter. And to take greater risks in the act.

At first it's just knocking over marsh tomato plants with a dead tree limb. The reddening globes spilling their golden seeds on the soil thrill him. He's too young for any overt sexual excitement in the act, probably; but to see the skintight vessel forced to reveal its luscious wet interior is perhaps not always a masquerade of sexual violence. It's just violence, maybe.

The same holds true for eggs. They downright want to be smashed, otherwise why are their shells so frail?

The problem with tomatoes, eggs, spiderwebs, is that they offer too little resistance. When with a knife he's lifted from Lei's kitchen Shell manages to sever the melon from its stem, hacking it to bits so that ants can swarm it all over before some human gardener comes back to salvage segments, well, that's more gratifying.

But not gratifying enough.

Maybe this is just another kind of hexing, a kind that even a boy could do. Ruin things.

His father is deep in rumination. Nanny sinks into the most comfy wicker chair. She holds her mending in her lap so she can pretend to be industrious. Lei flutters about in increasing desperation. Shell's sisters are occupied with various exploits outside the Lei's home. So Shell takes to mayhem with talent and a precision so quickly honed as to seem divinely given. If the Unnamed God don't want me to break the latches in that goat pen, why do I get the idea to do it? The goats don't mind. I'm a liberator, Papa.

He never needs to say that, though. The goats go running wild, ruining scores of gardens in an afternoon. No one has seen Shell at the goat paddock. Maybe the gate has just broken open? No, the knife-sliced strips in the bark show ill intent.

Then two of the goats who wander far enough out of town to be enjoying a rural holiday are set upon by savage teeth sharper than Shell's knife. The boy himself comes upon the corpses. He's able to run back to the center of town and deliver the sorry news. No one suspects him, no one could. He's a kid. And those aren't *his* teeth imprints upon the throats of the goats.

Maybe they're Ski'ioti bitemarks. Just wondering aloud here.

Other touches of mischief follow. Someone's pet cat has been lowered in a bucket into the well. The cat survives but is disagreeable company ever after. Four bright yellow birds have been tricked into a net somehow and their little necks wrung. Feathers are glued with rice paste to spell a word on the side of the rice house, but no one can read the word as the blood artist is not, apparently, a gifted speller. The corpses of the dead, twisted on the ground with their little claw feet drawn up, spell out quite enough.

The townspeople begin to murmur more loudly. Frex hears about the rash of mischief. He shoehorns the outbreak of vandalism into his sermons, a metaphor about the devil's sleight of hand. Then someone breaks into the home of Pari'isi Ma'ani, the father of Pari'isi To'or. A portrait of the Initial Pari'isi, by all reports a soft and congenial paterfamilias, an advocate of civil courtesies, has been abused with a knife. The man's soft eyes removed, like stones from cherries.

This awakens in the people of Ovvels a suspicion of witchcraft. What can anyone want with such dedicated vandalism, abducting the eyes of the long-dead head of one of the ruling families? What will be next? Who will be next? What if it isn't the rare portrait featuring eyes, but the eyes themselves? Crows have eaten the eyes of the goats, eventually. Who else needs eyes? Witches need eyes, to spy with; that's why witches keep crows in the first place.

Lei Leila'ani is the first one to assess the vigor of the mounting threat. To her credit, she doesn't toss the Thropp family out on its ear. Instead, she sees an opportunity. They should all go away, if just for a while. "If we leave and the vandalism continues," she says, "it will be proof that no one in this house is responsible."

"And," says Nanny blandly, "if we leave and the troubles stop?"

Lei chokes back a sob. "Then we'd better not come back."

"Oh my," says Nanny, "there's no 'we' in this business, Goodwidow Lei Leila'ani." Using the formal title is possibly the cruelest thing Nanny has ever said to the landlady. "You couldn't possibly think of joining us. They'd think we kidnapped you. In any case, I doubt Frex would think of leaving. An appearance of guilt. Frex?"

Frex won't comment. Meanwhile the instances of outrage continue unabated—nothing more dreadful in nature, but no slackening of alarm, either. The citizens of Ovvels rarely lock their doors, and most of their windows are covered only with netting. If that. Townspeople are also not avaricious as a rule, so few of them keep precious items around. The luxury items in the more prosperous households are those panels of fabric stripes, framed and hung or freestanding on folding screens. Any number of these delicate pieces are found slashed with a single slit, which puckers, showing mud plaster or bamboo lathes through the surgical scar.

But everyone has a store-pot of coins someplace. Dead birds and ruined cabbages are one thing; when money starts to disappear from various hidey-holes, the disgruntlement becomes more public. At one meeting, after Elphie has sung the crowd into a somnolent moment but before she's managed to disappear for her colloquy with Pari'isi To'or, she sees the mood change. When the basket begins its circuit for the daily pennysworth, it collects more commentary than cash. "Our money is already disappearing," grouches one miserly old biddy. "Why should we surrender what is left?" More than one other voice concurs. The usually docile congregation, a hive about to swarm.

"We'll take a day of reflection at home tomorrow," says Frex to his flock. He cuts the meeting short without referring to the collection basket again. With a chop of his hand he freezes Elphie in the act of stealing away. "We're going home, Elphaba," snaps Frex. "No discussion. Collect Nessa from whatever classroom she's bothering." Elphie doesn't dare object.

Frex is noisily upset. At the rooming house, both Lei and Nanny try to calm him down. It doesn't help that Pari'isi Menga'al, Pari'isi To'or's uncle, chooses that morning to make a personal visit to Lei's aerie. In other circumstances this would be the peak moment of

Lei's life, confirming her as a prominent member of the community. Now, it's scandal. Lei allows the magistrate in but Frex won't come from the other room to recognize his authority. "My calling is from the above, not from you," he shouts.

"I have no doubt," says the well-upholstered official. "But it is I who have come calling, not the 'above.' I have jurisdiction over the citizens here, and also the visitors. We need to discuss the recent upsets happening in this community. Words are being spoken."

The anonymity of the report is fearsome. *Words are being spoken.* Elphie might speak some herself had she a mind to.

Her father will not emerge from the rooms the family has occupied. He begins to pray loudly while smashing about with the old wicker suitcases and leather trunks that have been hiked up in the rafters of Lei's storeroom. The class and status of the Pari'isi elder holds no sway here, and the magistrate leaves in a distinctly bad temper.

"They won't even know who they are anymore without me," says Frex; and "If they can so quickly conclude the worst, what good have I done?" Elphie sees her father batting against airy grievances, adrift in a river-flood mist without bearings, without navigational instinct.

Nanny and Lei bow out and go to fix a distracting meal in the larder. In the family room, Nessa weeps softly and no one wipes her nose. Elphie says, "Tell me what to do so I have something to do, it's useless to just stand here." And Shell goes and stands in a corner with his back to the others, ostentatiously giving himself a punishment, though nobody takes time to question him about it. Frankly, all four of the Thropps would like to stand in four corners of the room, backs to their kin, ignoring the inevitable. But there is the work of packing to manage.

Lei bullies herself to Elphie's side. "You will keep this family afloat," she whispers. "But you can't do it alone. I will help. You can trust me. You like me well enough—that's all it takes."

"I don't know what you're talking about. And why do I like you? Remind me."

"I am one of those who haven't moved to the other side of the path when they see you coming." Lei ducks her chin several times, driving her point into the floorboards.

"Is that all it takes to make people likeable? That they haven't picked up a stone and chucked it?"

"You're putting it crudely. I'm on your side, Elphaba Thropp."

Elphie shook her head. "Liking people, not liking them—I don't really get it. But I don't think it has anything to do with me anyway. Can you move, you're standing on the hem of my skirt."

Lei won't move her foot. Elphie nearly takes pity. In a voice of flat affect she says, "I wish I could cut you a set of your own wings, so you could fly yourself into a better life." Lei, insulted and hurt, lets out a little gash of sound and gives way.

Frex tells his children and Nanny that they'll abandon Ovvels tomorrow, unbowed and unashamed, at the height of the market morning, through the crowds. To prove their lack of shame. Tomorrow! Elphie throws down the handful of toiletries she's been assembling. She reaches for the last item of clothing in what had been Mama's trunk. She pulls it out, leaving at the bottom the oval looking-glass that Mama had taken from Colwen Grounds all those years earlier. "If it's not to break, it'll need something soft to be wrapped in," she barks at her father. "Take care of it yourself. I'm bringing this cloak to Unger as a good-bye present."

Her father is in too fraught a state to forbid her, but she does see him take a prayer shawl of his own and wrap up the mirror. He cannot not let it go yet. "Eventually it will come into your possession, Elphaba. It'll be a keepsake for you. It held your mother's face, once upon a time."

She hurries with the last tawny garment. Of uncertain function, it's trimmed with scraps of dingy white fur and lined with rotting silk panels. Climbing the steps of the clothier's shop room she feels an unfamiliar pang, but she doesn't take the time to question its character. There's too much to do.

"Ah," says Unger when she hands the item to him. He behaves as if she hasn't been gone for months, as if her reappearance is timely and expected. "I believe this must be what's called a lying-in robe. Or a morning jacket. For the expectant mother who has the luck to have staff attending her needs in the final months. Not often seen in this climate, what with the ermine tippets. A bit overdone. Of course, I could be wrong."

"But do you want it? You can just have it," she says. "It seems the time has come for us finally to hunt down the family of Turtle Heart. Father is determined that we flee before we're run out of town. They've turned on him. We're leaving in the morning."

"Not a good look, to run away," says Unger. "Gives legitimacy to the accusations. Still, he's taking care of his family, something I do, too, though in a much less dramatic way. Yes, I'll take this off your hands. I'll even pay you for it."

"I don't want any payment."

"You're getting it. Listen. It's this: a piece of advice for you."

The new window glass has been installed and it is an oval like her mother's mirror, though at a scale of several orders of magnitude. The orientation, mostly vertical, tips up at one parabolic point. The light falls upon Elphie, and she knows she is pitiably green. She stands there with stone-hard eyes. She hates advice. "What," she finally says, to get it over with.

He props his rump upon the high stool behind the counter, folds his arms over his chest, and tilts his head back, examining her down the bridge of his nose and the slopes of his sallow cheeks. The hair in his ears wants trimming. "Recently, I've done some work for Pari'isi people," he tells her. "It's common knowledge among them that their stricken young To'or admires you for your ability to learn."

"Stricken?" she says, before she remembers, oh yes, Pari'isi To'or isn't expected to live long.

"It doesn't surprise me, Pari'isi To'or's opinions. They corroborate my own. But the young master has had more formal training than I ever did, and *he's* impressed by your quickness, the vivacity of your mind. Maybe your retreat from Ovvels isn't untimely after all."

"The Pari'isi chieftain isn't so fond of us, we've learned."

"That's all public relations. He has to be seen to be taking a stand against the unknown. Never mind about him. Pay attention. In truth, Elphie, our self-approving society here in Ovvels will soon grow too provincial for one of your interests and capacities." He sees that she is fretting, wanting to leave before this gets too personal. "My payment for this memento of your mother's? For all I know she wore it when she was carrying you. In any case, it buys you this piece of counsel."

"I have to go," she says, preparing to escape.

"Exactly so. Elphaba Thropp, you need to challenge yourself more than you've done so far. You were busy making little wings for the festival of Se'enth. You have farther to go, and on a separate model of wings. You might sit an entrance exam for one of the universities in Shiz. *Are* you listening to me? Shiz is the center of learning in all of Oz, as far as I've ever heard. A real city, compared to which Ovvels is only a town. North of us by travel that takes days and days. North even of the Emerald City. In the province of Gillikin."

"What are you blathering about, we're going to look for Turtle Heart's survivors and, I don't know, bring them marsh plums or something."

"Stop trying to be witty and listen to me. Talk your father into sending you there. You deserve to do something more than trail after him. Yes, of course, now you're a child, you aren't what, fourteen yet? Fifteen maybe? Something like that? I'm bad at ages and I can see you are, too. But you've changed in Ovvels during the time you've spent here. You're getting ready to launch into your own life. If you were still working for me I'd fire you, just so you would *have* to find something more challenging to do. Don't let your father, that mysteriously good man, hold you back. Your way is not his way, and his way is not yours. Are you taking this in?"

"You've lost your mind," she says, "he'd never let me."

"Don't ask him then. Just do it yourself."

"I'll say it again, you've lost your mind."

"Ah well," he says, turning from her, tucking up the morning jacket, brisking into busy work, "who cares about that, as long as you have found yours."

# 53

She ought to head back, what with the household in such a state. But before she turns her steps toward Lei Leila'ani's, Elphie sidles toward the lagoon, then takes the shortcut, threading her way across the watered allotments to the far side. She hurries up the slope. Where usually she would move from blind to blind, those stands of bamboo and giant fern, today she makes the shortest path, out in the open, to the grove of cedars that has been her private study. Hers and Pari'isi To'or's.

The right thing would be for To'or to be waiting for her as usual. But perhaps his uncle has caught wind of the secret tutorial and forbidden To'or to attend. The hill is bare of consolation. Of any sort.

Elphie whirls in the breeze lifting off the water, stretching her arms out on either side like the whirligig seed of the swamp maple. Winged seeds, able to fly on the breeze. Could she make herself a pair of wings, she could find—find what? Go high enough to see the world, see where Neri-neri and Lollo-lollo went? See where To'or is hiding from her, and call him out, if only to say good-bye? She has no wings to fly, no lift—only ambition.

The gymnastics of whirling in desperation, they blur everything; she is dizzy. Life reduced to a set of edges streaking past in colored ribbons. Tears come and she lets them, and hang the hurt. Hurting helps.

When she stops, Elphie becomes aware of a new sense of isolation. The landscape, unraveled into fuzzed belts of color, has come back together. It now seems a glassy globe. She isn't peering into it, to see the future or the past. *She* is inside, she is the one locked inside the world. She gets this for the first time. From the cedar branches above her, to the rice terraces, the agriculture, the humming hive of Ovvels, and the marshes and riverines and jungles from which the family had emerged and to which it will soon return: This is her prison. With a high blue lid, the sky, and a deep reflective floor, the water of the lagoon.

Caught inside the world and inside herself: a double prison. She may never escape.

Realizing this in a profound way, perhaps the first existential thought she's ever articulated for herself, she realizes there's no point in waiting for the feelings to lift. The next job of life is to live with these feelings. To work, then, toward the next brave thing.

When she gets back to the house, she corners her father in his prayer cell. She speaks in a low voice. "You aren't seriously thinking of letting Lei Leila'ani come with us when we go tomorrow?" she asks him.

She wonders if he is drunk. He is something. Wracked, to say the least. His eyes are fringed with glue and redness. He can't bring himself to put his arguments into words.

"Look," she says. "If Lei leaves with us, her fellow Ovvelians will conclude she *was* part of the problem. She'd never be able to come back. This is her home; we aren't her home. For her sake, we have to leave without her knowing. It's the right thing to do. We can't steal her security from her."

Frex isn't so far gone in distress to catch this insincerity. Elphie, concerned about the kindest thing to do? He raises an eyebrow and runs a hand with dirty fingernails through his beard.

"She might think she belongs with us," Elphie continues. "You might even think that. But she doesn't. She can't begin to manage Shell. The best course of action is to slip away in the morning before she is up. She sleeps very heavily as you know. Otherwise, we'd have breakfast once in a while. We'll get up before dawn. This is one time Shell will behave. He doesn't want her as a fake mother anymore than—that anyone else does."

"She's a good woman," says Frex, hopelessly.

"You let her come with us, you take her goodness away from her, for she's only good in the eyes of her neighbors."

"You're ferocious and ungenerous, Elphaba. You have no reason to be jealous of her."

"You'd be miserable if you stole her good name from her in exchange for her company. While she can always rent out her house to other lodgers after we are gone. She's good at looking after her own interests."

They stare at each other for a while that goes on too long, but neither can break the gaze.

The landlady is snoring softly behind her half-opened door when Frex leaves behind the final item once belonging to Melena, a brocaded purse in which he tucks a small fold of bills as a final payment. He doesn't notice Shell wheel back and pocket half of the cash.

The roofs tilt and wink, lifting above a sea of lagoon vapor.

Frex and Nessa refuse to turn to look at Ovvels one last time. Too proud. Shell and Elphie turn, though. Elphie can't make out Lei's house, only the clot of trees that mark her neighborhood. Shell says a bad word. Elphie holds his hand. Nanny walks with surprising vigor, restored to purpose now that Lei Leila'ani is out of the picture.

An unfamiliar sense of family purpose and conviviality.

"I know you did it," says Nessa to Shell, when their father has strode far enough ahead to be out of earshot.

"Did what?" Shell's retort is brave and taunting.

"Broke that porcelain tea set," says Nessa. Elphie looks away.

"I didn't, you did," says Shell. "You hexed them over the side of the rail because you were angry you couldn't pick up a teacup by yourself."

"I never would," says Nessa, "and my great moral strength is that I don't lie, either. A paradox: I may not have arms, but I am armed with the truth."

"Oh, please," mutters Elphie.

"Even if I did," says Shell, "you prolly hexed me to do it. You can't deny that. Even if you don't 'member. You coulda hexed me in your sleep."

The arrogant little kid has got his sister cornered. She bites her lower lip until it bleeds, and Nanny has to come over and clean her chin. "If I didn't have to love you, I would so hate you," Nessa says to Shell.

"Too bad," he says cheerily. He's deflected attention from the possibility that he had committed all those other small crimes, too, and he goes skipping ahead on the path, free as sin itself.

# 54

ut it proves more difficult than they've guessed, to follow the clues that Ta'abi, the master glassblower, had written out for them on the back of Unger's bill. Imagine a spider trying to describe which radial thread it just took to acquire the breakfast bug near the web's vortex. Same problem. The family is looking for a stretch of river with an unusually dense mangrove overhang. But the nameless braided rivers are mostly free of permanent settlements, and nearly identical. Only the grace of fate will lead them to Turtle Heart's kin. Or it won't.

Still, they keep on, in bark canoes and on foot, in monsoon rains and in rarer dry dusty days. And they ask everyone they meet for advice, and sometimes follow it.

It's tricky. For one thing, the name Turtle Heart being a translation of Chelo'ona, too many variants proliferate. In the fungal-like relationships of small hamlets and knock-'em-up seasonal posts, people with names something like Stah Chelo'ona, or Heart of Turtle, or Chelo'ona Goah, Turtle Pulse, are always cropping up. The Thropps have only a clue; they don't have a map.

As the weeks turn to months and the months drone on, and Frex goes back to that more hardscrabble life as a traveling preacher, they discover that the more efficient question to ask isn't about Turtle Heart, or Stah Chelo'ona, but this: Does anyone even *remember* a disappeared young man, a handsome young man who had been both glassblower and prophet? One who had sounded an alarm about the miners of rubies swarming down from the Emerald City? Who had gone away, to protest and to petition for cease-and-desist?

Since the Quadlings are in general such a complacent type, compared anyway to striving Munchkinlanders, Turtle Heart's personality type stands out more in local memory than his name does. Some of the older members of the communities nod sagely. But he always seems to be from a different clan, one that has upped and moved, north is it, or maybe south. As Frex has no other ambition but to preach until he dies, and his family has no recourse but to stick with him, their meanderings are discouragingly random. Maybe they will eventually find someone who had known Turtle Heart, and then Frex will ask forgiveness for the prophet's murder in the forecourt of Colwen Ground all those years ago. Or maybe they won't. Meanwhile they're doing the work of the Unnamed God. Perhaps the wild goose chase nature of this enterprise is a divine plan. And they should just shut up and stop complaining about it.

It might go on like this for the rest of Elphie's life except that one day, a sweltery day in which gnits and gnasties swarm, the mission party is hiking into a new enclave when a familiar voice rings out. Their names are being languorously announced. "Cattery Spunge and Frexispar the Godly. And that scrap of fern now grown to a beanpole, Elphie-Fabala-Fae herself!" From the shadows of a beaded curtain behind which she's been squatting, protected from the biting insects, their erstwhile, sly cook pokes her head. Boozy herself.

She must have been very young back in those days, thinks Elphie, because she hardly seems middle-aged now. A few lines on her forehead and around her memorable mouth. Her hips are broader, but her posture is much the same, and the vigor—or lack of it—brings back memories that Elphie can't place. But those sensations of unseen memory, oh, they're strong indeed; she feels lifted by something invisible.

This, maybe, is the antidote to her epiphany of loneliness in the cedar grove. It's a first for her: reunion.

"Nessie-nessie, walking like a holy maiden. Miracles happen. And this the little prince, coming up fine," Boozy says of Shell, looking him up and down. "I thought they'd drown you for the trouble you gave to your mother."

"Apparently not," says Shell, chin up. He doesn't know who Boozy is but he can recognize the dangerous tone of intimacy.

"As I live and breathe," says Frex, limited joy at this happenstance.

"You'll be a big help." Nanny mops her brow and shoos away the insects. "For one thing, you can tell us where in the mucklands we actually are."

"Oh, this place has no name, too ugly," says Boozy. "But this someplace between Ovvels and Qhoyre, more or less. Maybe closer to Qhoyre. Bengda to the that-way, and on the other arm, you get to the wide salt fields and the white wild wheat. You not still looking for the folks of that nobody your in-laws done in?"

"Turtle Heart's kin. Yes," says Frex. "Or Stah Chelo'ona, as we've heard it said. Or some such wrinkle."

"Well, you come to the right place," says Boozy. "They here the last little somewhile. At least I think it's them."

"You knew? And you could have told us?"

"I don't know where you go after I leave you." Boozy isn't as easily scared as she'd been when she was a younger cook. "Besides, I forgot all about you."

The family sets up the single tent. They've become used to rather too close quarters, so they're happy that Nanny agrees to doss down in Boozy's little cabin. The children want to join her, just for the change, but Boozy will have none of it. "You all got diseases I don't need," she declares. While she won't elaborate, Elphie assumes Boozy means the birthmarks, apparent in the case of the sisters, and probably hidden somewhere in Shell's cranky trouble-maker soul, too.

They discuss strategies over a simple supper Boozy serves up—a kind of spicy mud stew, by the look of it. The clan they are hunting for—if it's the right people—camps a morning's journey north-ish of here, in the direction of the salt fields but not as far. If they haven't upped and moved on, she warns them. Nobody sticks around anyplace very long unless they live in a place like Ovvels or Qhoyre, where buildings are more solid than tents and too much trouble to move. Still, Boozy will lead the missionary family out that way and wait for them and lead them back again. But they can only stay one more night at the edge of her home because she doesn't want to get a reputation for harboring witches.

"Again? What *is* this witch thing?" says Frex. "An ugly new anx-iety. We are pious folk who bow down before the Unnamed God."

"You can't see your god, can't even give him a name," says Boozy. "So how do you know which way to bow? I never understand that part."

"Some of us are partial to Lurline, the fairy queen," insists Nanny.

"Codswallop and pigspittle," says Frex.

Still, Elphie thinks the domestic rancor has a convivial aspect to it. Elphie misses Unger, and she almost admits to missing Pari'isi To'or, so to bump into Boozy in the middle of nowhere is sweet accident. And that Boozy is still disagreeable! What weird consolation. Frex even allows Shell to enjoy a small glass of river-grape wine, thinking it's Shell's first taste of such.

They raise a toast to times past and times yet to come. Nanny warbles a soft little hymn to Lurline, and for once Frex doesn't shush her. They all float off on rafts of sleep in a state that comes as close to something called happiness as Elphie has ever really dared to think possible.

Overnight, of course, the world inches back to its ordinary vexatiousness. Tranquility is but a fleeting guest, and under scrutiny it dissolves, shy as a ghost.

# 55

First comes the question of who will join Boozy on the expedition. The end in sight: to ask pardon for the ways that Frex and Melena, delaying Turtle Heart in his quest, may have set him up for danger. Frex, the lead plaintiff in this campaign. But who else? Shell is too abrasive, too unpredictable to bring along, also to leave behind. "I'll take on that charge," says Nanny, theatrically, "as was ever my burden." She's relieved to be let off the hook.

Frex wants Nessa to join the delegation. At first the girl agrees. But when Nanny brings out Nessa's shoes and kneels down to affix them upon her feet, the first shoe drops a glistening beige scorpion upon the earth. The second shoe does the same. Creeped out by this, Nessa changes her mind. The docile girl refuses to oblige. (She's growing up, too.)

"All this is a sign," she insists. "The Unnamed God has sent two sacred poisoned messengers to show me that my coming with you is risky, maybe fatal."

"Fatal for you, or all of us?" Elphie muses innocently. "Makes a bit of a difference."

"I'm not going to be paraded for my deficits," Nessa continues. "Father, if you're to blame for arranging Turtle Heart to be in the right place at the right time for his own death, that's your problem. I'm not going to march around for sympathy so you can be let off the hook. I'm not putting on the bloody poison shoes. Go without me."

A ferocity of conviction in her mood, and—such clarity. "I

didn't raise you to be so authoritative," her father mumbles—but he backs down. "Well, *you* can help Nanny and watch Shell."

"She's not the boss of me," says Shell, who at eight is a fire-cracker of increasing combustibility. Frex slaps Shell across the mouth.

"I know you're wound up, but that's uncalled for, really," says Nanny softly. "Get a hold of yourself, sir."

They set off from the nameless hamlet, along a track crowded on both sides by murkweed. Boozy, Frex, and Elphie. She knows why she's included in the party. Melena is dead and Elphie is the minister's oldest child. It's her job to stand behind him in a moment like this. The unspoken obligation of the senior child.

The path leads through a sameness of new-growth forest, low and scrubby and damp. Boozy remarks that this part of Quadling Country had been drained by Emerald City engineers. By now the mineral seam of ruby has been played out, leaving wreckage of the vegetable pearl plantations. The fish and waterfowl upon which the migrant Quadlings rely had all disappeared, and they're coming back only slowly. "Oh," says Boozy, recounting this tale in her languid way, "but the water table dropped, of course, and what should emerge from the shrinking riverbank but the carcass of that old perqu'unti."

At first no one knows quite what she is talking about. Elphie has forgotten, and Frex had been largely absent on that long-ago morning of confrontation with the armed Quadling men.

But Boozy rattles on. "And to think, Boozy find it, of all people! The usual feasting little grubbies never dare demolish it. So it a whole preserved corpse."

"How far away was that?" asks Frex flatly, not really interested.

Boozy raises an eyebrow. "You still a bit of a puffball. Don't you recognize where you are? *This* the old riverbank. Where you slept

last night is where you were camped a dozen years ago or whenever suchlike. Now we walking along the old riverbed. Up ahead
the water is refreshed again, where dikes and berms got built to
contain it. But now, you hiking on the ghost of water." And Elphie
sees this must be true. The track is in a declivity, and older, wilder
forest thickens on either side of them as they stumble forward.

Frex mutters, "I certainly hope there are no more crocodriloi to
pester us today."

"They died out for now," says Boozy, but adds cheerfully, "if
your no-name god powerful enough, maybe he bring them back to
life by your atonement."

They continue in a silence that grows more spiteful and more
welcome the longer it lasts.

At a ferry slip of sorts, three men are squatting in a group,
throwing bones and smoking. They stand as Boozy approaches.
She addresses one of them as Ti'imit, and introduces him to the
missionary party as her husband. Frex gives no sign of having ever
met him before. Ti'imit returns the nonchalance. Caution on both
sides. Boozy browbeats Ti'imit into leaving the game of chance
and taking take them down the river, which here is shallow and
sluggish. "Mangrove thicket," she tells Ti'imit.

"A raft," says Elphie, blanching—to the extent she can blanch.
"Not even a boat with sides?"

"Oh, right, you shrink from the wet. But this a raft sits high on
the water."

"Not high enough," says Elphie. She refuses to step aboard
while it rides so low. Frex insists. So a stool is brought forward and
Elphie can perch on it, putting her shoes on the rung. Little sheets
of riverwater wash over the boards in sinuous curves. By holding
her breath and doing mathematical constructions in her head, Elphie is able to endure.

It's not a long trip by water, probably not half an hour. Soon enough they're delivered to the other side, a break in the mangrove defenses large enough to beach the raft. "The crocodrilos, its back busied like that," said Boozy, waving a hand at the fractally complicated fretwork of roots and stems. "Smart. It disguise itself as mangrove till supper swim along."

Ti'imit stays with the raft as the others go inland on foot. Frex begins to fret. "You don't mean to tell me that this clan of Turtle Heart's was here all along, when I started my ministry to Quadling Country, and you didn't even say so?"

Boozy shrugs. "No, of course not. Our people move, they camp, they leave camp, they camp again. The ruby thieves unsettle everyone. This clan we visiting been here only a year. I mean this time; they been here before."

Up the slope, along a sort of chalky ledge, through a grove of limp-looking baby oaks, and then down into a small settlement of tents erected on bamboo platforms set about four feet off the ground. "The land still angry," says Boozy. "Sometimes it just flood with old water to make its opinion known. Higher floor better."

"Works for me," murmurs Elphie. "Where's a mountaintop when you need one?"

Boozy bids them to wait while she arranges an introduction. When she comes back, she looks a little drunk. That long forehead of hers is a ruddier brown. "I do not know how it work," she says, "but the someone who remember Turtle Heart, whether yours or some other one, will see you. Briefly. Did you bring tribute?"

"Oh," says Frex. "What will he do if we didn't think of tribute?"

"The chieftain is a her. Chaloti'in. Come forward, both of you." Boozy leads Frex and Elphie to a clearing behind the tents. A small group has assembled. Men summoned from their chores stand in a half-circle behind a woman about Frex's age. She is seated in a folding chair with X-shaped legs. Chaloti'in, apparently. A woman of nervy expression. Her hair looks unnaturally black though her face shows the lines of time and tragedy. She holds in one hand a white porcelain object. It takes Elphie some time to recognize it as the skull of a small monkey. Were she back in Ovvels she'd be measuring it for wings.

The matriarch gestures the guests to approach. Boozy stands to one side, ready to translate if needed. But after all these years in Quadling Country, Frex and Elphie between them manage the dialects pretty well on their own.

"Explain," says Chaloti'in, her voice holding everything back but suspicion.

"Elphaba," says her father. "You sing first. That can be our tribute."

So the green girl stands forward, what else can she do, after all this time what else is she there for but to help her father buy some pardon? Frex doesn't identify a sacred tune, and Elphaba closes her eyes and lets her voice out, afraid to go far at first. She extemporizes. Coaxes forward a melismatic loop of wordless melody clustered around a root note. Slowly extends it up and down the scale. Her drawn-out vowels, unbuckled from consonants, seem tentative. She files a melodic petition before this wizened, middle-aged queen of the swamp on behalf of her family, and perhaps of the whole world. What can anyone ever do but ask for mercy.

Frex may be startled at his daughter's instincts but he doesn't post any opposition. He watches Elphie with gratitude, but she doesn't know that, because she closes her eyes as the melody ventures abroad.

When she draws the voluntary to a whispered finish, neither high note nor low, just there, she drops her hands to her sides. She keeps her eyes down and hears her father bring forward his petition pertly, as if guessing that Chaloti'in won't stand for embroidered rhetoric. But Chaloti'in cuts him off and speaks to Elphaba. "Singing is only for our ancestors," says the striking woman. "Who are your forebears?"

Elphie indicates Frex. "My father is the seventh son of a seventh son."

"I don't mean him." Chaloti'in curls her upper lip, the first sign they have that this interview might not land Frex his absolution. "I mean *your* forebears. Where does your instinct come from?"

"Well." Elphie doesn't glance at her father for fear of how offended he might be at attention paid to his daughter over himself. "I suppose, then, my mother? Who died seven or eight years ago."

"A start," says Chaloti'in. "But ancestors go back and back, and far and far. We cherish them and are wary, too. They are the beaded net that collected our souls and brought us forward into light. You have a strange provenance."

"My father is a minister in the unionist faith—"

"I am not talking about that man." Chaloti'in sounds fed up. "Is what you sang a funeral song for the lands of the Quadlings? For all of us? You give us a longing but we do not recognize for what." Now she sounds bereaved, as if Elphie has arrived with bad news. "I am a seer," Chaloti'in continues, "like many of my family. It comes in our blood and breath. The one you call Turtle Heart and that we call Chelo'ona Stah was a prophet. And a glassblower. Yes, I knew him. Tender and flighty, but he could see threats and provocations. He warned us. Long ago he went off to the imperialists to tell their military to stop sending troops to build that highway of yellow steps. To stop draining the wetlands for the crystallized blood of the land beneath us. He went away and he never came back, and the ruination of the earth continues until this day. We are crowded off of the marshes beyond Qhoyre, we are made to wander for our sustenance farther than is easy to manage."

She's left the subject of Elphaba's talents and weirdness, for which the girl is grateful. Elphie takes a step back and extends a wide-open palm to her father.

"I have news of your clansman," says Frex. When Chaloti'in tries to cut him off he keeps going. "No, I will be heard, Madame Seer. I'm partly to blame for what happened to Turtle Heart. Your prophet left Quadling Country and meandered into Munchkin-land. I suppose because the houses of the Eminences there are nearer than the court of the Emerald City. Along the way, Turtle Heart stopped for sustenance at our outback outpost. Mine and my wife's. Stone cottage. I was not home at the time. My wife took him in and they became friendly. When I returned from my labors, I also took up with him. We cherished him as a member of our family."

Elphie steals a glance at Chaloti'in. The chief looks as if she thinks stories of affection are a waste of time, and untrustworthy. But at least she's now listening to Brother Frexispar the Godly.

"Our attentions delayed Turtle Heart from his mission," concludes Frex. "Had we been less smitten with him, had my wife merely given him a meal and sent him onward, had I not been entranced by his foreign mystique, he might have arrived where he was going at a more advantageous time. It was only bad luck that a human sacrifice was needed—a peasant response to the drought, and a family response to decisions my wife and I had made. But there he was. He showed up. Bad timing. And so he was killed. And I am partly to blame. I have stumbled through life ever since, making amends, trying to bring news of the Unnamed God to your nation—"

Chaloti'in has had enough of this. Without looking around. she opens and closes her free hand. An attendant comes forward and slips into her grasp a crozier of river rushes, perhaps eight feet high. Chaloti'in nods Frex forward. He obliges, descending to one knee as before royalty. With confidence in his god he keeps his chin high and his forehead reared back. Before Elphie can protest, Chaloti'in has whisked the rushes down upon her father's face, striping blood from skin. It beads in vertices. "We don't shrive, we don't shrive," she says calmly, as if concluding a business deal with a river merchant. Which perhaps she is doing. "And not for Turtle Heart. What's done is done. You find your comfort some- where else, not from us. Go away from here. Stay away from here." She glares at Boozy, and the former cook seems taken aback. "You are tainted by your association with these monsters. Shame on you." But she flicks one reed in the air toward Elphie, not as a whip but as a pointer. "Except for her. See her safely to where she is going next."

Frex crumples on his hands and knees, blood in his eyes. His visible wounds will heal but the scar of shame beneath them will remain. Chaloti'in gets up and walks away, munching on a seg- ment of marsh plum that someone has handed her, perhaps as a palate cleanser after such vitriol.

# 56

With her familiar insouciance, Boozy agrees to join the family party as they depart from the unnamed hamlet where she now lives. What Ti'imit thinks of her plans doesn't seem to matter. Her tenure will last only for the time that the family takes wandering through the lowlands, northeast, in the general direction of Qhoyre, capital city of Quadling Country. Once Boozy can deliver them into a place where the nighttime streets are lit with oil lamps, she'll have had enough, she tells them. Perhaps, Elphie later thinks: That harridan called Chaloti'in had privately ordered Boozy to escort the family out of the region. Or even hired her to do it. Boozy doesn't sweat the details, however, or not out loud. Not in front of the Thropp family.

In those weeks, or are they months, probably, Boozy becomes the majordomo of the outfit. While Frex has managed to put away a small bankroll from his earnings, he isn't working now. His confidence in his calling has been shattered for the second time in his life. He becomes a hermit in the marshy wilderness, praying for his own salvation, or begging for strength to live until his children grow up enough to survive his death. He makes little effort to summon a prayer meeting. Instead, he relies on Boozy to buy or barter food for the family. He hands over cash so she can pay the occasional landlord for the relief of a roof instead of a tent over their heads, especially in a rainy week. Boozy and Nanny between them manage the household, Boozy cooking with her easy indolence, Nanny fretting and laying down the law.

Ah, but it isn't easy for Nanny, either. Elphie guesses that Nanny has become somewhat paralyzed in this stifling humidity. Sensing, perhaps, an eternity of punishment for her, too, adjacent her employer, with no possibility of parole.

Meanwhile, Nessa grows serene and self-admiring, or at least seems to—who knows what she really feels, now that she has learned to govern her expressions more strictly?

And poor unparented Shell, he remains the juvenile scofflaw, an afterthought in the family history, betrayed by both his dead mother and his absentminded father. He's growing up without anchors, Elphie thinks. Once she sees him poking open the wallet where Frex keeps the reserve funds. She is about to squeal on her little brother until she realizes that he's taking some funds from a satchel hidden inside his tunic, and he's adding coins and notes to the depleted stash her father had taken when they'd left Ovvels. Probably Shell pickpocketed the cash from Ovvels parishioners, but even so.

Before Boozy does leave, though Elphie doesn't see this as a goodbye conversation, the cook offers her the corpse of the crocodrilos as a souvenir. "A souvenir of what?" asks Elphie. Boozy just shrugs. She shows Elphie the thing. No, it isn't a skeleton. Boozy explains that the thing was pulled from the water and buried for a while in a bog, where its skin leathered up, its bramble-hedge of cresting armor withered off, and its expression settled into a grimace of reproach. It has shrunk, or it never was as big as Nanny remembered it. In fact, it fits into the bottom of a reticule made of leather of reptile, a cruel touch or a fitting one, Elphie can't decide.

Elphie's curiosity about Animals makes the bizarre souvenir attractive to her, but how can she agree to babysit a sack of ribs and preserved organs capped by what is left of its dorsal phalanges? What does Boozy expect her to do, bring the creature back to life? Elphie bites her lip, considering. It might have stopped there except

Nanny has been listening across the wooden platter of rice and pepperstems.

"I'll take it," says Nanny. "Elphie, I'll hold it for you while I can manage it, and I'll spring it on you sometime as a curio of your childhood. Surprise!"

"This is what I have to prove a childhood in Quadling Country," says Elphie. "A bag of bones and intestines. Who needs a toy porcelain tea set? I wish I were back at show-and-tell at the lodge, and allowed in the door. I'd show them this gristle, and then I'd tell them about it."

"You can make something out of this someday," says Frex, a rare instance of his paying attention to what someone else is talking about.

"I can make sense of it, maybe," says Elphie. "If I learn how."

"Make Nessa some crocodrilos arms," says Shell, filching the ripest of the pepperstems from the serving board. Nanny thwacks him with a wooden spatula. "Hex them up for her. You think you're so smart, figure out how to do that."

Elphie doesn't answer. She is ever more aware of her limitations and of her needs, too. The answers don't lie in prayers or in magic, though, not as far as she can tell. She's inept in both departments. The troubles in her mind are beginning to weigh upon her. It isn't easy to say, then or ever after, what she struggles with except trying to survive being young. She wants to know more, however heartbreaking it might be. She is impatient with not knowing. Unger Bi'ix and Pari'isi To'or between them have a lot to answer for, shaping in her an appetite that she is impatient to slake. But she does not know how.

## 57

Boozy disappears again, leaving that sack of reptile carcass with Nanny, after she's delivered Frex to Qhoyre. The capital city of the province of Quadling Country, that sunken, subordinate quadrant of Oz.

Though on their odyssey the Thropps have lived here once before, Elphie has few memories of it. The city is four, six, eight times larger than Ovvels. The advantage of a busier street, Elphaba learns, is that there is more hubbub to distract the pedestrian. She can pass by provoking only a sidelong glance, if that. Well, look; here are other Munchkinlanders doing trading, and they're paler and taller than the native Quadlings. People with different traditions of dress and with different features and skin colors, and sometimes different accents or even different tongues. There's nobody else green, to be sure; but green seems less outrageous when there are so many other distractions on the street.

Frex tries with limited success to establish another congregation in Qhoyre. Perhaps his heart isn't in it. Or the people of Qhoyre already know that, in the nativist practice of ancestor reverence, there's sufficient to sustain them while they practice enough life to become, all in good time, ancestors themselves.

Shell takes advantage of the busier alleys, the torpid marketplaces. He is ever quicker to disappear in a crowd. Slipping his hand into pockets is a cinch in a bigger city. Nanny despairs of him but she can't be expected, at her age, to bounce along behind him through market stalls, trying to keep him law-abiding.

As for Nessa, poor Nessa. Something about that experience

with the scorpions in her shoes has spooked her, but good. She takes to going barefoot, which gives her the appearance of a saint's statue from which the arms have been hammered away. Humility at its most distinguished. She seems somehow to enjoy being just faintly repulsive. Elphaba can't work it out, but then the curious mechanics of character don't mean as much to Elphaba as other topics. Such as how the lungs work, and the mind, and where sits the soul, if you even believe in such an entity. And if you do, can Animals be said to have souls, and if not, why not? None of her father's homilies ever engaged with this question, which makes her cross.

On an overcast afternoon in the autumn of the following year, Elphie is on her way home from a halfhearted attempt to sing a little audience toward her father's washtub sermon. Her mind is on herbs and music and homiletics. As she stands back, trying to avoid a splash of puddle while a carriage passes, she is poked on her shoulder blade. She turns to gripe at the interruption. She has onions to deliver for the evening pottage, and Nanny will be waiting.

A man stands there in a rather fine cape of arresting distinction. She doesn't recognize him, but the cape is ornamented at the collar with ermine tippets. Her heart lurches. "Why are you bothering me?" she barks, as soon as she's certain it isn't Unger.

"I know you," says the gentleman. His manner of speaking and deference is almost courtly. "I couldn't mistake you for someone else."

"You don't know me, nobody knows me." *Not even myself.* She doesn't understand why her reaction is sudden outrage. Or is it fear.

He explains. He is the uncle of her former tutor, Pari'isi To'or. He doesn't say "your friend," and that is sublime courtesy, for

Elphie has never decided if studying things together constituted a friendship or merely commerce.

The uncle identifies himself as Pari'isi Menga'al. Elphaba remembers him. One of the most influential citizens in Ovvels. He sort of ran them out of town?

Pari'isi Menga'al asks Elphie to join him for a cinnamon tea at a nearby café. She's never dared tiptoe into such an establishment, but she's too curious to pass by the chance to hear from To'or. The uncle steers Elphie, the lightest of touches only, toward a table. Someone comes over and asks her what she wants.

She's never known how to say what she wants.

Pari'isi Menga'al orders for her. "I must get home, I'm not on a holiday here," she tells him as they wait for cups of tea to be brought over.

The hot drinks arrive. Cinnamon threads its cajoling odor up from a porcelain teacup set in a fretted basket made of twisted wires. She closes her eyes to absorb the warmth on her skin, but she's suddenly shaken with grief about how time is passing, and there is so little left of her life, really. Every porcelain teacup gets smashed sooner or later. The stinging wet at her eyelashes must be the condensation of tea. She brushes it off. "What is it you want with me?" she hammers at her host.

He tells her that the boy has died. As expected. Maybe three seasons after her family disappeared from Ovvels. Pari'isi To'or had spoken of Elphie only in respectful tones, and had hoped, as Unger Bi'ix had hoped, that she wouldn't be stymied by the limitations of her origins.

"Limitations?" Elphaba gets stroppy. The nerve. "My mother was the Thropp Second Descending of Colwen Grounds, I'll have you know. While we don't keep track of what's gone on in that family, I've advanced to being the Thropp Second Descending. At least. Not that I want such a distinction, or need it. But, um, I'm not as shabby as all that. *Limitations!*"

"And your father, who raised you?" It is the softest of insinuations, but in the tender hesitancy of her host, she can infer that he thinks she's been failed by her father. Frex hasn't taken Elphie into account. His holy calling has blinded him to the reality of his daughter's needs.

Maybe Pari'isi Menga'al hasn't meant to suggest all that, but the conclusion registers in Elphie's mind with the clarity of a theorem proof. The flush of her understanding blocks out the sound of Pari'isi Menga'al's voice for a moment. Hey, she's just grown up, in that one instant. It hurts. Liberation inflicts its scars, too.

"My father did what he could. Tell me: Did Pari'isi To'or suffer?" But then she shakes her head and holds up both her hands, revoking her question. She doesn't want to know. "Why did you stop me? Just because you knew me? Is that reason to hold me from bringing supper to my family?"

The man laughs. "Of course not. You had a reputation for being strong-minded, and I can already see why. No, Miss Elphie—as I was saying—"

"Elphaba," she says.

"Miss Elphaba. No, I stopped you because happenstance is as valid as fate is. As prophecies are. You stepped in front of me as I was waiting to cross the street. Lucky me, that I was alert enough to recognize you."

"It can't have been that hard. I'm not easily mistaken for someone else."

"But you've grown up quite a bit. Have you seen anyone from Ovvels since you left?"

"Never."

"See? So here we are, be it luck or destiny. I'm in the capital this week on municipal business for Ovvels. I stumble upon an opportunity to make good on the story of Elphie—Elphaba. My nephew died before being able to see to its next chapter. But here I am instead."

"If I remember correctly, you pushed us to abandon Ovvels. No?"

"No," he said firmly. "I paid an obligatory call to register a complaint, but I had no intention of taking other steps. But now I am, in a different direction. Toward the next chapter, as I said."

"Fancy that you think there might be a next chapter. I think I'm stuck in this one."

"Well, maybe you are. Or perhaps you aren't." He leans forward. "As you know, our household does a lot of business with the fabric merchant. Unger Bi'ix. That's where my nephew first met you, I think? We're in and out of his shop several times a year. Frequently Unger has mumbled some hopes that certain recommendations he made to you might come to pass."

"I don't think it was any of his business. Anyway, I don't recall them."

"I do. He suggested he thought you might sit for exams to enter Shiz University. He believes that despite your lack of formal schooling, you have a zealous mind and a canny one. Perhaps attending a school might be a way to break you free from the limited expectations of your family. He's mentioned this to me more than once, and wistfully. I'd be pleased if I could go back and tell him that you walked right into my path in Qhoyre, and I raised the matter. I'm only here on business for a few days, but I can make enquiries on your behalf."

"Father wouldn't approve. Anyway, the family needs me."

"Don't give yourself airs." If his tone is kindly, there's a remonstrative edge to the thought. "Do you know other people any better than you know yourself? It doesn't strike me that you do. Give them the chance to surprise you."

So she allows this biggywig to come home with her. The boardinghouse above a stable isn't far, and it's still not yet dusk. Father will turn him out on his ear, no doubt, offended at the meddling man, and a foreigner at that.

But Frex doesn't send the Quadling grandee packing. Whatever resentment Frex might harbor about having had to flee from Ovvels, it brought him to the fulfillment of his long-standing goal of confession. And maybe Frex is impressed that a highborn member in good standing in Ovvels even wants to take the time to seek him out.

While Pari'isi Menga'al doesn't accept an invitation to stay for wheat pottage, he does take a small glass of ambrosial cordial from a hidden stock of Nanny's, of which no one has ever been aware before this.

Frex listens to the visitor's proposals and his offer to help. Pari'isi Menga'al explains. Since Qhoyre is a regional capital, albeit a shabby one in the poorest part of the country, far-off Shiz University maintains an office in the commercial center. Here, in this city.

Elphaba isn't sure she wants to follow up the suggestion, even when Nessa speaks up and says *she* would be happy to sit for an entrance exam. "He came to talk to *me*," snaps the older sister. "Of course there are cautions and concerns," says the visitor to Frex. "Your daughter is a humble country girl. There is much that will be arresting and strange to her in a big city. Some of the scholars will be from well-placed families—"

"Elphie is the Thropp Second Descending," huffs Frex, glancing at his unkempt oldest child. "Though she needs to grow into the practices of refinement. She has had so little guidance since her mother died. I worry about her proper comportment."

"There are separate schools for girls and schools for young men," continues Pari'isi Menga'al. "Supervision is strict, so you needn't be too alarmed. Still, it will be a challenge. Society is different there. Many different sorts of people from all over Oz. I understand there may even be Animals on the faculty. That alone would take some getting used to."

"Animals?" Elphie is intrigued and doesn't try to hide it. "Educated Animals to whom I might be expected to—to talk?"

"I wouldn't worry about it overmuch," counseled the visitor. "I think the practice of hiring Animals for professorial and research posts is on the wane at the moment. You ought to be safe enough."

Elphie sits up straight and squares her shoulders. "All right, if you can arrange an interview, I'll do it. That is, if Father allows."

She glances at Frex. "I'm beyond claiming the power of allowance," he admits. "You aren't yet grown up, Elphie, but you are most assuredly not growing down. I have managed to keep you alive these sixteen years or so. You owe me nothing."

For some reason this is one of the most searing things he has ever said to her. She can't work out why this stabs her. Surely she owes him something.

Or maybe not. She can't yet know. Maybe the answer is unknowable, or maybe whatever the answer is doesn't really matter.

# 58

She muses over how she came to be here as she sits in a still, nearly empty question hall one morning, with a proctor at the front of the room, glaring a little dangerously at her. "What?" says Elphaba.

"I said you could start. This is a timed test. Are you afraid to begin?"

"No," she says. All of her life trembles on the tip of a pencil. "I was just thinking." She lowers her head and turns to the first question.

# 59

This is nearly all I am going to tell you about.

All the palaver, the arrangements, the saying good-byes, the questions about funding. An endless series of knots to unravel and to tie up again. It is some months before the day arrives.

Nanny is to stay behind in Qhoyre with Nessa and Shell. Nanny has been weepy, Nessa brilliantly envious, and Shell bored by it all, and pissy. Elphaba has been busy stomping away in a new pair of thick leather boots, the type that miners wear. Breaking them in. Who is paying for what, she doesn't know for sure and doesn't ask. Maybe there are stipends for poor students. Or Pari'isi Menga'al, who has come by once or twice more, might have ponied up some funds in honor of his nephew. Perhaps Unger Bi'ix cashed in those vegetable pearls of Pari'isi To'or's that Elphie had once given him. Whatever. The fees are taken care of, and Elphaba doesn't worry about it. Money doesn't interest her at all, neither glad of it in hand nor vexed when it's in short supply. Such a bother.

On the final visit of Pari'isi Menga'al before her departure, he hands her a good-luck gift. A vegetable pearl kitted out with the kind of hooking apparatus suitable for attachment to an ear lobe. It belonged to Pari'isi To'or. A token of friendship, perhaps.

Elphie has learned enough manners to say thank you—just in time before she's considered rude as skunk cabbage and her bursary is reclaimed by the offended donor. But after the uncle leaves, Elphie strolls down to the river and she drives a sharp, sparkling arc through the sky, delivering herself of the need to husband souvenirs of friendship. The vegetable pearl sinks back toward where it grew. She has no appetite for friendship and she wants no obligations of affection.

The past promises us nothing but this: it will abandon us. Leave us orphaned. Unless we abandon it first.

On the day of departure, Nanny is beside herself dispensing teary advice, blessings of Lurlina, cautions and promises and doomy predictions. Finally she throws her apron over her head, a well-timed means of stifling herself because Elphie has been about to do it for her.

Shell goes into hiding and won't come out, and he may not even be on the premises. She can't blame him. Elphie is abandoning him, after all. She'd feel just as ornery. Probably.

But Nessa, Nessa comes forward in her bare feet, and stands in the light of the window. The steam of horse manure from the stalls below wreaths about her and is somehow relieved of stink. Elphie, her heart torn, thinks: this is what holiness can do, maybe: denature the world.

"I should give you a gift," says Nessa in a fake, formal voice, "but all I have are my wounds."

"Well, I don't want those," says Elphie, not able to help herself.

"The wounds in my heart," explains Nessa.

"Oh." Outside, a clock in a tower chimes. "It's okay. I wouldn't know how to care for them. But I have something for you." She reaches in the pocket of her traveling apron and pulls out a small stone, easy on the palm, a perfect black egg of a stone. "I found this one day on the shore near the lagoon. Does it remind you of anything?"

"Should it?"

"The black stone in the water that we turned into a marsh plum overnight. The hex that probably wasn't a hex. Don't you remember? Or were you too little?"

"I can't pick it up," Nessa reminds her sister. "Are you going to push it in my throat to silence my prayers for you?"

"Nessa, I'll take any prayers you have to spare, I guess. No, this stone—it's something inert and yet full of, um, possibility. You could still hex your own life, Nessa."

"You know I don't look kindly on—"

"I don't mean hex with magicks. I mean change. Follow in my footsteps, or someone else's. Get out. When it's your turn. Make the black stone into something worth biting into—like a marsh plum. I don't know. It's a *token*. Get it? I thought you'd remember."

Nessa's smile is wan and watery; that's the unwelcome tears on their way. "It doesn't matter if I was too small to remember. You have done it for me. You took care of me. I don't need a symbol to remind me of that."

Elphie sets the stone down anyway on the windowsill. She would clasp Nessa's hands if—if. Instead she circles an arm around her sister's waist. They are not embracing, they are just walking together, back and forth in front of the window, into the sunlight and out of it, silently. Parallel shadows on the floorboards.

Now, most of what I say next is conjecture.

Frex and Elphaba will travel by coach on a rural route that bows west to avoid the capital of Oz. Frex will say he doesn't want Elphaba to come up against the snares and temptations of the Emerald City. While this may be prudent, Elphaba will think her father is hiding his own uncertainty about a city even larger than Qhoyre, one where as a Munchkinlander he would be an unwelcome foreigner yet again.

The capital city. One day perhaps she will go there. On her own.

But now, after ten days or more of traveling in silence, Frex praying in the corner of the carriage and Elphaba trying to read the texts that the admissions committee has recommended, the unpainted country trap drawn by the hired horse will arrive at its destination. Shiz will be a perky place, brisk and sunny. The climate will be dry, something almost entirely new to Elphaba, raised as she's been in humidity. The lofty trees will spread their limbs farther apart, and the leaves will be more plentiful, more pliant, smaller. There will likely be movement of wind in the branches, a dry current rather than a wet one, blundering noisily in the air all around them.

Shiz University having sent instructions on how to locate the welcome hall, the bewildered driver will navigate city boulevards and lanes and get there at last. Impressed with itself, the four-square granite building will squat heavily on a napkin of lawn littered with colorful red and yellow leaves. If the green trees can turn colors here, thinks Elphaba in a rare moment of metaphor, maybe I can, too.

Her father will help her down from the trap with a hand accustomed to assisting his other daughter. Where Elphaba will refuse to cry, he will blow his nose. He will pull down her reticule. He has given Elphaba permission to take her mother's old valise, the one that once held all Melena's clothes. Also the oval mirror. The clothes have all been given away by now, but the mirror will rest at the bottom of Elphaba's folded garments, and papers, and books of her very own.

"Don't be lonely," her father will say. "If this works out for you, perhaps in time I'll be able to send Nessarose along as well. Will you write to us?"

Elphie looking about. Other members of the college congregating. On the pavement, in dark scholarly robes, stand three distinguished-looking older men and—sweet Lurline!—what seems to be a Goat, balanced on his hind legs, in conference with an Ape in high regalia. They turn to regard her with a cool skepticism. This isn't going to work. She should get back in the carriage and return to the marshland. She almost reaches for her father's hand.

The five professors, if that's who they are, will be interrupted in their scrutiny by another carriage arriving. The faculty members pivot, blocking Elphie's view. She can't quite see, but she infers a bright golden presence, a student with a trilling voice who emerges and descends from the carriage—she will declare as if delighted with her own competence—*So here I am, I* did *make it on my own, straight from the station, Doctor, imagine!* Their attention to some mesmerizing newcomer is discomfiting, but welcome; this gives Elphie a chance to take a deep breath and summon her nerve.

She turns her sharp chin away from the new arrivals. Time enough for all that.

"Don't be daft. Of course I will write, Father."

"A piece of advice."

"No. Thank you, but no. Anything you could teach me, you've already done. I won't forget it. But I am here to learn something else."

She'll stand back a step. She won't kiss him or embrace him, but I imagine she will touch him lightly on his forearm. He will watch her stump up the paving stones to the front steps of the hall. How she will be hurrying, as if he might change his mind! The building's high windows will gleam, reflecting a candied blue run through with strange thin clouds. The skies of a foreign climate. One that will become hers. There she will stand, in a dark traveling frock that draws no attention to itself, as befits a minister's daughter. The doors of the hall will swing open before her. She won't look back. What happens next will be her story, not his, so he will turn away as she flies forward.

That's how I see it anyway. But what do I know, really? It's all conjecture. An assessment totted up by the inchoate witnesses of these rough years. We are the wet wind, the lazy, refulgent river-ways, maybe the gazing globe, maybe the polter-Monkey. Watching. Watching from the dark past toward the green dawn. Waiting to see how it plays out.